Francis James Finn

Harry Dee or Making it out

Francis James Finn

Harry Dee or Making it out

ISBN/EAN: 9783741189067

Manufactured in Europe, USA, Canada, Australia, Japa

Cover: Foto ©Andreas Hilbeck / pixelio.de

Manufactured and distributed by brebook publishing software
(www.brebook.com)

Francis James Finn

.

Harry Dee or Making it out

HARRY DEE

OR

MAKING IT OUT

BY

FRANCIS J. FINN, S.J.

NEW YORK, CINCINNATI, CHICAGO

BENZIGER BROTHERS

PUBLISHERS OF BENZIGER'S MAGAZINE

CONTENTS.

CHAPTER IX.

CHAPTER X.

CHAPTER XI.

CHAPTER XII.

CHAPTER XIII.

CHAPTER XIV.

CHAPTER XV.

CHAPTER XVI.

CHAPTER XVII.

HARRY DEE.

CHAPTER I.

*IN WHICH I FEEL COMPELLED TO TALK MUCH ABOUT MY
EARLY YEARS, AND TAKE A JOURNEY INTO THE
COUNTRY TO SPEND CHRISTMAS NIGHT IN A VERY
MYSTERIOUS HOUSE.*

I HOPE the reader may not be bored; but I find it
necessary to begin my story with a great deal
about my insignificant self.   I am not the hero; and
yet, owing to a strange run of circumstances, am so
wrapped up with the characters and events which are
to figure in my narrative that I find it impossible
to make any sort of a beginning without telling
somewhat of my own early history.

And, to begin with, the reader must know that
when still a very small boy I succeeded in throwing my father and mother into a state of terror by
an extraordinary piece of conduct.   One night my
mother, who had a habit of stealing to my little
bed to tuck me in securely and repeat her good-
night kiss, found my bed empty.   Not a little startled, she instituted a diligent search, and to her
horror discovered me walking, fast asleep, up and
down our garden walk.

Of course the family doctor was called in at once.

He asked me all sorts of questions and made me so nervous that I put an end to the examination by bursting into tears.

"Madam," he at length said in grave tones to my mother, "you needn't be at all alarmed at Harry's somnambulistic propensities; he'll probably grow out of them. It's a—in fact, it's an idiosyncrasy."

For which he charged the usual fee.

The doctor's learned opinion of my case was on the point of bringing my distress to a climax, when my father led me from the room, and informed me that "somnambulistic propensities" merely meant that I had a tendency to walk in my sleep, and that its being an idiosyncrasy of mine was another way of saying that it was very odd on my part to do so.

"But," added my father, "you needn't bother about it. Some people snore in their sleep; others talk in their sleep; that's the sort of idiosyncrasy they have. Yours is to walk."

My father's way of putting it not only dispelled my alarm, but even made me somewhat proud of myself. I at once looked upon sleep-walking as an accomplishment. Even at this moment I cannot without smiling recall my conversation with Willie Styles, a very small boy with very large eyes, who lived within a few doors of us.

"Willie," I began, hastening over to his house, "do you snore in your sleep?"

"No," said Willie.

"Do you talk in your sleep?"

"No."

"Do you walk in your sleep?"

"No."

I looked on him with something akin to contempt

as I added, "Willie, you haven't got any iddy-sink-racing."

"What!" gasped Willie.

"I can walk in my sleep, Willie, and that's an iddy-sink-racing."

Proud both of the fact and the declaration, I departed to communicate the news to our cook and house-maid, leaving Willie in a state of perplexity not to be described.

The doctor's opinion, however, did not reassure my mother. Thenceforth she rested but little at night. Seated in an arm-chair beside my bed, she would clasp my little hand in hers and sleep as best she might. Night after night she took her station beside me, and with sweet sadness do I remember how often that soft, caressing mother's hand would gently stroke my brow; how often the mild, sweet face of my mother would bend down to mine as I awoke with a start from some troubled dream, and how, as her loving eyes fixed themselves on me, her lips would touch my cheek, while her soothing voice would charm my dream-haunted fancies into peace.

One morning—it was in my ninth year—I awoke bright and early, and, as was my custom, kissed the hand that clasped mine. But the hand I had ever found so gentle, so quick to answer my slightest touch, was cold and irresponsive. I raised my eyes to my mother's face; the smile I knew and loved so well still lingered about her features. But there was something in her face which I had never seen before, a weird beauty not of this world, which caused me to leap from my bed and clasp her in my arms and call her name. My dear mother gave me no answer. God had called her away.

I pass over in silence this, the supreme sorrow of my life.

Even during the first sharp agony of loss, it became evident to my father that it would not be prudent to leave me unguarded. The death of my mother had a very disturbing effect on me, and my restlessness during sleeping hours grew more alarming. The question then arose as to the choice of a night-watch. My father was not easily satisfied. He sought for some fit person throughout the city, but apparently to no purpose. At length he resolved to advertise in our daily paper, the *Sessionsville Democrat*, and accordingly the following appeared in its columns:

WANTED—A night-nurse. Must be steady and thoroughly reliable. Apply for further information to John Dee, 13 Madison St., Sessionsville, Missouri.

Quite promptly that morning the applicants came pouring in. My father and the doctor made short work of some, found great difficulty in putting off others, and finally, through sheer desperation, chose the least of many evils, as they thought, in the person of a woman giving her name as Mrs. Ada Raynor. As I say, it was for lack of a more satisfactory applicant that they chose her; for her evidences of a "character," as the saying is, were dark. To their searching inquiries her answers were vague and unsatisfactory. Whence she came, what were her past circumstances, they strove vainly to ascertain. The words into which she put her answers, while giving evidence of a good education, and, indeed, of no little refinement, only served to thicken the mist that obscured her past.

For all that she was duly installed, though my

father frowned and the doctor shook his learned head. As for myself, notwithstanding the fact that I was at an age when inquisitiveness is keen, I was not so difficult to please in the matter as my elders. What does the small boy care for the past when the present is so full of novelties and delights, when the future is brimming with unknown wonders and magnificent possibilities? Here was Mrs. Raynor bright and smiling, with pleasant answers to all my questions and many a gorgeous Eastern tale to while away an idle hour. Her past was nothing to me. In brief, I came very shortly to love her much; and though my father and the doctor could not be brought to believe it, she certainly seemed to return my affection. She had a soft, gentle way of calling me "Harry" which brought back vividly the tones and accents of my dear mother. There were other gracious resemblances, moreover, which I discovered for myself; and it came about quite naturally in course of time that I began to call her mamma. There was no doubt about the radiant smile which greeted me when I first addressed her by that endearing name. Nor at the time did it seem as though I had in anywise misapplied the term. To me she was in fact a mother; in her I placed all the confidence of a child's innocent, unsuspecting love. That love, as after-events go to prove, was within a little of wrecking my life. Every term of affection was afterward to be paid for in days of sickness and sorrow.

Beyond doubt Mrs. Raynor was a faithful nurse. It was her wont to sleep from early morn till noontime. But afternoon and night she was my constant attendant. Whenever my "iddy-sink-racing" threatened me, she was at once beside me to soothe me and restrain my wanderings. My love grew with the months, and served to take off much of the bitterness of that first sharp grief.

And now let me begin my story proper. It was about sundown of the 21st of December, the day after my eleventh birthday. I was lying on a rug close to the glowing hearth-fire in our sitting-room, reading for the tenth or eleventh time the absorbing tale of "Ali Baba and the Forty Thieves," and had just reached that exciting passage where Morgiana pours boiling water into the jars wherein the thieves have hidden themselves, when a brisk, firm step without brought me to my feet. Well did I know my father's footfall, and I hastened from the sitting-room into the hallway to meet and greet him at the door. To me his return was ever one of the pleasantest moments of the day. As he opened the door he always found me waiting within; and raising me in his arms would give me a fatherly kiss. That was all. He rarely spoke. On this occasion, however, he did speak.

"Harry, I've great news for you," he began as he returned me to the floor. "Of course you remember your Uncle James, don't you?"

I shivered at the name. Uncle James had been the bugaboo of my life. He had been face to face with me only once, but that was enough. The interview was a short one, yet short as it was my uncle had spoken so harshly, frowned so forbiddingly, and made such ugly faces that I had retired that night with my fancy at the complete mercy of all manner of hideous pictures.

My fear and aversion were not astonishing inasmuch as my uncle seemed to inspire the like feelings into all who came in contact with him. The old man was universally detested. From all I had heard he was very rich and very ugly, very harsh and very miserly.

"Remember Uncle James, papa? Indeed I do!"

"Well, something strange has come over him—poor James!—he's a diamond in the rough; for he's really making a show of being genial. Look at this!"

And unbuttoning his overcoat, my father took out a large yellow envelope, from which he produced a letter.

"See!" he said, holding it before my eyes.

"Read for me, papa; you know I can't read writing."

"Listen, then; I won't skip a word."

TOWER HILL MANSION, December 20, 18—.

Mr. John Dee,
DEAR BROTHER:—

Here my father paused, while the muscles of his face twitched; from after-experiences I infer that he was unable to reconcile his knowledge of my uncle with the warmth of affection implied in the term "dear." He went on reading, however, without comment:

I want your son Harry, my nephew Harry, to come to my house Christmas eve and stay over night. Important business.
Your brother,
JAMES DEE.

If my father counted on my being gratified by the wish thus curtly expressed in this letter, he was certainly deceived. The thought of passing a night under my uncle's roof was unbearable.

"O papa! I don't want to go."

"Why not, Harry?"

I must confess that at this stage of the conversation I blubbered.

"B-b-b-because he's an ugly old man; and he lives away out in the country—and—and "—here my grief grew more intense—"I c-c-c-can't b-b-bear him."

"Well, Harry! I didn't imagine you were such a coward."

This put a check to my tears.

"And to think," continued my father, a trifle sternly, "that a son of mine should speak of my brother as an 'ugly old man.'"

I began to feel uncomfortable. I realized that I had put myself in the wrong. After all, he was my uncle.

"Can Mrs. Raynor come along?" I asked concessively.

"Of course. That's understood. I'll speak to her at once."

But, no less to my surprise than to my father's, upon his asking her to accompany me, she showed the greatest agitation.

"Is it necessary for me to go?" she asked, after a moment of reflection.

"Well, it's not absolutely necessary," answered my father.

"Then I'll not go."

My father changed countenance.

"Mamma," I cried, catching her hand, "will you let me go alone to that house in the country?"

Mrs. Raynor drew me close and her face softened.

"My dear Harry, I'll miss you very much while you're gone; but it will be better that some one else go with you."

"But, mamma, I want you. Won't you please come?"

In a voice strangely agitated, Mrs. Raynor answered:

"I'll go. Yes, for your sake, Harry, I'll go."

On the 24th of December, accordingly, we took the morning train for Tower Hill, and I must say the day passed very pleasantly indeed. Toward nightfall we reached Tower Hill station, where we found awaiting us a rusty carriage under charge of a rusty driver, who shut us in with a sullen jerk and drove us off at moderate speed to my uncle's mansion.

That night proved to be an eventful one in my life.

CHAPTER II.

IN WHICH MRS. RAYNOR AND MY UNCLE HAVE A PASSAGE AT ARMS, A WILL IS READ, AND I GO TO SLEEP IN AN UNHAPPY FRAME OF MIND.

TOWER HILL MANSION, though a stately pile, was cold and forbidding. "Keep out" seemed to be the dominant note of its front. Nor did the interior belie the exterior. The furniture from hall to library and from library to sleeping apartments was severe, massive, and gloomy.

I shivered as the surly driver rang the door-bell; I shivered as a surlier servant threw open the door groaning on its hinges; and you may be sure that I clung to my nurse's hand from the moment of our entering through the gloomy portals to the moment that we were conducted into the gloomy, heavy-curtained library, where, surrounded by long, gloomy shelves, filled with dark, ugly, musty, forbidding books, sat my old uncle, gloomiest among the gloomy.

As I entered, my nurse gave unmistakable signs of agitation; her face worked convulsively; and I fancied that she was stifling a rising sob. How her hand trembled in mine as we came face to face with my uncle! He raised his cold, heavily-shaded eyes and glanced at me long and sternly. Yet more sternly did he stare at Mrs. Raynor.

He had not changed in appearance since I last met him. His face, from the pointed chin to the wrinkled forehead, was yellow and sombre, and his long, thin nose and thin, bloodless lips were as cold as of yore. His sunken eyes seemed to dwell in a region of perpetual frost, and his neglected hair, falling about his shoulders, appeared to be whitened not so much by the touches of old age as by the polar atmosphere he carried about him. As I gazed at him in fear and trembling I wondered whether it were possible for him to smile.

"Boy," he began, while I was still ruminating upon this remote possibility, "who is that woman with you?"

"Mrs. Raynor, Uncle James. She has my mother's place."

"Your mother's place!" he repeated, and his voice was as the movement of an ancient door upon historical hinges. "Pah! You're too old to be cod-

dled, boy. Your nurse wasn't invited here. Woman," he added, and all the rusty rheumatic hinges
of his voice now came into full play, " go about your
business. "

Previous to the first mention of my uncle's name
to Mrs. Raynor, my father had thought her a woman
whose passions were conquered and dead. Her
agitation had undeceived him. And now that she
stood face to face with this forbidding old man,
she manifested that there were other smouldering
fires in her bosom; for the flash of anger which shot
from her eyes as my uncle addressed her filled me
with awe.

"God knows," she cried, still holding my hand,
"this is the last place upon the earth I would come
to, Mr. James Dee. I know you. So does my
husband—so did he, rather. For he died penniless,
a victim to your treachery."

At Mrs. Raynor's first words my uncle gave a per-
ceptible start. As she went on, her voice gathering
passion and volume with each word, his yellow face
grew paler. There was that in the words of this
woman which seemed to pierce his very soul; and
when my attendant had uttered these, the first words
in which I had ever heard her make allusion to her
former history, my uncle gave a gasp—was it fear
or anger?—rose from his chair, raised his skinny
hand, and pointed with his skinny finger toward the
door.

"Go away, woman, go away! Leave this house
at once!" he snarled.

"I'll go, too, uncle, if you please," I stammered
forth.

"No, boy; you remain."

2

I was terrified beyond measure. Catching my nurse's arms, I cried out:

"Mamma, I'm going to stay with you. If you go, I go too."

"Come on, Harry," answered my nurse, resuming the gentle tones my ear knew so well. "We'll leave this wretched house together; there's a curse hanging over it, and some day it will fall." And turning, we were leaving the library.

"Hold on! Stay! One minute!" How the old rheumatic hinges of his voice rasped as he called out to us in these words.

Mrs. Raynor paused and faced him; her bosom heaving and her eyes still sparkling with anger, she stood like a deer at bay.

"Since you stick so close together," he went on, "I'll have to give in for this time. Woman, you may stay."

"But I won't stay," returned Mrs. Raynor, her voice trembling. "It is not enough, O my God, that he should have brought ruin to the husband, but now he must insult the wife!"

"I'll not stay either," I cried. "Mamma, take me away from this awful place."

The old man lifted his hand to secure our attention. His face had changed again. He endeavored to look benevolent; there was a contraction of the facial muscles which in itself had the appearance of an attack of paralysis, but which, under the circumstances, I took to be an attempt to smile. He might as well have tried to fly.

"Madam," he said, with a bow as stiff as a recently-rinsed towel in midwinter, "I ask your par don. I was harsh. I see that you love that boy. For his sake, I ask you to stay."

Mrs. Raynor hesitated.

"I assure you that to-night I have something to settle which is of great importance to the boy's future career; and I have made up my mind that Harry is to spend the night here and take his Christmas dinner with me to-morrow."

I hope I am not mistaken, but I thought, even as my uncle spoke, that a little of the Christmas spirit of peace and good-will shone in his cold, hard eye. In the light of after-events, it is consoling for me to believe this much of that wretched, loveless man.

After a short pause Mrs. Raynor made answer:

"For Harry's sake I will stay."

"Very well," said my uncle calmly, though I thought that he was secretly pleased. "Sit down then."

We complied with this abrupt bit of consideration, whereupon my uncle pulled a bell-rope beside his desk.

In there came presently the hideous, scowling servant who had admitted us into the house. In the matter of downright ugliness he set my uncle in quite a favorable light.

"Caggett," rasped my uncle, returning that gentleman's scowl of inquiry with a scowl of impatience, "tell the cook to come here at once."

Caggett gave a grunt, took his leave, and presently returned accompanied by a portly woman who entered the room with her arms akimbo.

"Caggett," growled my uncle.

A deep, guttural grunt from Caggett gave evidence that that giddy servant was all attention.

"Caggett, leave the room."

There was no doubt about Caggett's versatility and power in the way of growling and scowling now. He departed with a snarl which brought into play his ugly yellow teeth; he backed his way out of the room, and after bestowing a look upon me which forced me to hold my breath for fear, shut the door upon himself with a bang.

"Now," continued my amiable relative, "women both, and you, boy—are you listening?" The last three words he brought out with a burst—a sound as of unmusical cymbals brought clanging together by a furious hand.

"Yes, sir," I answered timidly, almost frightened out of my senses. I was clasping my nurse's hand, and even in my excess of terror could not but notice that the strong tempest of passion was yet raging in her bosom. She was muttering to herself, inaudibly for the most part, although once or twice the words "wretch," "villain," "scoundrel," and the like came hissing from between her set teeth. I felt that I was growing in fear of her too.

"Are *you* listening, cook?" said my uncle.

"I'm a-listenin', sir."

"That's what I want. Now listen closely."

He took up a paper from his desk. It was apparently yellowed with age. He held it for some time in his hands, then, without further prelude, read aloud something to this effect:

"I, James Dee, being of sound mind, do hereby devise and bequeath all my money and all my pos-

sessions of what kind and value soever to my serv-
ing-man, James Caggett."

The old man here raised his eyes and threw his
gaze upon me.

"Your father and I, boy, had a quarrel once," he
explained, " and I made up my mind that he should
not get one cent of my money. Caggett struck me
as the man who'd see to that. But blood is blood.
Caggett's not of my family and you are. Besides,"
continued the old gentleman, in the same strain of
simplicity and candor, " I hate Caggett."

"Look!" continued my sensational uncle. He
tore the paper into bits and threw the pieces upon
the gloomy, smouldering hearth-fire.

"Listen again." He selected another paper from
his desk and read in substance:

"I, James Dee, being of sound mind, do hereby
devise and bequeath all my money and all my property and all my possessions of what kind and value
soever to my nephew, Harry Dee. There! Have
you all heard?"

"Is that all?" asked Mrs. Raynor.

"Yes," snapped my uncle. " The rest is for the
lawyers."

"I do not speak on my own account," said Mrs.
Raynor, "for there are others to consider, Mr. James
Dee. If I tell you who I am, will you promise to
make some restitution to me for the wrongs you once
inflicted upon my husband?"

"We'll talk about that another time, woman."

"But look! You are in my husband's debt for
fifty thousand dollars. I claim that money, and I
will get it, too."

"Another time, woman."

"Now's the time," continued Mrs. Raynor, in a solemn voice. "Can you promise yourself a long life? You're an old man."

My uncle looked at her quite mildly.

"Yes," he said slowly, "I'm an old man—an old man. Boy," he continued, turning to me, "I want to see you alone for a moment in my room. But business first. Women both, please sign this will as witnesses."

The "women both" complied. Whereupon my uncle turned to me with, "You're a rich man now, boy."

Then he pulled the bell, in response to which Caggett entered.

"Caggett, show this woman the boy's room, and see that the fire is in good order. Breakfast at seven, woman, dinner at one."

Then, taking my hand, he conducted me up the broad stairway and into the room at the head of the stairs, leaving Mrs. Raynor in charge of Caggett.

He drew a chair beside the hearth-fire, and seating me in it, stood looking down on me not unkindly.

"Harry," he said at length, and I was awed by the softness of his voice, "you're the picture of my mother."

I looked up into his face. His eyes were dim and there was a faint quivering about his lips.

"I was a little boy like you when she died—poor mother! If she had lived I might have been different."

As I continued to gaze at my uncle I wondered how I could ever have called him an ugly old man. Now he looked quite like my father.

"Harry, I'm getting old, and if I die soon you must get your papa to see to my accounts and to make it right with any people who have claims upon my money."

"Yes, Uncle James."

"I've been mean, Harry. And—and—to-morrow's Christmas. You're an innocent child—won't you—won't you pray for me to-morrow?"

"O uncle!" I cried, jumping to my feet and catching his hand.

In an instant my uncle had stooped down and kissed me lightly on the forehead. He straightened up at once and veiled his face in his hands. For a moment he was silent. Then, with an effort, he spoke:

"Breakfast at seven, boy; dinner at one. Go to bed." And before I had recovered from my surprise at this abrupt change he was seated at his desk, and with the old face set into its habitual frown, was writing as though I were a thousand miles away.

I made my way into the long corridor, and perceiving light streaming from an open door at the further end, hastened toward it. Mrs. Raynor was awaiting me. Her agitation was extreme, and I could see that she had been weeping.

Mrs. Raynor was communicative that night. In a voice broken with emotion she related something of her past history. It was a tale of sorrow and wrong, a tale that involved a very dark chapter in my uncle's life. I do not feel at liberty, nor do I consider it pertinent to my narrative, to enter into that sad story. As I have since learned, there was no word of exaggeration in her account, and as I listened I was thrilled with horror and inflamed with

indignation. Alas! the affecting scene with my
uncle was driven from my memory like a dim dream
and—as I write I ask God to forgive me for it—I
allowed my feelings of hatred toward my uncle full
play. On that night, hallowed as it should have
been by the sweet sentiments of peace and love, I
yielded to such passions as I humbly trust I shall
never yield to again.

It was late when I fell asleep, and I regret to say
that I carried into a troubled dreamland my bitter
thoughts against the brother of my father.

CHAPTER III.

IN WHICH I AWAKEN TO A SAD CHRISTMAS.

I WAS habitually an early riser. On this Christmas morning, however, it must have been full
seven o'clock when I awoke.

I shall never forget that awakening; for it was
not the slow transition from unconsciousness to semi-
consciousness, where sleeping and waking join
hands. No; I passed from sound sleep to perfect
wakefulness with a start, jumped from my bed and
uttered a short gasp of terror. I was alone. For
the first time in years I awoke to find myself alone!

As I threw a hasty glance about the room, my
heart gave a sudden jump, my very blood seemed to
congeal, and the sweat of agony started upon my
brow. For a moment I was dumb with horror;
then I broke into a scream of agony.

An awful discovery! There was a stain upon my
coverlet, a stain upon the floor, a few crimson stains
upon my night-shirt, and beside the chair on which

Mrs. Raynor had been seated the night before lay her glove, crushed and crumpled.

"Help! help! Murder!" I screamed; and in an ecstasy of fear I made a dash for the door. In the helplessness born of terror, I tugged at the knob in vain. Convinced that I had been locked in for some dire purpose, my terror passed beyond all limits. For the moment I became a maniac. I threw myself upon the floor and shrieked and screamed. Happily for me, even in this passing frenzy, the sweet words of my poor nurse—whom I now believed to have been foully dealt with—came forth from the chambers of memory and fought hand to hand with the sombre terrors of the present. Was not God present? Could bolts and bars lock out my angel guardian? My cries died away. Gradually I became calmer, and arising from my grovelling position on the floor, I fell upon my knees and prayed to God for help. Then I breathed a short ejaculation for the welfare of my poor nurse, dead or alive. Had she really been murdered? By whom? This was an awful question. I feared to assent to that answer which my mind suggested again and again: "Your uncle is more than a swindler and a thief; to make his title to fifty thousand dollars good he has become a murderer."

While absorbed in these reflections, a hand was laid upon the door without. I sprang to my feet, and waited in breathless anxiety to learn what new terror was upon the turn of events.

The door opened sharply and revealed Caggett—gloomier, uglier than he had shown himself the preceding night. His conduct was singular. Catching me roughly by the arm, he hurried me from the room into the corridor, along nearly its whole length, till he stopped before a door.

"Boy," he growled, "do you know whose room this is?"

"My uncle's."

"Were you here last night very late?"

"No, sir."

"You lie! you were. Now, boy"—here he drew me to the door and laid his hand upon the knob—"now, boy, look and see what you've done."

And he threw open the door.

I took one look, gave a scream of horror, and—what happened after that I know not. For the first rough glance had been enough. Vivid as the picture still is in my memory, I have not the heart to reproduce it in all its ghastly details. My poor uncle had been stabbed during the night and lay dead upon his bed.

No wonder I fainted. The sight had conjured up a terrible tale of wickedness.

Into that thrust I saw gathered the hatred of the wronged wife and the revenge for a husband dead of a broken heart.

O my nurse! you to whom I had, in all a child's unstinted love, given the sacred name of mother!

CHAPTER IV.

IN WHICH I HEAR BAD NEWS, HAVE BRAIN FEVER, AND AFTER THREE VERY GLOOMY YEARS ENTER UPON A NEW LIFE.

WHEN I came to my senses I found myself in my little bed at home. My father was bending over me anxiously.

"O papa!" I cried, "do they think I did it?"

"No, indeed, my dear boy. No one but that wretched Caggett even suspected you. The whole thing seems to be now quite clear. The police have examined into the case. You must know there was a robbery, too. A large sum of money was taken, and that circumstance has helped to clear the matter. It's almost beyond the shadow of a doubt that your nurse—I always distrusted her for her dark, mysterious ways—committed the murder, partly out of hatred to your uncle, partly with the desire to make away with some money which she claimed he had swindled from her husband. Your uncle's cook gave a very clear account of Mrs. Raynor's conversation with my dead brother after he had read the will. Your nurse, after dabbling your night-shirt with blood, so as to lead us to believe you had killed him in your sleep, fled the house. But she'll soon be found. The police all over the country are on the watch for her."

"Papa, how much money was stolen?"

"Well, it seems that the miserable old man had a habit of sleeping with a large sum of money by his side—under his pillow, rather. Caggett, who knew his ways, testifies to his certain knowledge the sum in my brother's keeping on that night was fifty thousand dollars."

Fifty thousand dollars! The very sum Mrs. Raynor had claimed.

.   .   .   .

Nevertheless, Mrs. Raynor was not found. For what light could be brought to bear upon her whereabouts, the earth might have swallowed her.

Nor was Mrs. Raynor the only one to disappear.

The cook, housemaid, and coachman could with difficulty be persuaded to remain till the funeral rites
had been performed.   The two nights they spent in
the house after my uncle's death had been nights of
terror.   Each had a tale of strange groanings and
mocking laughs and weird sighs.   As for Caggett,
he continued to frown and snarl, but said little.
Even after the others had taken their departure, Caggett prolonged his stay in the lone house for several
days.   He had received permission from my father
to put the interior in order, and to make out an
inventory of the furniture, books, and general state
of the house.   How Caggett went about this work
nobody knows; but the gossips of the country made
much of his bravery in remaining alone in a " haunted
house."

Haunted house!   That was now the title of Tower
Hill Mansion.   Days passed into months, but from
the hour Caggett locked every door and brought the
keys to my father no sign of happy human life, no
sweet prattle and silvery laughter of childish voices,
no light steps of little feet, nor bright faces peering
from the open windows softened the gloom of that
dismal house.   The doors were locked, the blinds
closed, and around its gloomy gables the wind
sighed and moaned its mysterious requiem for the
well-nigh-forgotten dead.

People shuddered as they passed it by day and
prayed as they passed it by night.   Strange tales concerning it flew from mouth to mouth; and in course
of time my uncle's name ceased to be uttered and
his dwelling came to be called the " haunted house."

Many of these details were made known to me
long afterward, for at the time I was in no condition

to learn them. After the short conversation with my father set down in the beginning of this chapter I suffered a dangerous relapse. Brain fever set in, and for some weeks I struggled blindly in the arms of death. I came off the conqueror—not without loss. My sleep-walking habit, it is true, disappeared with the brain fever; but in its stead I found myself robbed of my strength and enveloped in a nervous gloom which, it would seem, doctors' skill could not dispel.

The three years that ensued were the unhappiest of my life. The memory of Mrs. Raynor—so kind to me, yet so cruel—haunted me; the face of my uncle, now as it quivered in kindness, now as it blanched into the horror of hideous death, came and went in sleepless hours of the night. Life, so gay and hopeful and joyous to most boys, offered me little to look forward to. My father, as the years went on, grew more and more distressed at my condition. He counted on time to cure me, but he was disappointed.

Finally, after much thought and consultation, he concluded that the active, stirring boy-life of boarding-school might prove the best remedy. Accordingly he sent me at the age of thirteen to a college which, as he had been led to believe, combined in happy proportions study, piety, and healthful out-door exercise.

On the 13th of October I took the train for St. Maure's.

CHAPTER V.

*IN WHICH I FALL OUT WITH A YOUNG RASCAL, FALL IN
WITH NEW FRIENDS, ONE OF WHOM FALLS UPON SAID
YOUNG RASCAL, AND ENTER THE COLLEGE OF ST.
MAURE'S IN THE BEST OF SPIRITS.*

"ST. MAURE'S!" shouted a railroad official as
the train stopped before a small depot on the
outskirts of a village.

Jumping to my feet, I grasped my valise, hurried
out of the car, and as the train moved away took
a hasty view of my surroundings. I had been told
that St. Maure's College was near the village, but
was ignorant of the direction. My first glance took
in many things, though it failed to discover the college.

I turned toward the west and followed with my
eye the fast-receding train: no college building
loomed up before me from this point of view, but
my attention was aroused for all that by the sight of
three boys advancing along the track. Two of
them were of about my own age, as I judged; while
the third was taller and appeared to be older than
his companions. Each of them had a gun upon his
shoulder, and the larger carried in addition a game-
bag, which seemed to be pretty well filled. I divined at once that they were college students.

While I stood looking at the approaching trio
and endeavoring to nerve myself to address them,
my valise was suddenly jerked from my hand; and
on turning I was confronted by a rather roughly-clad
boy of sixteen or seventeen, with as ill-favored a
countenance as one would meet with in a year and a
day's journey.

"You're a college kid, ain't you?" he remarked. "I always carry their baggage. Come on, youngster: I'll do it for fifty cents."

I was at the time a very timid boy, but this was too much for me.

"Give me that valise!" I cried.

"Yah!" ejaculated the young man, swinging the valise behind his back and facing me, with one eye closed and his tongue sticking out in unmistakable derision.

I stepped forward and endeavored to snatch my valise from his hands, but the disdainful youth dexterously swung it round. I reached after it, and made several circles about my tantalizing acquaintance, only to find that things were in precisely the same situation as when I began; if anything, one of his eyes was closed more tightly, and his tongue stuck out at greater length.

"Give me a quarter, sonny," continued the jocular young gentleman, "and I'll hand over your gripsack."

I stood still, not knowing what to do. It had seldom fallen to my lot to deal with such rough personages,—Caggett, indeed, was the only one I had ever brushed up against,—and though my outraged sense of justice prevented me from considering for a moment the idea of giving the fellow a quarter, yet I was extremely annoyed.

I again made a dart at my valise.

"Naw, yer don't," observed the amateur highwayman, running aside. "No quarter, no grip-sack, bub."

"I say, hand over that grip!" exclaimed a new voice

I turned, and to my joy I found that the young huntsmen, most opportunely for me, had come upon the scene.

The speaker, a dark-complexioned, somewhat chubby, merry-eyed lad, was the smallest of the three. He gave me a cordial nod, as did his larger companion, while the third surprised me with a salutation bordering closely upon a profound bow.

On hearing these words my victimizer backed away from us with notable signs of haste.

"Do you hear?" continued the jolly-faced boy. "Drop that sack."

"Yah!" answered the baggage-thief, making derisive signals with his fingers, with which expression of his feelings he turned west and started off at a run.

I was about to give chase, when the larger of my sympathizers thrust me aside, letting his gun drop in the act, and exclaiming as he dashed forward:

"Leave him to me, Johnnie; I'll spike his battery."

"That's all right, Johnnie," added the first speaker; "you needn't worry about your valise. John Donnel means to get it, if he has to bring back the fellow's scalp with it."

"Hadn't we better run on after them, Tom?" suggested the other. His voice struck me as he spoke with its wondrous sweetness.

"Come on, then," replied Tom.

Without further ado we ran forward in the wake of pursuer and pursued.

While, on the one hand, Donnel was handicapped by the game-bag, this disadvantage, on the other, was counterbalanced by the valise which encumbered the runaway. As to the issue, it was evident at a glance that Donnel's overtaking his opponent was only a matter of a few minutes. Slowly but surely Donnel was nearing his quarry. The question was not how to catch his hare, but how to cook it. All the difficulty would be in the meeting. This seemed to occur to the smaller of my two companions, for he cried:

"Come on, boys, as fast as you can. Maybe John will need our help."

At the word his companion shot on ahead, and soon left us many yards behind.

"It does me good to see Percy run," continued my companion, talking with as much composure as though he were going at an ordinary walk. "You should have seen him when he first came here last year. You'd have thought he was a girl in disguise; and now there isn't a nicer nor a better boy in Kansas. Hallo! John's taking off the game-sack. He'll run him down in no time, once he's got that off."

John, who was now within a few feet of the runaway, had indeed released his shoulder from the strap which supported the game-bag. But instead of throwing it aside, he suddenly swung it round and brought it with no little vigor about the legs of the fugitive. That bold young gentleman was almost lassoed. He plunged and fell to the ground; and before he could pick himself up John Donnel had clutched my valise, while the rest of us had ranged ourselves by the side of our champion.

"Will you fight?" exclaimed the fallen highwayman, picking himself up and directing a savage look at Donnel.

"How much a side?" asked John.

3

"Dollar a side," he answered after a pause.

"How much time will you give me for training?" continued Donnel, tranquilly.

"You'd better sneak off," suggested the smallest of my friends.   You're talking to John Donnel."

"Oh!" exclaimed the pugilist, changing countenance, and without more ado he shambled off.

My companions burst into a hearty laugh.

"Excuse us, sir," said Percy, controlling his mirth, "but the village boys are awfully afraid of John Donnel since he thrashed their champion last year—on my account, too.   By the way they talk of him, you'd think John was a fire-eater; whereas he's just as nice as can be.   And now allow me to introduce you to Tom Playfair."

"Glad to see you," exclaimed my stout little friend, extending his well-browned hand and shaking mine heartily.   "That red-haired boy," he continued, "who just made the speech——"

"It isn't red; it's gold," put in Percy.

"Is the awfullest dude in the college; and his name is Percy Wynn—and he's got ten sisters and still lives."

"Don't you mind that Tom," said Percy, taking my hand and bowing again; "he's always poking fun at me."

In the matter of hair, there was no doubt that Tom was poking fun.   Percy's hair was indeed of a beautiful gold, a fit setting for a face delicate, refined, and wearing an expression singularly engaging.

John Donnel was a fair-complexioned boy, with a countenance remarkable for its sunniness and frank, open expression.   Somehow I felt at once that I

was in the presence of three very remarkable boys;
and I may add that the passing of many years has not
weakened that impression.

"I'm ever so glad to make your acquaintance," I
said. "My name is Harry Dee. I've been unwell
for a long time; and my father thought that the
bustling, active life in a boarding-college might
give tone to my nerves."

Hereupon Tom Playfair, with a smile, caught
hold of me, turned me completely around, and then
stood off and gazed at me critically with his arms
akimbo.

"What you want is an extra layer of fat and lots
of laughing. You ought to make it a point to smile
before and after meals," he said good-humoredly.

I must admit that Tom's remarks were to the
point. At this period of my life I was intensely solemn and very thin. My face was noticeably pale,
and my lips and eyelids had a trick of quivering in
and out of time, due no doubt to the state of my
nerves.

"You'll grow fat on Kansas beef fast enough,
Harry," said Donnel. "But suppose we celebrate
the occasion. We don't get a new boy every day.
Tom, it's your time to treat."

"What shall it be?" asked Tom. "Pies?"

There was an unequivocal murmur of assent from
John and Percy.

"All right. You fellows walk on at your ease.
I'll run ahead and get them," and away darted
Tom.

As we walked smartly through the village we
chatted pleasantly, and I could hardly conceal my
delight with my new friends. Their natures were as

sunny as the brightest of days in spring; they talked and laughed with an abandon, a freedom from care, that was something new to me. Neither of them said one word smacking of piety, and yet I could not but perceive that I was in an atmosphere of holiness and innocence.

Just as we were passing out of the village Tom rejoined us in a way that was playfully abrupt. He came upon us at a run, and brought himself to a stop by plunging into Percy, who incontinently sat down.

"Here you go," cried Tom, tearing open the package he bore, and offering no apology to his prostrate friend. "Pies for the million. My friends, eat pie while you may, for to-morrow it's cakes."

He referred to the college-dinner dessert; pie-day alternated with cake-day; and, it goes without saying, the boys were sufficiently interested in the matter to know what was forthcoming each day as regards that part of the *menu.*

Not a little to my astonishment, Tom presented me with an entire pie; and on my remonstrating, he in turn was still more astonished.

Each of my friends took a pie without any objections; and I must add (model boys though they were) that they were considerate enough to help me dispatch my own.

"I say," began Tom, as we resumed our road toward the college, "how are you on baseball?"

"Not much," I answered. "You see, I'm too weak for hard batting or throwing or fast running. But I can curve a ball down and in and out, and place it pretty well."

"Couldn't you train him for our nine, Tom?" asked Percy.

"I don't see why not. He's not near as hopeless a case as you were, Percy, when you first came here. Why," he added, addressing himself to me, "you should have seen him. He had girl's hair, and used to walk about taking short steps like a pigeon, and the first time he threw a ball he hit John Donnel on the neck, and then he yelled like a woman when she sees a mouse. But now he's our left-fielder and holds everything—and my! you just ought to see him on the run when he goes after a ball. And as for base-stealing—he'll be a terror if he's not afraid to slide. He can run farther in less time than any fellow in the yard."

Tom, I could see, always became eloquent when speaking of his friend Percy, who on this occasion blushed violently and looked about him as though he were desirous of hiding himself.

John Donnel, who had been watching me intently during Tom's panegyric, now said:

"Percy, I agree with you. Harry has the right sort of build for a baseball player, or I'm much mistaken. All he needs is filling out; he'll get that soon enough. And we need a pitcher for our Blue Clippers, anyhow. Harry Quip's arm is too sore for regular work. Tom, you'd better undertake to train Harry Dee."

Tom and Percy listened with great respect to Donnel. And certainly on this point he had a just title to their regard. Though still in the small yard, John was looked upon as one of the best second-basemen in the college. Close upon John in authority came Tom Playfair, whose training and executive abilities were rated so high that on joining the Blue Clippers at the beginning of the present school year he had at once, mainly owing to the influence of Donnel and Keenan, been elected captain and manager.

"We'll make you a member if it can be done, Harry," said Tom, "and we'll have you in trim within a month."

I was surprised and delighted at the kindness and cordiality of my new friends. Why they should at once have taken me so fully into their confidence is a question I cannot answer to this day. Boys are marvellously quick in their likes and dislikes; and as far as I have had opportunity of noticing, they seldom judge amiss. By a sort of intuition they form lasting friendships where the older and wiser are wont to pause, weigh, and consider.

He should deem himself fortunate who finds it an easy matter to win the love and confidence of the young; and, looking back, it strikes me that the friendship shown me by Tom, Percy, and John is something of which I may well be proud.

Tom and Percy! How I wish I could paint them to the reader as I saw them on that red-letter day of my life. Tom, stout, brown, ruddy, with his face ever serene, with mischief twinkling ever in his eyes. But if fun proclaimed itself on his open face, decision asserted itself with even greater force. His mouth was of the firmest, his chin of the squarest.

Percy was equally handsome, but in another way. There was a certain delicacy about his person, form, and feature—even his clothes seemed to lend themselves to the expression of this capital point. His skin was very fair and white, save where on either cheek a slight touch of the rose lent an exquisite beauty to his exquisite complexion. His eyes and brow bespoke intelligence, and his whole face, regular in every feature, was mobile, refined, tender beyond any boy-face that has ever come under my notice. Like Tom, he was dressed in polo shirt and knickerbockers. I lay down my pen to gaze upon them again, and as I gaze my eyes grow dim with gracious memories, and I cry from my heart, "God bless them!"

The conversation on our nearing St. Maure's, by a natural school-boy transition, turned from baseball to class matters.

"Percy and I are in First Academic," said Tom, "our third year of Latin and second of Greek. I wish you could get in with us; we've a splendid teacher—Mr. Middleton. He's our prefect, too. Do you know any Latin, Harry?"

"A little; I've studied it about two years and a half under a private teacher. In fact, I've studied hardly anything but Latin, Greek, and arithmetic; and I went through everything in the morning hours from nine to twelve and had the afternoon free."

"Gracious!" exclaimed Tom; "what a nice daily order—half-holiday every day."

"How did you go about Latin?" put in Percy. "Did you begin with reading *Historiæ Sacræ?*"

"Yes; for seven months I was kept on nothing but the accidence and *Historiæ Sacræ.* I declined and conjugated till there was no sticking me. Then I began translating Cicero's letters. My first lesson was half a line; but I had to know everything that could be known about it, and I studied syntax in reference to each lesson. What I translated I learned by heart. Then I was made to put some English sentences into a similar style of Latin —that's what you call theme-work, isn't it?"

"Exactly," said Tom; "you've just been going on the lines Mr. Middleton sets for us. We learn by heart everything that we translate. How far did you go in Latin?"

"About five hundred lines of Cicero—mostly his letters. But I know it all, so that were I to lose my book I could put every word on paper."

"That's the system in St. Maure's, pretty much," observed Tom. "They are getting closer to it every year. But how about the *Copia verborum?*"

"Well, besides learning the inflection and meaning of every word I came across in Cicero, my teacher put four or five new words into each of my daily themes. In that way I got in about five or six hundred extra Latin words."

"It's a great plan," put in Tom. "Percy and I are terribly interested in Latin. You see, it's this way. Next year, when we get into Humanities, we've a chance to compete for an intercollegiate gold medal to be given to the one who writes the best Latin theme; now we want to hold up our end here at St. Maure' against the other six colleges that are in it."

"And besides," added Percy, "we count on Mr. Middleton's teaching us next year; he's very anxious for us to come out well in the contest, and that alone is enough to make us work for it."

"Just so," resumed Tom, "and it's his last year of teaching. After that he will go off and study theology and come back a priest. And if we don't give him a send-off next year it won't be our fault. You'll work for it, won't you, Harry?"

"If I'm able to get into your class," I replied, "I'll do my best."

"Shake hands on that," said Tom, grasping my hand. "We're none of us particular who gets the medal, provided it comes to some one in our class. But if we all work close together we'll help one another and maybe carry off some of the honors."

"There are nine places of honor, and there are seven boys in our class who are going to work from now till next April, one year, to get in their names. There's Percy and myself, and Joe Whyte and Harry Quip, and Will Ruthers and Joe Richards, and yourself."

If I had been pleased with our few words on the subject of baseball, I was both pleased and astonished at the eagerness with which my companions took up the question of Latin. They were real ideal boys; boys who loved work and play—an unusual combination.

On further talk we came to an agreement to help each other in this wise: The "big six," as Tom called the aspirants for the Latin medal, were to coach me in the part of Cæsar and Sallust which they had seen during their two years' study, while I in return was to go over with them the particular letters of Cicero which it had been my lot to review with my tutor.

With the ratification of this compact on our lips we entered the college grounds; and thus, auspiciously surrounded by the truest of friends and already spurred on to emulation in my studies, I made my entrance into St. Maure's.

CHAPTER VI.

*IN WHICH THE BLUE CLIPPERS GET A NEW MEMBER AND
THE COLLEGE BOYS A HALF-HOLIDAY.*

TOM PLAYFAIR conducted me to the room of
the president. At first view of the Father I
was somewhat dismayed. He was tall, dark, thin-
faced, and wore a pair of sombre spectacles. He
was writing at his desk as we entered, and before he
looked up I obtained a good view of his face in
profile. I took him to be a man of books and of a
somewhat saturnine disposition.

"Father," said Tom, "here's a new boy, and his
name is Harry Dee."

The president laid down his pen and turned
toward us. His face, harsh and austere before, became illuminated with a smile, genial and winning;
and as he advanced to greet me all my fears vanished.

His greeting was indeed cordial. After-experi-
ence proved to me that I had been deceived by first
appearances. Not entirely, perhaps; for I am convinced that by nature Father Delmar was severe,
but grace had triumphed over nature, and he had
won the secret of sweetness from a life of self-
denial.

"Now, Tom," said the president, after the first
greetings had been exchanged, "in what class shall
we place Harry?"

"In our class, Father. He's been studying Latin
and Greek the last two years."

"Indeed?" There was a gratified look on Father
Delmar's face. "Well, to make sure I'll examine

Harry. You can wait outside for a moment, Tom, and then I'll put him into your hands."

On Tom's going out the president said very gravely: "Harry, I congratulate you on meeting Tom. He's a good boy, a *very* good boy, but he's not alone in the field. There are others."

"Percy Wynn?" I suggested.

Again a bright smile of gratification lighted up the president's face. He looked more than beautiful when he smiled.

"Ah! you know him. You're lucky. In some respects Percy is marvellous, and, what's best of all, each thinks nothing of himself and all the world of each other. But now for your examination."

The president was an expert at this sort of work; and in five or six minutes he contrived to find out nearly everything I knew, and, to be frank, an infinite number of things of which I was dismally ignorant. For all that he seemed to be satisfied, and I felt more gratified in exhibiting my ignorance to him than my knowledge to others.

"Well," he said at length, "I'll have to stand by the verdict of your first examiner: here's a ticket for First Academic. You are strong in Latin and Greek, fair in English, and somewhat wanting in history and geography, which you must make up by private study. Now, my boy, go, and may God bless you."

Tom met me without and proceeded to guide me over to the small yard. As we drew near the gate between it and the large boys' division, I noticed that Percy, Donnel, and half a dozen of the students were grouped together.

"Hurrah!" said Tom. "Percy and Donnel have

spread the news of your coming and got our fellows together. That's Mr. Middleton over there; he's— well, he's just the best teacher you'd want to meet. There's not a boy in our class who wouldn't stand on his head for him."

Even as Tom spoke Mr. Middleton advanced, smiling a welcome as he neared us.

"What class is it, Harry?" he inquired as he caught my hand and gave it a cordial squeeze.

"First Academic, sir," I answered.

"Splendid. Welcome to St. Maure's, welcome to the small yard, and welcome to the First Academic."

In very deed Mr. Middleton seemed to rejoice over my being in his class fully as much as Tom and Percy. It struck me at once that there was something of the boy in Mr. Middleton—a certain freshness, vivacity, and breeziness of youth. He was a man in every sense of the word and a boy in its best sense. In all his dealings with us little lads he never seemed to forget that he, too, had once been a small boy; his sympathy for us took the edge off his severest punishments.

"Now," pursued my new professor, "come and take a look at your companions."

Within a few moments I was as much at home with my new friends as one of my temperament and experiences could well be. I was taken with them all, especially with George Keenan and Harry Quip. While engaged in conversation with these two a very small boy approached me, took me by the hand, led me apart, and said:

"I'm glad to see you. Percy Wynn likes you, and that proves that you're all right. What do you think of Percy?" As he asked this question this

very small boy turned upon me a pair of piercingly
earnest dark eyes.

"I think he's one of the nicest boys I ever met;
he's—he's charming," was my answer.

"Charming—charming," he echoed. "That's a
good word. Why?"

He almost threw this monosyllabic question at me,
and I must confess that I grew so nervous that I
was unable to give him answer.

This very small boy perceived my embarrassment,
and proceeded to relieve it by putting me another
question.

"Do you like mathematics?"

"Not much, I'm sorry to say."

Whereupon the serious little lad sighed, but immediately brightened up and added: "Well, lots of
good fellows don't like 'em, but I do—awfully. I
like things proved. You're a Catholic, ain't you?"
he went on.

"Yes."

"So'm I. I'm a convert, and I converted my
father, too. You just ought to have seen me at him."
Here he broke into a smile. "I proved him wrong
and he couldn't wriggle out of it."

"All by yourself?" I inquired.

"Well, no; not exactly. I had a catechism along.
My name's Frank Burdock; your name's Harry.
Don't you think Frank is a pretty name?"

"Indeed, I do."

"Why?"

To my great relief I had a fit of coughing at this
juncture, and the small interrogation-point went on
in this wise:

"I want to tell you that Percy Wynn is the best boy

in the world. I don't say anything against any one else, you understand; but all the same I'll put my money on Percy every time. Now don't you forget that, please," and again breaking into a smile, this very serious small boy walked away.

Few youngsters on first coming to boarding-college escape the ordeal of being teased. Nervous and timid, I had looked forward with no little dread to this stern novitiate in my new life. But, to anticipate, my classmates by some agreement, tacit or otherwise, thoroughly sheltered me from any rough usage.

After an early supper Tom, intent upon business, brought me over to the "blue grass."

"I got permission to bring you here," he remarked, "because I wanted to try your hand at pitching. We've a strong nine; the only thing is we're weak in the box. If you've got it in you, we'll be just right."

Tom produced a "boy's league," and retiring to the proper distance, asked me to pitch the ball.

I gave him an out-curve.

"Very good!" he cried. "That was a big one. Now let's see your in-shoot."

Tom misjudged the ball and dropped it.

"Let it go again," he exclaimed, returning me the ball; "same way."

This time he held it.

"Goodness! but that's the wickedest in-shoot I've seen in the small yard. Send in another."

Tom kept me at the in-shoot for several minutes. His eyes glowed with excitement, and candor compels me to admit that I was not a little proud of the impression I had produced.

"You'll do, Harry; that's certain. You've no idea how glad I am. Now let's try your drop. That's good enough, too," he remarked as he caught the drop, "but you can improve it with practice. How long can you hold out?"

"At present," I answered, "not for more than five or ten minutes."

"You're not very strong yet, Harry, but we'll get you at the parallel bars and the dumb-bells and the boxing-gloves, and in three weeks you'll be able to pitch for nine innings twice a day."

Just as Tom ceased speaking Harry Quip came running over breathless with excitement.

"Oh, I say!" he bawled. "It's two hundred and fifty!"

Both of us stared at Master Quip, who was now dancing.

"In the shade?" asked Tom.

"Who's talking about the weather?" shouted Quip. "It's two hundred and fifty."

And Quip resumed his jig.

"If you'd like to go to a lunatic asylum," Tom observed, "we'll certify that you're a fit subject. Stop your wobbling and talk sense."

Thus adjured, Harry Quip, supporting himself on one leg, roared forth:

"Two hundred and fifty *boys*. Harry Dee fills the number."

Upon which communication Tom became fully as insane as Quip and joined the dance.

"Hurrah! We'll get a half-holiday, sure. To-morrow's Wednesday, and we'll have a swim in the river."

Both young gentlemen, now equally breathless,

deluged me with a torrent of words, out of which I gradually fished the meaning. I was to return to the small yard and, accompanied by a delegation, was to repair to the president's room and there, it was confidently believed, obtain a holiday as being the two hundred and fiftieth boy of the college.

Before I had fairly taken in the situation each grasped an arm and began hustling me unceremoniously back to the yard.

My arrival was greeted with a cheer. Other enthusiasts joined themselves to Tom and Harry, and in a trice there were some twenty of us, panting and breathless, outside the door of Father Delmar's room.

Here we all paused to recover our breath.

"Who'll make the speech?" asked Joe Whyte.

"Percy!" suggested several.

"All right," said Percy, who was the calmest one of the party. In fact, he rarely lost his breath or his flow of words. "Come on, boys; I'm ready," and he knocked.

"Father Rector," said Percy, when all had entered, "we've come to congratulate you."

The boys laughed. Frank Burdock threw his hat in the air, but missed it coming down, whereupon he blushed and retired into the obscurest corner.

"Indeed!" exclaimed Father Delmar; "on what?"

"On the fact that you now have two hundred and fifty students."

"Yes, sir—yes, sir—yes sir," came a unanimous chorus of voices.

The president smiled mischievously.

"Well, what about it?" he inquired.

"A great deal," answered Percy. "When you

became president of this college, I am told, there were not one hundred and twenty-five boys in actual attendance; and it is to your energy and efficiency we owe it that the number has been doubled. So permit me to say again, reverend Father, that we, the small boys, congratulate you with all our hearts."

"Well, my dear boys, I thank you for your congratulations; and in return for Percy's pretty speech I am tempted to make one myself."

Here the boys became very serious.

"But I am convinced that you do not want a speech just now."

The momentarily solemn faces of his auditors again quivered into smiles.

"So instead of a speech, which you do not want —now be sure not to shout till you get back to your yard—I'll grant you a half-holiday for to-morrow, which you do want."

There was a multitudinous "thank you, Father," from every boy in the room, and, presto! twenty-odd lads, their eyes shining with pleasurable excitement, scurried lightly through the corridor and broke into the yard with a cheer, which at once spread the good tidings throughout the college.

CHAPTER VII.

IN WHICH WE GO SWIMMING AND MEET WITH AN AD-VENTURE.

IN the dormitory that night I was pleased to find that my bed was next to Percy Wynn's. I retired thoroughly exhausted from the varied excitements of the day, and, contrary to my wont, fell

4

asleep almost at once, to wake only at the sound of
the bell next morning.

Mr. Middleton, my professor, more than equalled
the expectations I had been led to form of him.
The boys of his class to a man (excuse the bull) were
all absorbed in their work.   So was Mr. Middleton;
for their sixty per cent of enthusiasm he returned a
hundred fold.   The hour of Latin seemed to fly on
golden wings; and still not a second was lost.   The
thoroughness displayed by teacher and pupils was
something   extraordinary.   The   theme-work   and
translation seemed to possess all the charm and fascination of the play-ground.   Greek class was conducted much in the same way.   Mr. Middleton was
equally enthusiastic; the boys, too, were attentive
and wide-awake, though they lacked somewhat that
spontaneity of enthusiasm which had distinguished
the preceding hour.   Very quickly, indeed, noon-
time came, and with it our half-holiday.

At three in the afternoon some forty of us, accompanied by Mr. Middleton, took the road through
the village leading to the river.   It was to be the
last swim of the year.   The mornings were already
growing chilly, and in the fall months the river was
considered rather unsafe.

Frank Burdock, Percy, and Tom were my companions.   Presently, as we passed out of the village,
Keenan, Donnel, Quip, Whyte, Richards, Ruthers,
and a number of other boys whose names I did not
know at the time joined us.

"You see," said Frank to me, "we've got up a
little society to say the Litany of the Blessed Virgin whenever we go out swimming; that's to prevent accidents.   It's a good idea, isn't it?"

"It certainly is," I replied.

"Percy and Tom got it up," said Frank trium-
phantly.

Frank was about to add something further, when
he was interrupted by Percy, who called out:
"Ready, boys?"

"Let her go," answered Tom, imparting to the
words a seriousness which took away all their ob-
vious levity.

Then, in his clear, sweet, silvery voice, Percy recited the litanies, while the others, with every sign
of reverence, responded "Pray for us" in low, earnest tones.

The spirit of true Catholic faith and devotion was
alive in the college. It was a little world in itself
—but a Catholic world. Prayer and piety lent a
radiance to the atmosphere of play and study. At
noon-time I had been not a little astonished when,
at the sound of the bell, the scene of bustling life
and play in the yard was at once changed to a tableau. The batsman dropped his bat, the pitcher his
ball, the game of tag came to a sudden pause and
the small boy's shout of triumph to a premature end;
every head was bared, and each boy, where the an-
gelus had fallen upon his ears, stood stock-still
while reciting the angelical salutation. Presently
"the charm was snapt, and all the pent-up stream
of *play* dashed downward in a cataract." The pitcher
pitched, the batter batted, the tagger tagged, and
the gay-innocent life went on all the more merrily
for that sweet interruption.

The same spirit showed itself in the recital of the
litanies. All joined in with a will; and thus in
prayer we came within sight of the river.

"Look!" exclaimed Frank; "did you ever see such a yellow river?"

"Looks as if it had the jaundice from smoking too many cigarettes," commented George Keenan.

"It reminds me," said Tom, "of a man I knew who had a liver complaint, I think it was."

As the conversation went on we selected a place for undressing.

"I'm afraid it's pretty cold," pursued Tom, throwing off his jacket. "Are you a good swimmer, Harry?"

"No, Tom, I'm hardly able to take a dozen strokes."

"Well, you'd better be very careful to-day. Don't go out of 'bounds'—I'll point them out for you; none of us is allowed to go beyond them; and be sure, by the way, to keep pretty close to the bank."

"Yes," put in little Frank, "that's the way I always did till I learned how to swim well. So did Percy."

"We've had plenty of practice this summer," Percy explained. "You see, several of us went rusticating in Wisconsin on the shore of the prettiest lake one could wish to see. We went in swimming once or twice every day, and now we're all of us quite proud of our skill in the water."

"But Tom and Percy are the best," said Frank, with his mediæval smile.

"Come on there and hustle," exclaimed Tom, who, arrayed in his swimming-tights, was impatiently awaiting the laggards.

In a few minutes we were all plunging about in the water; and there rose upon the solemn air the mingled sounds of splashing and happy laughter.

But for all that the water was intensely cold. It was hard to refrain from shivering.

We were soon engaged in a game of tag. I was "it" for a few seconds, but succeeded in catching Tom Playfair napping. Next to Tom, and standing a little more than waist-deep in water, was Frank Burdock. Tom made a dart at him. With a gay laugh Frank took a leap backward, and as he leaped I gave a cry of dismay. My fears were realized. A huge drift-log had just floated within a few feet of little Frank, who was ignorant of its vicinity. His head struck against the end of it and, to my dismay, he went down.

I struck out at once, never reflecting that it was all that I could do to take care of myself. With a single stroke Tom was beside me.

"Go back, Harry, go back!"

I obeyed instinctively, and felt at once that Tom was indeed a boy born to command. His whilom happy face was now aflush with energy and determination as, with a magnificent overhand stroke, he made for the place where Frank had disappeared. Suddenly there arose another form at his side, as it were from out the very heart of the water. It was Percy Wynn, who had taken a long dive and thus put himself abreast of his brave friend. Just then, twenty feet or so further down the current, emerged the face of poor little Frank. His eyes were closed and his face was extremely pale; there was an ugly gash below his temple, and even for the moment that the cut was free from the washing of the water a stream of blood marked his sinking for the second time.

A clear voice now arose.

"Percy and Tom go on, in God's name! Every one else out of the water."

All of us hastened to the bank, in obedience to Mr. Middleton's command, while Tom and Percy made bravely on. Both used the overhand stroke, and breast to breast cut the water. They were magnificent swimmers. One would almost think that they were racing for a wager.

Suddenly they paused and, treading the water, gazed around and about them. But seemingly they discovered no sign of Frank's presence.

Then, as with one impulse, they dived. The place whither Frank had been carried was far out of bounds and very deep.

All this had come to pass within a few seconds. Mr. Middleton had not been idle in the mean time. Throwing off his coat and shoes, he now plunged into the river and came toward the scene of action with powerful strokes. He was a royal swimmer; for speed I had never seen his like.

As Tom came to the surface Mr. Middleton was at his side. Tom's quest in the underwaters had been fruitless. In another second Percy appeared alone.

There was a groan of dismay from the shore. Many of the boys sank upon their knees as Mr. Middleton, after saying something to Tom and Percy which we could not hear, dived down.

The next few seconds were seconds of agony. The sun went behind a cloud—a deathly stillness came upon the scene. Second after second passed. The only sign of movement or life came from Tom and Percy, who were treading water side by side.

Oh, those terrible seconds! It seemed an hour.

At length there was a ripple and a splash; and a great cry of joy arose as Mr. Middleton broke through the surface with little Frank supported on his strong right arm.

Tom was by his side at once, and catching one of Frank's hands, helped his prefect shoreward with the unconscious boy.

Then, as the party reached shallow water, a cheer arose from the shore, such as nothing but excitement and enthusiasm at highest pressure could arouse.

Eager hands were stretched out to them and helped them ashore.

There never was such hand-shaking since college began, and there was reason for our joy, since no one was harmed and Frank had recovered consciousness before reaching land.

CHAPTER VIII.

IN WHICH WE FIGHT OUR BATTLES O'ER AGAIN AND SPEND A PLEASANT EVENING IN THE INFIRMARY.

"THAT Mr. Middleton is one of the pluckiest men alive," observed John Donnel as we took our way home.

"He can swim with hands and feet tied," added George Keenan. "My! it was a sight to watch him making for you, Frank. You'd think he was running in the water."

"By the way, Tom, what was it he whispered to you and Percy when he dived after Frank?" inquired Donnel.

"'Say a Hail Mary, boys,' that's all he said; but

I tell you, it worked me up. While he was down in the water I think I got off more genuine praying in those few seconds than I did since the morning I made my First Communion. I said the Hail Mary only once, but when I got to the words, 'Pray for us sinners now and at the hour of our death'—oh! didn't I mean it!"

"Yes!" put in Percy. "That was my prayer, too; and, really, I never knew before what a beautiful prayer it was."

"Look here," cried little Frank, "perhaps you won't believe me, but it is a fact, even if I can't prove it. After that log struck me I forgot all about myself. I was—what do you call it?"

"Unconscious," suggested Percy.

"That's it, exactly. The next thing I knew I found myself lying on the sandy bottom, and there was a rumbling sound, like thunder, in my ears. Now, boys, wasn't I frightened? I felt that I was choking and that I'd be dead in less than a minute. I was awfully frightened—just crazy—you understand? Then I remembered, all of a sudden, that I had said the Litany of the Blessed Virgin, and—would you believe it?—I didn't feel one bit scared. No, sir; I wasn't afraid of death, and I just began saying the Hail Mary to myself, and when I got to 'now, and at the hour of our death, amen,' I felt a hand clutching my arm, and that's all I knew till I found Mr. Middleton and Tom towing me in to the shore."

"Singular!" murmured Percy. "It looks as though all three of us said the same sweet prayer at the very same time."

"That's just my opinion," added Tom, and

fell to thinking. Miracle or not, it came home to us that prayer was a practical part of life, and that the Mother of God had not been deaf to the wishes of her loving young sodalists.

Shortly before supper Mr. Middleton called Tom aside.

"Tom," he said, "you remember the time Percy crippled himself in running you down out toward Pawnee Creek."

"Do I? Oh, don't I!"

"And the supper in the infirmary?"

"Yes, indeed, sir."

"Well, a good thing will stand repetition. You and Percy and Frank need a good rest this afternoon and a late sleep to-morrow. So you needn't mind your night studies. Don't get up till half-past seven. There's a priest here staying overnight who will say mass at half-past eight. And by the way, your nervous friend, Harry Dee, might go along with you. Such a scene as he has witnessed this afternoon may have a bad effect on him. ' So just as soon as the bell rings for supper, all of you go quietly over to the infirmary. The Brother has promised me to give you a good supper."

And Mr. Middleton cut short Tom's ardent thanks by hurrying away.

I was standing beside Tom as he received this pleasant communication. I had come to look upon Tom as a hero, and I looked at him with some anxiety to hear what he would say.

"I hope there'll be lots of buttered toast!" ejaculated my hero, with no little ardor, saying which he dashed off to communicate the good word to the others.

And now for that supper! The reader must excuse me, but I can't bring myself to narrate how these life-rescuers demolished the viands. It's too prosaic; and I am tempted even to draw my pen through Tom's remark about the buttered toast. Suffice it for me to say that as they had shown bravery at the river, so they showed appetite at the table; and it struck me with much force that because a boy is good one has no right to grudge him health and appetite.

I had been tossing restlessly in bed for half an hour, when some one touched me on the arm. I turned and perceived by the dim light of the lamp that Tom was beside me. His face was beaming with sympathy.

"Old fellow," he began, "you can't sleep, can you?"

"No," I whispered, "though I'm very tired."

"You've got a shaking up from that river business. I'm sorry for you. The very first minute I saw you I guessed what was the matter."

"I don't understand you, Tom."

"Well, simply this: You've been an eye-witness to something terrible—or something in that line—a *murder*, maybe."

I almost leaped from the bed.

"Pretty good guess, wasn't it?" Tom went on calmly. "But it's all simple enough. You've got the ways of Jimmy Aldine. Poor Jimmy! He's dead now, my best friend. He had seen a murder. I'll tell you the story some day, and you'll tell me yours, won't you?"

"Indeed I will, Tom."

"All right, Harry. I'm told your mother is dead

—is that so?" And Tom gazed down into my face with a sympathy rare and strange in one of his years.

"Yes," I said softly; and as I thought of my mother dead and of her who had filled the place of mother far worse than dead, my eyes filled.

"Same way with me," said Tom gently. "I just remember my mother's face. My father says she was a saint. I believe him; and I'm sure she looks out for me. But, Harry, old fellow (that's between me and you), I have asked another mother to take the place of the one I've lost. You take her too."

For a few moments we were both silent.

"Now," resumed Tom, "I guess I'll turn in. I'd have gone to sleep at once only it occurred to me that the excitement had rattled you, and so I watched and saw you tossing and tumbling about, and then I thought we might as well have a little talk. I want you to feel that you're among friends."

I thanked him in broken words. What a wonderful power of happiness goes forth in a little kindness. But Tom was even more considerate. His kindness rose to the height of invention.

"I'll tell you what," he pursued; "I'll wheel my bed right alongside of yours, without disturbing the other fellows. Now, if you get nervous or scared, just bang me across the chest—hit hard, or I won't know the difference."

"How can I thank you for your kindness!" I exclaimed as Tom brought his bed within a few inches of mine.

"By going to sleep," Tom made answer. "You look as though you thought I was doing something extraordinary. Not at all. There's not a boy in the place, almost, who wouldn't have done the same thing if they'd known you were so nervous. You see, I came to notice it because I know how it is myself. A little before the time of Jimmy Aldine's death I had the horrors every night nearly, and I tell you I haven't forgotten it, either. Well, good-night. Remember, we'll try our hands on Cicero's letters to-morrow."

And making the sign of the cross, Tom closed his eyes and very, very soon gave evidence by the regular breathing that he was fast asleep.

His presence had a calming effect upon me, and I felt so happy for all his kind and considerate words. Yes, Tom *had* "ministered to a mind diseased." His kind words hovered brightly in my memory, and soon conducted me into the very brightest and pleasantest spot in dreamland—the spot consecrated to love, and purity, and innocence, and ever hallowed by their priceless presence.

CHAPTER IX.

IN WHICH I HAVE A BAD NIGHT AND PRODUCE A SENSA-TION IN THE DORMITORY.

ACCORDING to orders, we all arose at half-past seven the next morning, thoroughly refreshed. After a substantial breakfast we heard the late mass, and came from the chapel in time to get our books for class.

At noon-time Tom and I had a long *tête-à-tête*. I told him the dramatic incidents of my life, to which he listened with no little astonishment. When I had concluded my tale he fell into a brown-study.

"I'll tell you what I think," he at length said. "I think that there's not an end of this business yet, by any means. You loved your nurse pretty much the same as though she were your mother. Now, that's in her favor. From what I've seen and heard during my three years in boarding-college, I've come to believe that a small boy seldom misses it in the matter of likes and dislikes. Now, if your nurse killed your uncle, I'm willing to bet my head that she didn't do it merely for the sake of the money."

"You think not?" I exclaimed, with a great feeling of relief. The reader should remember that what had given me the greatest shock was the thought that one I had loved so much should prove so base.

"Honest," answered Tom. "Now, another thing: did your nurse ever act queerly—that is, did you ever notice anything in her conduct which might lead you to think that there was something wrong about her head?"

Before replying, I considered for a moment.

"No," I at length made answer. "She was reserved and distant with others, but with me she was ever kind and loving. I can't say that she at any time acted queerly."

"She might have killed him in a moment of insanity," observed Tom. "At all events, I'm quite sure that she didn't kill him in cold blood."

I was inexpressibly soothed by this opinion of Tom's.

"Another thing," he continued: "what about that house? Do you honestly think it's haunted?"

"I can't say for certain, Tom. No one goes near it, but everybody says it is."

"Well, we mustn't take a thing like that for granted. Now, I've got an idea which it won't do any harm to carry out. Who knows but it may throw some light on the subject? It's the same way in life, I reckon, as in books. We make lots of bad blunders simply because we take one little thing or another for granted. Now, I really don't see what that house being haunted or not haunted has to do with the case; but maybe it has. At any rate, it will do no harm to find out. Now, here's my plan. Next vacation you and I will spend a night in your uncle's house. You needn't look so scared. Of course, you're horribly afraid now. That's because you're sickly. But you'll be all right by next summer, and you'll enjoy the prospect of that night in a haunted house just as much as I do now."

· "I won't make the promise, Tom."

"That's right," answered my romantic friend. "But next spring I'll ask you the same question, and I'm perfectly sure that you'll say yes."

"I doubt it."

"No matter; and, Harry, if you don't mind I'll tell Percy all about the matter. You can trust Percy a thousand miles further than you can see him."

"Certainly, Tom, tell Percy."

From after-knowledge I am now certain that Tom did not believe my uncle's house to be haunted. But my new friend liked anything that gave promise of adventure, and the prospect of passing a night in a lone house was something after his heart.

During the day my imagination, despite my endeavors to the contrary, kept running on the unlovely memories of the night I spent at my uncle's. Horrible pictures flashed before me, over and over again, without order and without sequence. It was as though I myself were haunted. The swimming incident had unstrung my nerves; and my long talk with Tom had freshened into vividness the details of a night vivid enough as they ever were without my recalling them.

With evening these haunting memories grew stronger; to use a bold word, they became aggressive; and when I retired to rest I was in an extreme state of nervousness.

There they came, as I tossed restlessly upon my bed—the gloomy house, my gloomy uncle, the scowling Caggett, my angry nurse. At once the picture changed, and I was standing, terror-stricken, gazing into my uncle's room and contemplating that sad sight. This picture stared at me for a few moments, then *vanished*—it did not fade away—and at once another picture was gazing at me. I say gazing at me, for I know no other form of words to give the reader an adequate idea of the manner in which these pictures came and went. This picture was of a little boy leaping from a bed, a scream of terror upon his lips. He looks about him wildly—at the blood upon his night-shirt, at the blood upon the floor, at that pathetic glove bathed in purple, and as I gaze at this picture and it at me, it becomes more and more vivid, clearer, distincter—no vision, but a reality, and reaching the last degree of vividness, I become a part of the picture, I become the little boy; I, too, leap from my bed just as on that awful morning, and again scream in an ecstasy of terror:

"Help! murder!"

And with these words the spell is broken: and trembling in every limb, with a great sob bursting from my bosom, I find myself standing in the dormitory surrounded by boys with faces white as a sheet and gazing upon me in awe and horror; and before I can realize where I am, a soft hand is caressing my cheek, a soft voice is whispering soothing words into my ear—as a mother soothes her frightened babe. It is Percy, the only one of all the boys who has not been disconcerted by my scream. He is perfect master of himself, and the only emotion upon his expressive face is intelligent sympathy.

"Wake Mr. Middleton," chattered one of the boys nearest me.

Strange to say, Mr. Middleton did not awake, even on this occasion. He was the soundest of sleepers.

"No, you don't," whispered Keenan authoritatively. "Just let him have his sleep out. He deserves all he gets."

"You are always considerate, George," whispered Percy. "We can arrange this matter ourselves. I'll take Harry over to the infirmary and stay beside him for the rest of the night."

"No, you don't, Percy," said Tom. "You've had your innings already. I'll take him."

Hereupon there arose a whispered discussion. Donnel and Keenan and Quip put in claims, too. At length it was decided that Percy should have the office, whereupon Keenan turned round and said:

"Now, boys, hop into bed. I'm acting prefect."

The boys, who had recovered from their fright, gave a little series of giggles and obeyed.

I shall say little of that night in the infirmary. It is a fragrant memory. Percy was not an angel, for angels are not made of clay; but as he bent over me that night with his tender smile and his gracious words, as from out his blue eyes there shown that unselfish love which is not of the earth earthy, I thanked God from my heart for this object-lesson in the sublime nobility of human nature.

CHAPTER X.

IN WHICH WE DIVIDE OUR ATTENTION BETWEEN BASE-BALL AND LATIN, AND ARE PREPARED FOR A CONTEST IN THE ONE AND AN EXAMINATION IN THE OTHER.

THE nervous attack of which I spoke in the preceding chapter was, I might say, the first and last that I suffered at St. Maure's. With each day I seemed to gain strength and vigor. Little by little my nervous facial twitching disappeared, and before Christmas the attentive physician of the college pronounced me well.

How calmly and peacefully these golden months glided on. During October and the early part of November baseball held its own in the yard. Tom was unwearied in training his nine. Although he seldom called upon me to pitch, and even then but for a few innings, yet he gave me many words of encouragement.

"Just wait," he said, "'till the flowers that bloom in the spring, tra la, give promise of merry sunshine.' Then we'll turn you loose in the box, and

5

we'll show the second nine of the big yard a trick or two."

Tom was ambitious. It was his darling idea to play and defeat the Junior nine of the senior division. To most of our fellows the proposition seemed a trifle wild. But Tom had some foundation for the faith that was in him. To begin with, he counted on a strong infield. Joe Whyte was first baseman. As a batter Joe was weak, nor was he reliable in stopping grounders; but for holding a thrown ball he was perfect in his way. At second base he had John Donnel, a faultless fielder—he was called the king of second base—and the strongest batsman on the nine. Indeed, it was generally held that John was superior in safe hitting to any of the large-yard Junior nine.

George Keenan covered short field. This very little fellow contrived to be everywhere; always in the right place and at the right time. Fairly strong at the bat, he was at his best when running the bases. He could twist and turn with such agility that it was almost impossible to catch him off his guard, although he played off further from base than any one of our players. Third base was covered by Charles Richards. He was a strong batter, excellent for running catches, but not over-reliable at stopping ground balls. As for the outfield, Quip at centre and Ruthers at right were fair catchers and excellent throwers, although both were weak batsmen. Harry Quip, however, redeemed this defect by excellent base-running. Percy was the left fielder; he had one weak point, and that was in throwing. He could scarcely put a ball on a line from his ordinary position to second base. But, saving this, he was a phenomenon. He had a knack, which few fielders possess, of being able to judge a fly almost as soon as it was knocked. And when he got hold of a ball he clasped it, as it were, " with hooks of steel," that is, with two small, delicate hands, large enough, however, to hold any ball that came within their grasp. As for running, his speed was something extraordinary. Tom, Keenan, and even Donnel had to give in to him in this; although he was not as quick in recovering himself as George. Thus far Percy, fair in his batting, had done little in the way of base-stealing. But it was just on this point that Tom founded something of his hopes. He counted on Percy's becoming a phenomenal base-stealer before spring; and he himself had Percy in private training during the winter.

Tom himself was our catcher; and he was as steady, cool, and reliable there as any captain could be. He never lost his head, never flagged in his attention, never missed a point in the game. In throwing to bases he was considered second only to Ryan, the best catcher of the senior students.

But now for our nine's weakest point. I was on the list to pitch. It was evident to every one that unless I gained more speed the big boys would knock out two and three baggers almost at will. On the other hand, it was admitted that my curves were very good and that my command of the ball was unusual. As to my general playing abilities, beyond doubt I was the worst of all the " Blue Clippers." My batting was wretched and my base-running of a piece with it. Worst of all, I was very unsure in catching those twisting flies that are so often popped up for the benefit of the pitcher.

But for all this, Tom protested that I'd be on hand in the spring with speed enough and endurance enough to face the heavy batters of the Juniors for nine innings.

As for the opposing nine, they were clearly our superiors in batting, and they were provided, moreover, with an excellent pitcher. So matters stood in the autumn, at which period 't would have been downright folly even to attempt a game with the boys whom we purposed defeating in the spring.

I should add that the Juniors were in blissful ignorance of our lofty aspirations. During the winter season they forgot their baseball and devoted themselves between study-hours to sports suitable to the changing months. Not so with us. Tom kept us all at a regular course of gymnastics; besides which training, he contrived to pay special attention to Percy and myself.

In the mean time studies went on briskly. How our set did soak themselves in their Latin author! We spent the whole of the Latin class-hour in trying to catch one another. In this Percy was the quickest and Tom next. As for knowledge of Latin, I was considered the best. This, I could easily see, was not due to any mental superiority on my part, but to the fact that I had had a private tutor to help me and more time to give to the study. It was clear to me that for taking in new matter Tom and Percy were easily my superiors, and I had no doubt that by the end of the year both would at the very least be on a par with me in actual knowledge of the language.

Nor did we confine ourselves to the class-work; once or twice a week we held informal meetings.

Then, under my guidance, the ambitious young students read my selection from Cicero's letters. Before Christmas, indeed, they knew as much of these five hundred lines as I did myself; so that during the holidays we were all casting about for something new. I was at the end of my tether; the others had all read the same authors. We would have liked to have Mr. Middleton preside over our Ciceronian meetings, but we knew that what with his teaching and his prefecting he had all the work he could possibly attend to. Mr. Middleton solved our dilemma.

"Get Keenan," he said, "to go over a bit of *'Pro Archia Poeta'* with you. It's true you'll see it again in poetry class; but even so, you'll not lose by it."

Keenan gladly assented to our request; and during the months of January, February, and March we parsed, translated, analyzed, imitated, and memorized one hundred and fifty lines of "*Pro Archia Poeta.*"

Of course we didn't do all this because we looked upon it as fun, but we really did like Latin; and we really did love Mr. Middleton; and we really did hope to make, at very worst, a strong fight the following year for the intercollegiate gold medal.

I suppose all of us felt weary and disgusted at times—I know I did. But there was a spirit of energy in us, a spirit, you may be sure, breathed into us by our enthusiastic teacher, and daily kept alive and nourished by his heartening words.

During the second half of the year we began to talk Latin in class. As an encouragement to talk at all, Mr. Middleton offered a prize for the first week to the one who should make the most blunders.

Tom Playfair won it easily, with Harry Quip a distant second.

After a month the prize was for the one who
should make the *least* blunders; and, if I may anticipate, in June he was to receive the prize who employed in his class-talk the greatest number of
classical idioms. Percy and myself were a tie at
the end, and received each of us a very pretty picture.

It was the morning of March 21st; the sun, which
had risen a few hours before in a burst of splendor,
was now shining with the bridal brightness of
spring. The sweet twitter of the early birds fell
welcome upon our ears; while the fresh green
grass just peeping out of the earth and the swelling
buds on the trees gave promise of beautiful blossoms
and joyous ramblings over the grassy prairies, of
wild flowers, and all the scents and sounds that are
connected with the prettiest time of all the year.

The small boy loves life; and therefore he loves
spring. To him there is a glory about the budding
tree and divinely-painted flower which is dimmed
or invisible to the eye of an adult. The wild
freshness of spring touches a wild freshness of sympathy in the heart of the small boy.

Tom was as gay as the season.

"Harry," he exclaimed, as his eyes feasted upon
the landscape, "it's spring."

"I've observed it," I answered.

"And how much did you weigh when you came
here?"

"Eighty pounds."

"And what is it now?"

"One hundred and three."

"And do you think you could stand nine innings?"
I laughed.

"If the batters can stand it I can."

"So, you see, I was right when I said you'd be well by spring. Now, remember, on or about the 15th of April we're going to play the large boys one game."

"Only one?" I inquired.

"Well, yes," answered Tom. "It will be too much of a strain on us to tackle them often; and besides, either we'll beat them the first time or we won't. If we do, we're satisfied; if we don't, we'll scarcely be able to do it this year; for we intend to put in our best licks in a lump."

"Well, you may rely upon it, Tom, that I'll do my best to help on. But isn't our class-specimen to come off about the same time?"

"That's what I've counted on," said Tom. "We're going to make that a success, you know; and then we'll be flushed with success, as they say. Six of the players are in our class, and if they can stand up before a board of reverend examiners successfully they won't be afraid to face a big boy with a ball in his hand."

Tom was of opinion that the same energy which could conquer difficulties in the classics could also conquer difficulties on the play-ground. To him the boy who was leader in the play-ground and dunce in the class-room was a freak, a *lusus naturæ*. As a matter of fact, all of his players were as quick with their wits as with their limbs; in choosing his nine he had selected those who were fair in sports and in studies, in preference to better athletes with muddier intellects.

Spring, then, passed on with even pace. She set
the birds a-singing and painted the flowers in all
their glory of color and scented the breeze with her
perfumes.   She brought the brightest of sunshine
and the bluest of skies and the greenest of swards.
But strong as was her charm she could not allure the
Academic boys from their books.   They studied right
on in hours of study, and then when play-time came
they breathed in the vernal glories all the more joy-
ously that they had done their duty.

And so the time flew till April 12th arrived—the
morning of the specimen.

CHAPTER XI.

IN WHICH PERCY WYNN MEETS WITH A FAILURE.

THE president, vice-president, and dean of the
faculty honored our specimen with their presence and attention.

Charlie Richards delivered a neatly-worded opening address, concluding his remarks by inviting the
distinguished visitors to examine the class in English, Latin, and Greek.

The Precepts in English Composition were first
taken as subject-matter for examination.   The boys,
thoroughly drilled as they had been all along in
memory work, answered with such ease that after
the lapse of fifteen minutes the president called a
halt.

"That is too easy for your boys, Mr. Middleton;
we'll take them on something where we'll get a
fairer chance of puzzling them."

Then came the tug of war.

Sallust, bristling with idiom, formed a splendid *pièce de resistance* for the acute examiners.

They put questions right and left, but the answers came from right and left with almost equal readiness. Presently translation was abandoned and the field of syntax was invaded. Here we held our ground; we had taken nothing for granted in getting up our position, and consequently had no unprotected points. The examiners were flushed and smiling; the more they asked, the more their smiling grew. But what pleased us most was the fact that Mr. Middleton was gratified. He himself had not counted upon such readiness.

Finally, the president turned to our professor: "Mr. Middleton, this won't do. We came here to see what these boys are lacking in, and here they've been parading their knowledge for over an hour. Can't you give us a hint as to where we can catch them?"

"I would suggest, Father, that you try them in off-hand theme-work, modelling your sentences on the passages they have seen in the text-book. I should state, in justice to the class, however, that they did not expect such an ordeal."

The president was pleased with the suggestion. "Well, I'll make compensation," he said. "Now, my dear boys, I promise to give a fine book to any one among you who holds out the longest in giving correct off-hand translations. Your own teacher shall be the referee; when any one makes a blunder Mr. Middleton will rule him out."

Playfair, Percy, Quip, Whyte, Ruthers, Richards, and myself were delighted with this plan. None of us had anticipated any such line of questions in the specimen, but, as a matter of private work, we had repeatedly gone over our author, each one of us in turn building sentences in English, and the rest of us rendering them into Latin similar in form and idiom to the style of Sallust. Others of the class, however, were dismayed, not that they were unfit, but that they lacked confidence.

Very soon the examiners were hard at us, pelting us with simple sentences. One by one we were asked in turn, and at the end of three rounds not a boy had been remanded to his seat. But now the examiners, following the initiative of the president, fell to introducing "kinks" into their sentences, whereupon the slaughter commenced. Ten of our twenty-five classmates succumbed at the first fierce onset, leaving fifteen of us in the field. At the next charge seven bit the dust. There were now left Percy, Tom, Quip, Whyte, Ruthers, Richards, and myself.

To the surprise and dismay of all, Percy tripped on an irregular verb and, blushing violently, went to his seat. We all pitied him, for there wasn't a better scholar or a more popular boy in the class. Whyte, Ruthers, and Richards soon followed him, and there remained Tom, Harry Quip, and myself.

But, as the saying is, we had gained our second wind. Tom was cool, as usual, and steadied us.

"Stick up for the honor of the class, boys," he whispered. "Don't answer till you're sure."

We followed the advice, and held our positions for half an hour longer. The clock struck eleven.

"Two hours are up," said the president. "The contest is at an end. My dear students, permit me to congratulate you on the very extraordinary speci-

men you have given. If it were possible to be
above the standard of the class—and that is an open
question into which I shall not enter—I would say
that in Latin you certainly are above the standard.
Your contest in off-hand theme-work is one in which
boys of higher classes seldom come off with honor.
Certainly, if you can write Latin as you speak it,
there's a chance, and a good chance too, for you to
carry off the collegiate honors. For the rest of the
day you are free."

That last sentence was the sort of peroration we
wanted; on this occasion, indeed, it was a surprise.

Of course, we had a pleasant time of it. Percy
made light of his failure. "I thought a little too
much of my Latin," he said. "It humbled me very
much to fail. But to my mind nothing succeeds
like failure." And then Percy congratulated the
three of us with a genuineness which showed us all
how defeat may be turned into victory.

CHAPTER XII.

IN WHICH IS BEGUN A FULL AND TRUE ACCOUNT OF A GREAT BASEBALL GAME.

THE sun rose in an almost cloudless sky upon
the long-looked-for day. I was wondering, as
I proceeded to First Academic, how our boys would
bend themselves to their work. Mr. Middleton received us with a smile more genial, if possible, than
usual.

"Now, boys," he said, after concluding prayers,
"will you be good enough to promise to pay close
attention?"

"Yes, sir! Yes, sir!" exclaimed many.

"We'll do our level best, Mr. Middleton," said honest Tom, "but-a—you know how it is, don't you, Mr. Middleton?"

Tom was almost pathetic in putting this question.

"So," continued Mr. Middleton, "you Blue Clippers are going to put on your baseball uniforms for the first time this afternoon?"

"Yes, sir!" cried six voices as one.

"And you're going to be beaten hands down."

"No, sir!" was the unanimous answer.

"Well, for the next two hours I want you to put baseball.out of your heads."

Mr. Middleton paused, while the boys gazed at one another ruefully.

"Because," continued the professor gravely, "I am going to read you a story."

I wish we could have been instantaneously photographed at that moment. Such a collection of genial smiles and sparkling eyes never yet, I dare say, fell under the camera.

"Isn't he a teacher and a half!" exclaimed Tom, *sotto-voce.*

The "teacher and a half" had selected a tale of absorbing interest, and he made what would have been the dullest and longest hours of the year a little jaunt through fairyland.

At three o'clock we Blue Clippers emerged from our dressing-room in all the splendor of our new uniforms. We came out in single file, with Frank Burdock in full uniform as mascot and scorer at our head. The other boys of the small yard, who had been awaiting our appearance with no little impatience, gave us a rousing cheer; and, indeed, I think that we presented a brave appearance. With the exception of myself all of us were strongly built. Percy was a trifle slim, but his erect carriage and grace of motion made him the most striking figure of us all.

Our costume was simple: white flannel shirts, with "Blue Clippers" lettered across the breast, white knee-breeches, blue stockings, blue belt, and a white cap.

Tom was proud of our appearance.

"You look like poems," he observed. "It's a pity," he added, turning to me, "that we didn't pad your legs a little bit, but you'll pass muster, any-how. You stand straight now, and have left your wretched stoop behind with your delicate health. Forward, boys!"

And forward we marched, escorted by a noisy fol-lowing, to the baseball field. The large boys were already at practice; but at a quarter past three sharp they resigned the grounds in our favor. We tossed the ball from hand to hand for a few minutes, then retired to the players' bench, satisfied that we could move about in our uniforms with all the ease that we had anticipated.

Tom won the toss, and at 3:30 Willie Tipp set himself to beating a tin can as an indication that we were to take the field.

On taking my place in the pitcher's box, I felt not a little nervous. I was to make my *début* be-fore the whole college. A large boy named Foley was the umpire. As he stationed himself behind the batter and threw me the ball, his call of "Game —Play" was lost in the shout of enthusiasm that arose from the spectators.

In order that the reader may follow the game, I append the batting order and the positions of the contending sides:

BLUE CLIPPERS.

Wynn, l. f.	Quip, c. f.
Keenan, s. s.	Richards, 3d base.
Donnel, 2d base.	Ruthers, r. f.
Playfair, c.	Whyte, 1st base.

Dee, p.

JUNIORS.

Cleary, 3d base.	Fox, c. f.
O'Connor, s. s.	Earle, c.
Drew, 2d base.	Hudson, r. f.
O'Malley, l. f.	Poulin, p.

Bennett, 1st base.

First Inning.—Cleary tapped his bat against the home plate and stood awaiting my pleasure.

"One ball," called the umpire as my first pitched ball curved away from the plate.

"One strike," as the second curved in and over it.

I next gave him a drop. He caught it close to the handle of his bat and sent it bounding to me. I fumbled the ball, then got a firm hold of it, and sent it in my excitement at least three feet over the first baseman's head. Donnel was behind him, however, and caught it. Cleary was safe on first.

Following Tom's directions, I gave O'Connor a number of incurves, and to the joy of the small boys he retired on three strikes.

Drew sent the third ball I pitched him bounding slowly toward short field. Keenan came in at a dead run, picked it up neatly, and threw it to Donnel at second, who in turn threw it to first base.

"Out at second—safe on first," cried Foley.

I threw an outcurve to O'Malley, and it seemed to be just the sort of a ball he wanted. There was a sharp crack as his bat met the ball, which went sailing far over Quip's head into centre field, and before it could be returned to the diamond O'Malley was standing breathless on second, while Drew, amid the plaudits of the large boys, had scored. Fox retired his side by striking out.

When Percy Wynn stepped up to the home plate there arose a loud cheer. With the possible exception of Tom, he was now the most popular boy in the college.

"Everybody likes Percy," said Ryan, who happened to be near me. "You should have seen him last year when he first came! He could hardly do anything except look pretty. One would never have imagined that he'd turn out a ball-player. He hasn't lost any of his gracefulness, but he's gained strength, and physical courage, and endurance. Some of the boys sneered at him a great deal when he first came; now they're shouting for him at the top of their voices."

Percy contrived to bother the pitcher a good deal. One ball and one strike were called; then two balls. Percy struck at the next and made a foul. The umpire finally gave him his base on balls.

There was a buzz of enthusiasm.

"What's the excitement?" I asked Ryan.

"The boys expect some great base-running from him. They know he's a good runner, and they know, too, that Playfair would not put so weak a batter first on his list without a good reason."

And now Tom stood near first base and began coaching.

"Double A, double E," he exclaimed.

Percy took more ground, while the hum of voices died away.

"Double E A E," continued Tom.

The pitcher stood in consternation, staring blankly at the coacher.

"Triple A," shouted our captain.

With the exception of the Blue Clippers, every one was nonplussed. This was the first time within the experience of any one that coaching had been done by algebraic formulas.

With the expression of consternation still on his face the pitcher sent in the ball for Keenan, and as he raised his arm Percy dashed down the base line with a speed and grace seldom found together. Earle sent the ball on a low line-throw to Drew.

"He's out, sure," said Ryan.

But just as he spoke Percy "took a header," and ploughed his way, as well as I could judge, full fifteen feet. He reached the base after the ball, it is true, but before Drew could touch him with it.

There was a great shout.

"That's the best slide I've seen here yet!" said Ryan, with enthusiasm. "It takes lots of nerve and dash even to try it. Who'd think that Percy Wynn would be the first to show us how to make the 'Comiskey' slide?"

Keenan drove the next ball bounding to the second baseman and was called out at first, while Percy took third. Donnel, after two strikes had been cailed on him, sent the ball on a fly back of the shortstop. Percy stood on his base till it fell into O'Connor's hands, then dashed for home.

"You 've got to slide!" bawled Tom as O'Connor threw the ball in to the catcher.

And Percy did slide. As before, the ball had beaten him, but the catcher did not succeed in touching him, and Percy emerged from a cloud of dust safe on home. Tom now came to the bat, and was easily retired on a foul tip. Score, 1 to 1.

Second Inning.—I had more confidence in myself as I resumed my place in the pitcher's box. Following Tom's signs, I easily struck out Earle and Hudson; Poulin sent a hot grounder to Richards, who fumbled it, and immediately after, as I pitched my first ball to Bennett, made a run for second. Tom threw the ball straight and low to Donnel in the nick of time to touch the runner. This was the first whitewash of the game.

For our side, Harry Quip died on a grounder to the third baseman, Richards struck out, and Ruthers was retired on a fly back of third base. Score at the end of second inning, 1 to 1.

Third Inning.—Bennett took the first ball I offered him, and as it rose into the air far, far out in left field, there was a groan from the small boys and a shout from the seniors. But almost at once every noise was hushed, and three hundred pairs of straining eyes were bent upon our left fielder, who was racing at full speed in the direction of the falling ball.

Will he get his hands on it? Hardly; and even if he does he will scarcely hold it. Now he is almost under it. Look! he takes a bound into the air—and then there's such roaring and shouting and clapping of hands as only a phenomenal play by a general favorite can excite.

"That's what I call fielding," said the second

6

baseman of the large yard. "That Wynn started for the ball before most of us knew it had been struck. He's got the trick of judging a ball as soon as it's touched. I've seldom seen as pretty a running catch."

For two or three minutes it was impossible to go on with the game. The spectators bawled themselves hoarse. At length, in obedience to a sign from Tom, Percy touched his cap, whereupon the noise died away and play was resumed.

Cleary drove a liner over the shortstop's head and took first. O'Connor followed up the good work by popping a fly into short right field, where no one could get it; Cleary made third on it. Things were now in a critical state. O'Connor started for second as soon as I pitched. Tom threw the ball with all his force to Donnel, and as he did so the runner on third made for home. Donnel lost no time; his catching the ball and touching the runner seemed to be simultaneous; then he returned it quickly to Tom in time to touch Cleary out on home, thus accomplishing a neat double play.

Our first baseman struck out and, I am sorry to say, I followed his example. But there was a revival of enthusiasm as Percy stepped up to the home plate. Percy was not a strong batter by any means, so he made it a study to get his base by other than hard hitting. He bunted the third ball pitched to him and easily beat it to first. He made second on a passed ball; then on the next ball pitched ran for third. It was an exhilarating sight to see his slender, supple figure bounding over the turf—his mouth firmly closed, his eyes dilated with excitement, and his fair, almost feminine face flushed with exertion. For the third time Percy accomplished his great "slide;" the ball and he were on third together.

"How's that, umpire?" called Cleary.

"Out on third."

Tom Playfair, who had been hopping about in an ecstasy on the coaching-line, turned about at these words, and, with his hands plunged deep in his pockets and his shoulders raised to his ears, walked off and disappeared behind the backstop. I concluded that he had gone aside to suppress his anger, for Tom had a high temper. But the crowd was not so heroic. Roars of indignation poured upon the startled umpire's ears.

"Get off the earth, Mr. Umpire," cried Ryan. His request was taken up by the crowd, and petition after petition was proffered him to the same effect.

The most furious spectator was Frank Burdock. With an expression on his face which would have rendered him invaluable to an artist as a model for a Gorgon, he advanced upon the alarmed umpire, and dancing with rage, hissed out:

"Get a pair of goggles, you mud-eyed freak," and then this small bundle of nerves, I am sorry to say, sputtered out an expression or two which astonished and dismayed his friend Percy. To put it plainly, he used some rather profane language. It should be remembered that poor little Frank's early training had not been of the best; and in this moment of supreme excitement old habits asserted themselves.

Without stopping for breath, Frank went on:

"Come on, you ugly mud-eye. I'll thrash you and your whole family."

This was too much for the umpire. He could

stand the shouts of the college, but quailed beneath the blazing rage of the very diminutive boy.

"Safe on third," he cried.

This proved to be the prelude to another storm of indignation, in the midst of which Percy removed his furious little friend and brought him, with a few kind yet reproving words, to a sense of his scandalous behavior. Drew, the captain of the Juniors, was now giving the umpire a piece of his mind, and Tom, who, with an impassive face, had returned from behind the backstop, sided with Drew. And indeed it was a plain case. Evidently the umpire had been intimidated into changing his decision. Tom poured oil upon the troubled waters; at his word our men stepped into the field, and we began the

Fourth Inning.—Drew led off with a bounder to our third baseman and was thrown out. O'Malley, after knocking several fouls, was sent to first base on balls. Fox hit safely into centre. There were now two men on bases and but one out. A slow grounder from Earle's bat to Whyte, on which he went out, advanced the two runners to second and third. Hudson came to the bat, receiving an ovation from the large boys, with whom he was popular. Tom gave me a sign for a low ball, but unfortunately I pitched a high one; and Hudson sent it on a line over our first baseman's head. Both runners made for home. O'Malley came in safely, and Fox was fairly on his way from third base, when an accurate throw from Quip nipped him at the plate. One run.

Keenan for our side knocked an easy grounder to Cleary, who fumbled it. He stole second and made third on Donnel's out at first. Tom knocked a fly into left field. O'Malley caught it, and recovered himself in time to throw out Keenan in his attempt to make home on the catch. Score: Juniors, 2; Blue Clippers, 1.

Fifth Inning.—This was an exciting inning. Poulin reached first on a line hit over second. He was advanced one bag by Bennett's out at first. Cleary knocked an ugly grounder to Donnel, who succeeded in throwing him out without allowing Poulin to take third. O'Connor knocked me a slow grounder; before I had picked it up Poulin was close upon third base. I made a motion to throw it to third, but seeing that it was too late I lost my head, and before I could recover myself O'Connor stood safe on first. Drew was determined to make a hit. The third ball I delivered him seemed to be what he wanted, for he sent it on a low line into short left field. Percy was playing deep, but he made for the ball at once. On he came at a dead run, making what seemed to be a hopeless endeavor to get his hands on the ball before it touched the ground.

"He's got it!" "No, he hasn't!" "He can't get it!" Such were the exclamations as Percy literally threw himself at the ball, lost his balance, and made a complete somersault; and loud were the huzzas as he rose, holding the ball in his hand.

"Batter out!" called the umpire.

"We won't stand it," bawled Bennett. "He didn't catch it on the fly; he got it on the short bound."

Drew, the captain, then came in and helped to make life unpleasant for the umpire. As for the crowd, their sympathies were with Percy. Many thought that he had made a neat pick-up, but the play was so brilliant that they were glad the umpire had blundered.

The squabbling went on. Every man on our nine came in save Percy and Quip and myself.

"I say, Percy," whispered Quip, "you didn't catch that ball on the fly."

"I know it," answered Percy; "I didn't say I did, either."

"Wouldn't it be honest to go and tell the umpire?" It was hard to say whether Quip were serious or not in putting this question.

"It would be absurd," answered Percy. "In baseball such candor would be sentimental. I read a story in *St. Nicholas* once, where a boy sacrificed a game by announcing to the umpire that he had caught a ball on the short bound when the umpire had already decided it a fly catch. The story was very nice; but the writer didn't understand the duties of umpire and player rightly. The umpire is to judge our plays by what he sees. If he decides me out when I'm not, through his own bad judgment, I grin and bear it; in the same way, if he declares me to have put a man out when I haven't, I grin the more."

Percy was good, but he was not goody-goody. His conduct in baseball, you will notice, was consistent. When the umpire blundered into calling him out at third, he submitted gracefully. When the umpire again blundered in giving him a put-out where he had made none, he said nothing. In both cases he acted on the principle that the umpire was umpire, and that so long as he stood within the letter and principle of baseball rules, his decisions could not be reversed. Despite the protests of the Juniors, the umpire clung to his decision and ordered them into the field.

We of the Blues did nothing at the bat. Quip and Richards struck out and Ruthers was retired easily at first.

But as this chapter is getting very long, and as the most exciting part of the game is yet to come, I think the reader will be willing to begin the sixth inning in

CHAPTER XIII.

IN WHICH IS CONTINUED AND CONCLUDED THE ACCOUNT OF OUR GREAT GAME OF BASEBALL, AND IN WHICH I MAKE AN AGREEMENT WITH TOM PLAYFAIR WHICH, AS THE READER WILL FIND OUT LATER, HAS AN IM-PORTANT BEARING UPON THIS STORY.

O'MALLEY got just such another ball as I had presented him in the first inning. It went further this time, and had it not been for Percy's promptness in chasing and fielding the ball he would have made a home run on it. As it was, O'Malley reached third, amid the jubilations of his fellow-players. Fox knocked a swift liner straight at Joe Whyte, who caught it and sent it to third to catch O'Malley. Unfortunately the ball came on an ugly short bound to Richards and went rolling beyond him. Before he could recover it O'Malley had scored. Earle followed with a single base hit, stole second and remained there, as both Hudson and Poulin struck out.

Our half of the inning was mercilessly short. Whyte batted a fly to Fox in centre field which Fox caught with ease. I struck out. Percy knocked a grounder and was decided out at first on a very close decision.

Seventh Inning.—Keenan accepted Bennett's chance for an assist on an easy grounder. Cleary, who as a sure hitter had a reputation to sustain, missed the ball three times and retired to explain how it all happened. O'Connor's long fly to left was caught by Percy.

For our side Keenan opened with a model base hit and made second, while Donnel took first on a difficult fly, which O'Connor muffed. Two men on base and no one out. We began to recover from the despondency into which we had been thrown by the events of the last inning. Tom went to the bat evidently determined to bring in a run. He struck at the first ball pitched him. There was a sharp click.

"Foul—out," ruled the umpire.

As a matter of fact Tom had not touched the ball. Earle had snapped his fingers as Tom struck, and the umpire had been deceived. For a few moments Tom was too angry to speak; he bit his lip, and at length recovering himself, called for time. Few if any of the spectators had detected the vile trick. I myself, as I happened to be standing near the home plate at the time, had noticed it.

"It's too bad," I said.

"Yes; but what can't be cured must be endured, I reckon. All the same I'll see it doesn't happen again."

Drew, to whom Tom had motioned, was now at our side.

"Look here, Dan," said Tom. "That was no foul. Your catcher has worked a rowdyish trick, and we don't want it to happen again."

Drew became as angry as Tom. He was an honest boy and somewhat impetuous.

"I'll put that fellow in the field and bring in O'Malley," he said.

"No, no, Dan," objected Tom. "I guess Earle acted according to his lights. But his lights are mighty poor. It's no use making a show of him; but if you'd just tell him that we'll stop playing if he does anything like that again, I think he'll take the hint."

"Leave that to me," said Drew.

He took Earle aside and said a few short, sharp words in a low tone to that worthy which brought the blood to his cheeks; then he returned to his position, leaving the audience to wonder what had been the occasion of the delay. Earle realized that it was to Tom's generosity he owed it that he had not been publicly exposed. The lesson proved a good one. Ever after he treated Tom with unaffected respect.

Nothing daunted, Tom set about coaching with more ardor than ever.

You never heard such a storm of vowels as he set flying through the air. Double A and triple E, and I, O, U, and what-not came volleying forth; and when Harry Quip hit safely he advanced his letters to squares and cubes till he drove the opposing pitcher desperate.

In vain did Drew call time to protest against this singular system of coaching. Our captain had prepared himself against such objections; and showed clearly that he was allowed any language which was not improper or indecent; "and what," he added, "can be more innocent, more impersonal than the sweet, full, harmonious vowels of our dear mother-tongue?" So Tom was permitted to continue his algebraic coaching. But for all his cries of double A square and triple E cube, Richards and Ruthers struck out, leaving three men on base, and the score 3 to 1 in our disfavor.

Eighth Inning.—I think I was now at my best. In no wise tired, the nervous dread consequent upon facing large boys for the first time had now completely disappeared; and I was determined to give my opponents the sort of balls that they did *not* want. Tom had taught me to study each batter. In playing among ourselves I had followed his advice, and had soon learned to measure any batsman's strong and weak points after facing him twice or thrice.

Drew struck out, O'Malley knocked me a baby fly, which, for a wonder, I held, and Fox followed Drew's example.

Joe Whyte succeeded in hitting the ball, but it was awaiting him at first. I, too, sent the ball rolling feebly toward short field. The shortstop, pressed for time, threw wide to first base. Percy again became a runner by securing his base on balls, thus advancing me to second; whereupon Tom began to invoke all the vowels of the English language in such wise that the pitcher lost his head and gave Keenan his base on a balk. So there we stood, three men on base, when Donnel stepped up to the home plate. Honest John was so nervous that he reached at every ball pitched him, and retired disconsolate, with three strikes charged against him.

Tom received a rousing cheer as he stepped up to the bat. He was calm and collected, and the small

yard was preparing to cheer as one man. He gave
the third ball pitched him a vicious blow, and a
great cry of exultation arose as it shot out into left
field. But O'Malley had been playing far out for
Tom's particular benefit, and with a side run succeeded in pulling down what might have been a
three-bagger. Score, 3 to 1 in favor of the
Juniors.

Ninth Inning.—Assured that the game was now in
their hands, the big boys batted carelessly and went
out in one-two-three order.

Quip opened for us with a single; and the large
boys' nine began to look very serious when Quip
stole second and came in on Richards' safe hit into
right field. One run at last; another, and there
would be a tie. Richards, following Harry's example, dashed for second on the first ball pitched.
Earle threw wild and he was safe. Ruthers knocked
a bounder to the second baseman and was retired,
while Richards was advanced to third.

The excitement was now intense. But one man
out, but one run needed, Richards on third—but,
alas! all our weak batters to follow.

"Hit it, Joe Whyte—knock the cover off!" implored Tom. "Keep cool and you'll do it, sure."

And Joe did keep cool. He knocked a long fly
into right field. It was prettily caught, but before
Hudson could recover himself Richards was half-
way home and the game was a tie. I came to the
bat and concluded the innings by striking out.
Score, 3 to 3. As every boy reader knows, a tenth
inning became necessary to decide the game.

Tenth Inning.—Bennett sent a very hot grounder
directly over second base. In what manner Keenan

ever got there no one could see; but, all the same,
he chased the ball on a dead run, and with his right
hand alone secured it far out in short centre field.
How he recovered himself so quickly and, as the
runner was within a few feet of the base, sent it like
a shot to Whyte, and how Whyte held the ball,
thrown as it had been, is something that the boys
discussed for days afterward.   It was a wonderful
play on the part of both; and the game had to be
stopped till George and Joe had each doffed his cap
to the applauding spectators.   Just as play was about
to be resumed there came another interruption.
Joe discovered that a blood-blister had formed upon
his right-hand index-finger, which had not been
accustomed to handle such vicious throws as George's
had been.   Tom, after some deliberation, ordered
Quip and Whyte to exchange positions, and play was
at length resumed.   Cleary struck out and O'Connor was retired by Tom on a foul fly.

Now was our chance.   We built strong hopes
upon this, the tenth inning of the game; for Percy
was to be first at the bat.   He advanced to the
home plate, blushing yet cool.   And well might he
blush!   There was a tumult of applause; the large
boys clapped their hands vigorously; the smaller
screamed and threw their hats in air and many of '
them actually danced.   Little Frank, who since his
outburst had been scoring with bent and averted
head to conceal his tears of mortification, now
jumped to his feet and offered to bet fifty dollars
that Percy would make a run.   He had no takers.

I think Percy's turn at the bat must have occupied
full five minutes.   It was a game of strategy between
him and Poulin; both were most deliberate.   The

pitcher, who now knew Percy's weakness at the bat, was determined to force him to hit the ball, while Percy was equally determined not to be forced.

"One ball," called the umpire.

"One strike "—Percy had made no attempt to hit at the ball—"Foul."

"Two balls."

"Foul."

"Three balls."

The next came straight over the plate, but as low as Percy's knee. He stood like a statue as it passed him.

"Two strikes."

The next ball promised to be decisive. There was a funereal silence. Frank Burdock's face was aglow with excitement. Many a boy held his breath to await the issue.

The ball at length came straight toward the plate and low. Percy was obliged to take it.

"Foul," called the umpire.

The suspense was renewed.

The next ball came wide.

"Four balls—take your base."

"Now, Keenan, keep it up, old boy," cried Tom.

At the first ball pitched Percy dashed for second. How he flew over the ground! Before he had cleared half the distance a hundred spectators, transported with enthusiasm, came crowding about the diamond. As before, Percy accomplished his great slide. He simply tore up the ground, and in his course sent Drew, who was still waiting for the ball, head over heels. Percy had clearly beaten the ball. But when he picked himself up after his collision with Drew he looked quite pale, although he wore his usual pleasant smile.   Our captain noticed the change.

When the spectators had been cleared off the field and the pitcher had taken his place in the box, Tom called for time.

"Frank," he whispered to Burdock, "get a glass of water and bring it to Percy while I'm talking."

Then for five minutes or more did Tom wrangle with the umpire and Drew about the legality of Poulin's method of pitching.   He quoted the rules, brought out "Spalding's Base Ball Guide," and fought every point he could raise to the bitter end. He gained nothing he claimed, but everything he wanted, namely, time for Percy to recover from the bad shaking-up he had suffered.

Of course Tom might have called time and given as the reason that the base-runner had injured himself.   But, with his rare tact, he divined at once that Percy, ordinarily cool and self-contained, would be put to the blush by the universal sympathy and suffer more keenly from the pity and attention of the spectators than from his physical injuries.   So Tom contrived to get his friend the needed rest, and by his flow of words to centre the attention of every one upon himself.   After an interval of some three or four minutes Tom gave in gracefully, and the game was continued.

Evidently Percy had fully recovered.   He worried the pitcher not a little by the manner in which he played up and down between the positions of second base and shortstop.   He had thrown off his cap, and with his head bent slightly forward and his eyes fixed upon the ball, he moved up and down with a suppleness, a lightning quickness to recover,

to turn one way or the other, that delighted the on-
lookers as much as it annoyed the Juniors. Every
time that Poulin sent in the ball Percy ran almost
half-way down to third; nor, despite the throwing
to base of both catcher and pitcher, could he be
caught napping.

On the seventh ball pitched, Percy ran down as
usual to the shortstop's position, keeping his eye
fixed steadily on the ball. He saw that it was over
the base and judged that George would strike at
it. So instead of stopping midway he threw back
his head, and looking straight before him, made for
third. He heard the sharp crack of contact between
bat and ball, and still running at full speed, turned
to see it bound into the hands of the shortstop, who
made a feint at throwing it to third, but seeing
that Percy was already within a yard of the base,
wheeled about and, with deliberate and careful aim,
threw it swiftly to first.

The umpire's "Batter out" was drowned by the
voice of Drew.

"Home! home!" he shouted, in an excess of excitement.

"Home! home!" roared out nearly the whole infield and outfield.

For Percy, with a boldness not looked for by any
one, had not stopped at third. Turning sharply—a
turn, by the way, that no other boy in the college
but Keenan could make—toward home, so as to
lose scarcely a foot, he was more than half-way in
before the first baseman fairly realized what had
happened.

Bennett saw that the game was in his hands, and
with full swing of the arm he sent it straight and

low toward the catcher, who, with his mask and cap thrown off, was standing upon the home plate, his eyes straining and his hands stretched imploringly toward the first baseman.   But even as the ball left Bennett's hand Percy, now about twenty-five feet from the home plate, sprang forward and took the most heroic of all his heroic headers.

Ball and Percy! which first? The ball certainly was in the catcher's hand while Percy was still shooting along the ground, but before Earle could turn and touch him Percy, with an effort quick and violent, had stretched out his right hand and touched the home plate.   The game was ours.

Tom was beside Percy at once and raised him gently yet quickly from the earth.   Our brave base-stealer was ghastly pale and staggered even as Tom bore him up.

"I—I—think I'll sit down, Tom."

Tom hurried him over to a seat, then 'ran for Mr. Middleton.

"Please, sir, Percy's hurt a little.   The boys will all want to shake hands with him, and he'll faint or something, and I know he hates to pose."

The prefect clapped his hands, and standing in front of Percy so as to keep the boys from seeing him, waited till all had passed into the blue grass save Frank Burdock, Tom, and myself.

"How do you feel, Percy?" asked Tom sympathetically.

"It's nothing—just a little scratch, I think," answered Percy.

He had become very languid. His hair was tossed upon his forehead, and as he leaned with his head resting against the back of the players' bench and his lips quivering, we all perceived that he was suffering keenly,

"Look!" said Tom; "he's bleeding."

The blood we saw was just beginning to enpurple his knickerbockers a little above the knee.

At the sight of the blood Frank was terrified beyond measure.

"Oh," he blubbered, "that's all on account of my swearing. Won't you forgive me, Percy?"

The sufferer smiled, and with the smile something of his color returned.

"I'm not going to die, Frank. In fact, I feel all right again; you see, I cut myself when I ran against Drew's spiked shoes at second. I didn't intend to slide again, but when I saw that chance to take a run, I thought I'd do it even if I had to be carried home. But that last slide did hurt."

"It was great," said Tom enthusiastically. "I've read about it, but it's the first time I've seen a boy make from second to home on an out at first."

"Now," said Percy, rising, "I think we can start for home."

"You can lean on my arm," said Tom.

"No, you don't,"exclaimed Frank, with a touch of his former passion. "I'll attend to Percy myself."

Tom, of course, submitted.

"Now, Harry," said Tom, turning to me with his most taking air, "how about spending a night in your uncle's house this summer? Will you do it?"

"Yes," I answered at once.

7

CHAPTER XIV.

IN WHICH FRANK BURDOCK CATCHES A BIG FISH AND MAKES THE ACQUAINTANCE OF THE HAUGHTY OWNER OF A YACHT.

A MONG the happy days at St. Maure's that still remain "beautiful pictures on memory's wall," I count the ensuing months of May and June the happiest. May, the month of Mary; June, the month of the Sacred Heart. The glory of heaven seemed to us students to blend with the earthly splendors of spring; and though, boylike, we all looked forward eagerly to the days of vacation, still, by the sweet practices associated with May and June our natural eagerness was, as it were, spiritualized.

And so when vacation came we were prepared for it; prepared to enjoy it, because we had done our duty in the matter of studies; prepared to enjoy it rightly, because we had entered fully into the beautiful St. Maure's traditions with regard to these latter months.

My father, who came on to attend the annual college commencement, could scarcely believe his eyes on seeing me.

He had counted on finding me healthier and stronger, but, as he said, " I was not prepared, Harry, to find you an athlete."

Tom, Frank Burdock, and Percy made it a point to win their way into my father's favor. They were, at my instance, engaged in a conspiracy; and I am glad to say that they succeeded. These three intriguers won over my father at a single sitting; in such wise that when they asked the burning question he said:

"Harry couldn't be in better company: of course he may go!"

Then we exchanged such hand-shakings, such glances of joy; and though we took our leave of dear old St. Maure's with sadness, yet the prospects before us and their discussion soon made us the happiest of lads on the eastward-bound train.

.   .   .   .

It is mid-summer. From the western rim of the heavens, where lies enisled an archipelago of glorified clouds, the sun is giving his parting benediction to the upper world. In the zenith are here and there gauzy bits of fleece, reflecting faintly, yet so beautifully, something of that blaze of glory which the sun has conferred upon their western sisters, and moving onward like stately, dainty ships of the air over an infinite sea of blue. Lightly they hover over the tranquil, well-nigh slumbering waters of a romantic lake upon whose quivering bosom the changing colors of the heavens reproduce themselves in mirrored splendor.

But the scene is not without its human element. At anchor within a hundred feet of a steep, grassy bank four lads are seated in a fishing-boat. Each is holding a rod in his hands, but their hearts seem to be otherwhere. The vision of the glory above has caught their eyes, and as they silently follow its changing splendors, they forget the object of their expedition and allow their lines to lie neglected in the water.

"Isn't it beautiful?" murmured Tom.

"Yes," answered Percy softly, "the beautiful day is most beautiful in its death."

"I hope we'll be that way, too," resumed Tom.

"There's a quotation from Shakespeare that would fit in here, but somehow I can't work it in; I'm no good at quotations."

"Something to the effect that nothing should so become us in our life as our leaving it?" suggested Percy.

"You have spoken," answered Tom.

"If Paradise were any prettier than this scene," I observed after a pause, "what a wonderful place it must have been!"

"I wish Eve had minded her business," put in Frank Burdock tartly. "She ought to have kept her husband steady instead of putting crazy notions into his head. If I marry at all," continued this wise-acre, "I'll find a girl who will keep me from getting cranky."

The twilight meanwhile had come upon us, and the clouds in the west were softening in color; a classic beauty succeeded the oriental splendor which had melted away with the sunset. A golden sheen now palpitated over the face of the waters, while a light breeze springing up carried its perfumed message of nightfall from shore to shore.

"I wish I were Joshua," said Frank.

"Yes? What would you do?" inquired Percy.

"I'd make the sun stand still. I ain't no poet like you, Percy, but I guess I know when I like a thing—and I like this."

Further observations were cut short by the sudden click of Frank's reel as his line spun out into the water. He put his hand to the reel, gave his line a jerk, and—

"I've got him!" he cried. "Just get the landing-net ready."

"Play him carefully; don't get excited," said Tom.

"Who's excited?" asked Frank disdainfully. "I'm not afraid of the biggest pike in the biggest lake in Wisconsin—ow!"

This exclamation was provoked by the apparition of a very large fish, which sprang furiously out of the water in a vigorous struggle to rid itself of Frank's hook.

So startled was our little friend that the reel escaped from his nerveless clasp, and away went his line, paying out at a rate which indicated that his fish was in a hurry.

"You've a curious way of showing your bravery," said Tom, as Frank recovered his control of the reel. "Here, you'd better let me play your fish for you."

"You just sit right where you are," snapped Frank. "When I want your help I'll ask you."

Anxious to redeem himself, Frank now gave evidence of coolness and skill. In and out he played his fish until he had brought it, thoroughly exhausted, to the side of the boat, where it was easily landed by Percy.

"A wall-eyed pike and a beauty!" exclaimed Tom.

"It's at least six pounds," added Percy.

"You don't say!" piped Frank. "Oh, won't I write a letter to papa to-night. It beats any catch he ever made—and I'll tell him so, too."

Having killed our fish at once—a merciful act, by the way—we applied ourselves in earnest to our ~~~. Fresh minnows were supplied, skilful casts made, and each of us set about reeling in our lines and throwing them again, according to the current style of fishing which obtained among the approved anglers of the region. Suddenly our attention was distracted by a novel sight, a new element added to the serene loveliness of early twilight. Around an arm of land to the east of us there swept, in all the poetry of bird-like motion, a milky-sailed yacht, gorgeous in flags and fresh bright colors, upon whose deck stood a boy and a girl. The girl was at the tiller—a pretty little child of seven or eight, every detail of her dress betokening the taste and care of a refined home; her unbound golden hair falling free upon her white dress, and reaching almost to her sash of blue, tossed alternately by her quick movement and the gentle breeze. Beside her was a boy of fourteen or fifteen. One glance at him would satisfy an observer that in gazing upon the boy he was gazing upon the owner of the yacht, and a proud owner he was! His pretty face—somewhat feminine; so feminine, in fact, that it could not with propriety be styled handsome—was marred by a disdainful curve in the lines of his mouth and play of his lips, while his head thrown haughtily back added to his appearance of superciliousness.

The little miss smiled at us in all the sweet ingenuousness of childhood. With that mobility of feature which is one of the pretty graces of innocent years, she conveyed in unspoken words the message of her own happiness in the possession of the graceful yacht and radiated her joy upon us. Not so the real owner of the *Aurora*. His brows took an additional turn upward as he surveyed us from the dizzy heights of his ownership.

"You'd think that fellow had a lien on the lake,"

whispered Tom. "But hold! his haughty majesty
is about to address us."

"Any luck, boys?" inquired his "haughty majesty."

"Look!" exclaimed Frank vivaciously, holding up
his fish.

"Ah!" exclaimed his "haughty majesty," passing
his hand through his hair with an æsthetic flourish,
whereupon Tom ducked under the seats to conceal
his laughter.

"Ah! what a be-you-ti-ful fish!" cried the girl.
"Did you catch it, sir?"

"Yes, ma'am, all myself," answered Frank, much
flattered by the "sir," and putting into the "ma'am"
an intonation which sent Percy's head down on a
level with Tom's.

"I—ah—I'll buy your fish if you have no objec-
tion," continued his "haughty majesty."

Percy was now under the seats. Frank was about
to return an indignant answer, when Tom came to
the rescue.

"Me lud," he said, with much impressiveness and
doffing his cap as he spoke, "your ludship's humble
servants have not put up their stall for selling fish
yet, but, me lud, when we have, me lud, we will be
most gratified to secure your ludship's distinguished
custom."

From the bottom of the boat came a silvery laugh
which there was no resisting; I broke into a roar,
and even serious Frank chuckled audibly.

As for the little girl, she joined in our merriment
through sheer sympathy, whereupon his "ludship,"
who had changed color, turned his wrath upon
her.

"Rose, if you don't behave yourself you'll never come out in my boat again."

Rose blanched at the very thought. "Me lud," having thus disposed of her, cast a cold eye upon us.

"You're vulgar," he observed.

"Yes, me. lud," answered Tom, respectfully but cheerfully; "for mark you, me lud, we have not had the pleasure, me lud"—here Tom gave a bow which would have won the approval of Chesterfield—"of your very improving company."

"I'm no lord."

"Oh, I beg pardon, most noble dook," continued Tom gravely. "We really——"

"Now, you stop!" cried the "duke" plaintively.

"Tom, Tom," giggled Percy, "do give his grace an opportunity to say a word or two."

His grace was not slow to speak.

"I'm neither a lord nor a duke," he said gravely, as though he expected to excite surprise by the announcement. "Are you boys staying around here?"

"Your majesty, we are. Yonder 'neath the shade of a wide-spreading beech tree—it isn't a beech tree, but that is no matter," Tom added in parentheses—"stands a little cabin, wherein, your majesty, we have, so to speak, pitched our tents. Furthermore, your majesty, be it known to you that our board is paid by our parents with regularity, for though not poor they are honest."

The yacht-owner was in two minds about us. It would have pleased him to swear at us, but he feared to compromise himself. The fact of the matter was that he doubted whether Tom was serious or in fun. So he adopted a middle course by scowling.

"Are you fellows Catholics?"

"And it please your majesty, we are."

"I don't like Catholics."

"Most of us can't help it, your royal highness; we were born that way. But it isn't catching."

The yacht was now almost beyond speaking distance, and as Tom uttered his last remark the haughty owner, yielding to his rage, stamped his foot, shook his fist at us, and spat into the water.

As if to make amends for her brother's conduct, Rose waved her handkerchief and sent a silvery "good-evening, sirs," across the dividing water; and as the boat went beyond the limit of distinct vision we saw, or rather inferred, that his lordship was scolding her bitterly, for the little lady bent her head and covered her face with her hands.

"Boys," said Tom, "I'm sorry I chaffed that fellow, not on his account, but on account of that little girl. The fact that he was her brother should have made me behave myself. Do you know, I've often wished of late that God had given me a sister. I'm sure I'd be a better fellow. She would have toned down a good deal of my roughness."

Percy laughed.

"If there's any roughness about you, Tom, I wouldn't have it removed for the world. But I think what you say is reasonable and natural. A good sister is a treasure to a boy—I ought to know, for I've just the best lot of sisters in the world. I don't know what I'd have been were it not for them."

"I have heard it said," I remarked, "that there is no earthly love so pure and elevating as the love between brother and sister."

"I believe it's quite true," said Tom. "It's a great pity—isn't it?—that many big brothers make

it a point to tease their sisters, to be cross and ugly
toward them. Lots of 'em are good boys, too;
but what is good in them is kept for outsiders, and
their poor sisters get the benefit of what's worst in
them. There, now, take his 'ludship,' for instance:
he doesn't seem to care two cents for the happiness
of his little sister as long as there's the least question of his own dignity. It's a pity!"

"By the way," said Percy, "that puts me in mind
of a strange remark Mr. Middleton made to me one
day. He was speaking of a boy who had been at
St. Maure's the year before you came, Tom. The
boy, it seems, was but a little over eleven years old,
extremely polite, amiable, and obliging. He gained
favor with all and soon rose high in the esteem of
the entire faculty. Yet before the spring had come
he was dismissed from the college as a student too
dangerous to be allowed to associate with the small
boys. Now, here's the remark of Mr. Middleton's
that surprised me. 'For weeks and weeks,' he
said, 'I could discover nothing out of the way in
this boy. But one day, in speaking with me, he
said that he was the only child, that he had no
brother or sister, and that he hoped he never would.
From that day I felt that there was a serious flaw in
his character.'"

"Why did he feel that?" asked Frank.

"I suppose," answered Percy, "because it showed
a cold, unloving disposition."

"One of that kind," observed Tom, "could become
cruel and wicked. I've heard it said that all the
great saints were very warm-hearted."

Our philosophical discussion was brought to an
end by an injudicious fish which made a bold at-

tempt to run away with Percy's fishing outfit. Percy was an expert, and with little trouble succeeded in landing a lusty four-pound black bass. Before he had it fairly in the boat Tom was playing another, and before Tom could announce the fact Frank was reeling in vigorously.

As for myself, I was kept busy with the landing-net. Tom's fish proved to be a three-pound pickerel, Frank's a two-pound black bass.

"Hurrah!" cried Frank; "we've about twenty pounds of fish. I guess we can start for home. It will be dark in half an hour—I'll row."

"No, no, Frank," said Tom, pulling up the anchor. "Why, just look at the sky; I shouldn't be surprised if we had to face a storm. Sometimes there are ugly squalls on this lake."

"That's an awful cloud in the west," cried Percy; "it's growing larger and blacker. Yes, we'd better hurry or we'll get a drenching."

There were two sets of oars in the boat. The seat in the middle was sufficiently wide to allow two rowers to sit together: on this seat were Tom and I, each using one oar. Percy was behind us wielding the other pair, while Frank, with the tiller-ropes in his hand, sat in the stern. We had not taken a dozen strokes when a low, dull, distant sound came upon our ears.

"It's coming, boys. The wind is storming among the trees on the western bank," I cried.

"Listen to it," whispered Frank in tones of awe. Momentarily the sound grew in volume; gradually, above the deep groaning and fluttering, arose a shrill shrieking like the exaggerated sounds of a million fifes. Onward swept the wind in its tyrannous strength till the waters on the further shore crisped, then reared their myriad white crests and broke into angry waves. Before these water monsters had made their appearance our vigorous united strokes had brought us almost midway between the eastern and western shores of the lake.

"It's no use, boys," cried Tom. "We may possibly make it, but our safest plan will be to turn back. What's the matter, Frank?"

For Frank, who was facing us, had become deadly pale and jumped to his feet.

"Look! look!" he gasped. "The yacht!"

CHAPTER XV.

IN WHICH THIS STORY IS WITHIN A TITTLE OF LOSING ITS CHIEF CHARACTERS AND THUS COMING TO AN ABRUPT END.

THE three of us turned our heads and saw a sight which chilled our blood. The *Aurora*, which, after skirting the eastern and southern shore, had taken its course northward along the western bank, was now with full sails set bearing the brunt of raging water and roaring wind. Yielding to the blast, she had bowed down, down, till her sails seemed to be lapped by the rising waters. Clinging to a mast with one hand, the boy was vainly endeavoring with the other to take in sail, while the girl, her hair streaming in the wind, was stretching toward us one little hand in pitiful entreaty. We scarce had time to take in this awful picture when a fresh veil of darkness seemed to drop down from sky to earth, and the storm burst upon us with full fury.

"To your oars!" shouted Tom. "We've got to save them; pull, boys, with all your might!"

Very fortunately for us, none of us was a novice in the art of managing a boat. Every day during the past few weeks we had practised at pulling together. And so, compressing our lips, we held an even stroke against wind and wave.

"Keep her toward the yacht, Frank," continued Tom; "don't let her turn one inch either way."

"All right, Tom. I'm not afraid; you can rely on me," answered our steersman, his eyes fixed upon the *Aurora.* "Pull, boys, pull hard. Oh, they're going to capsize!"

"Don't turn round," whispered Tom to Percy and myself. "We must depend on Frank for our course. Pull steadily."

"God help them!" cried Frank, despite his excitement keeping a firm hold on the tiller-ropes; "their boat is capsized!"

As Frank spoke there arose above the howling of the blast and the beating of the waters a piercing, heart-rending scream. That scream seemed to stop my heart-beats, and I noticed that Tom and Percy were beaded with sweat—the sweat of agony. Frank was sobbing.

"For God's sake, Frank," cried Tom hoarsely, "are the boy and girl in sight?"

"The girl has gone under; and there the boy goes. Oh, hurry, hurry!" And Frank was on the point of jumping up.

"Don't move," cried Tom. "If you do there's no chance of saving them. Quick! are they under water yet?"

"The girl is up again—poor girl! Ah! she's

caught hold of the yacht and is hanging on to it. There's the boy now. Good! he is clinging to it, too."

The three of us breathed a sigh of relief.

"If you hurry up," cried Frank, "we'll be able to save them; the yacht is drifting this way."

But pull as we might, it was slow work.

Still more disheartening was the gathering gloom. Shadows seemed to be literally rushing down upon us. Our every stroke was tallied by a deeper tinge of black, as though some genie of the air was scattering huge handfuls of darkness on our course.

"Don't be afraid," called Frank to us. "I can see the boat quite plainly. I've good eyes, and I'll keep that boat in sight till we get to it."

As he spoke there was a dazzling flash of lightning that broke zig-zag across the heavens, followed by a loud clap of thunder.

"Don't forget to pray," exclaimed Tom.

Then followed a series of blinding flashes and rumbling detonations, which, added to the fury of the wind and the lashing of the waves, impressed us, I am sure, with a sense of God's might and our own powerlessness. In the midst of it all we bent sturdily to our oars in silence, each of us praying for help and guidance from above.

Desperate as was the plight of brother and sister, our condition was not without its dangers. Thus far, it is true, we had shipped but little water; but we knew not at what moment the hungry white-caps would hurl themselves raging into our boat. We plainly saw, moreover, that should we succeed in reaching the yacht any attempt at rescue would be fraught with peril. In consideration of all this, the four of us, I think, had a great deal to say to Almighty God. None, indeed, was overmastered by fright. What boy not an absolute coward could yield to fear under so cool and plucky a leader as Tom Playfair? Presence of mind never deserted him, and such was his influence over all that in critical moments he infallibly became leader by common consent.

An exclamation from Frank roused us from our commune with God.

"Listen!" he exclaimed.

Again the clear, piercing cry of the little child shivered through the air.

"The little girl is giving out, I think," said Frank, in answer to our questioning glances. "Her hold has slipped—ah! she's got it again. Keep on rowing; we'll be beside them in a minute."

As Frank ceased speaking there came a lull in the storm. In the western sky appeared an opening in the clouds, through which streamed something of the twilight beauty, and the veil of darkness, routed by the western light, lifted as suddenly as it had fallen. The thunder grew fainter and fainter, the breeze died almost completely away, and nothing but the lashing waves gave evidence of the fierce elemental conflict so lately raging about us.

During this lull we heard what, should we live into the centuries, none of us shall ever forget. That sweet, clear, delicate voice came throbbing over the waters in trembling melody:

> "Jesus, Saviour of my soul,
> Let me to Thy bosom fly,
> While the angry waters roll
> And the tempest still is nigh."

And there the tiny voice, which had paused between some of the notes as though the child had lost her breath, quivered into silence.

Another voice was heard:

"Help! help! save us!"

It was the boy's.

As if in rude answer to his call the wind, which had changed a point northward, came howling through the trees and across the waters; and then our hearts were thrilled with pity as we heard the child cry: "Jesus, dear Jesus, save us; save us, dear Jesus."

"Pull, boys!" screamed Frank. "The girl has given out; she's lost her hold and is sinking. You're very near.   A few strokes more."

"Percy," cried Tom, "it all depends on you now. You've got to go it alone. Haul in your oar, Harry," and Tom almost tore his shoes from his feet.

"There," cried Frank, "she's come to the top."

Tom had arisen and caught sight of the child, some forty feet from our boat, just as her face disappeared.

"Keep the boat steady."   And as Tom spoke he plunged into the waters.   He emerged in a few seconds, quite near the spot where the child had gone down.

"Behind you! behind you, Tom!" rang out Percy's voice as the girl again came to the surface.

Tom turned at once, and in the nick of time; the child was just sinking.   He made for her with rapid stroke, failed of reaching her, and followed her down into the waters.

In a moment he arose with the child supported on

his left arm, and, by Divine Providence, within a few feet of our boat.

"Bring the stern round to Tom," cried Percy. Obedient to the tiller the boat turned broadside to the wind, shipping in the movement the crest of a large wave. Not without difficulty Tom caught hold of the back support above the rudder blade, and assisted by Frank lifted the half-drowned child into the boat.

We were now quite near the yacht. The boy, his cheeks blanched with terror, his eyes protruding from their sockets, was shouting to us inarticulately. Before Tom could succeed in climbing into our boat, the storm suddenly came down upon us with new force. The wind was blinding and sent the waves lashing against our frail boat. Panic-stricken, the boy, throwing out his arms toward us, plunged into the water and at once disappeared.

I foresaw what would probably happen and immediately threw off my coat and shoes. I was a poor swimmer; but as Percy was needed at the oars and Frank at the tiller, I saw that if worst came to worst it would be my duty to venture after my friend. No sooner had the strange boy thus madly tempted his own destruction than Tom, releasing his hold on the boat, made for the spot where he had gone under.

What ensued when the stranger came to the surface is horrible to relate. Tom reached out, caught him by the arm, and was about to assist him to our boat, when with a wild cry the drowning boy threw his arms about his would-be rescuer in a death-clasp. Tom struggled vainly to free himself; both went down together.

8

How long they were under water it is impossible
for me to estimate. Upon their disappearing I
whispered Percy not to leave the oars till I had
made an effort to assist Tom; and disposing myself
to spring to their rescue, watched eagerly for their
coming to the surface.

Oh, what a weary, long, long time it was while
we prayed for their reappearance! At length, still
clasped in the other's arms, Tom came to view. Even
in the moment, and as I plunged into the water, my
eyes took in a sight which stands out as vividly before my imagination now as it presented itself to
me in the awful gloom of that storm-beaten twilight.

The boy, in first grasping Tom, had clasped him
from behind. The violence of that clasp was revealed now. Tom's face was deathly pale. He
had managed to twist about somewhat in the grasp
of the drowning boy so as to face him partially, and
as he rose I perceived that he had freed his right
hand. But oh, the countenance of the stranger! All
the hideousness of terror had invested it; all the
mad rage of despair. There was nothing human in
the expression. It was a hideous nightmare of
God's image.

All this I noticed in one glance as I threw myself
from the boat. What happened while I was under
water was afterward supplied me by Percy.

As they came to the surface, Percy said, Tom, who
had freed one hand, made an effort to free the
other. With a wild, animal-like, muffled voice, the
drowning lad caught at the free arm, and would have
held it had not Tom jerked it from his grasp and
without delay struck him thrice with all his force

about the temple. With the third stroke both again disappeared.

When I came up there was no sight of either.

"Wait!" called Percy. "Watch!"

Just then Tom emerged, paler than before, bearing in his arms a senseless form.

"Quick! catch hold!" he gasped.

I took the body from the panting hero, and striking out for our boat, which Percy had contrived to bring within a few feet of us, reached the stern in safety. Violent as the storm had grown during the last few minutes, it was just then, I think, that it reached its height; just then, when the grave question of studying how to get three persons into a frail boat presented itself. Tom, swimming at my side—how feeble his stroke!—seemed to be equally perplexed with me for some solution.

"If the boat founders," he labored forth gaspingly in my ear, "all of you make for the yacht."

Then, with a painful effort, he said aloud: "Percy and Frank, pull off your shoes."

In a twinkling Frank was in his stocking-feet, but before Percy could lay aside his oars a huge wave swept into the boat, which at once began to sink.

"I'll take care of the little girl," cried Percy. "Look out for yourself, Frank. To the yacht, every one!"

Fortunately we had kept near the ill-fated sail-boat; fortunately for Tom, who was spent with his efforts in the double rescue; fortunately for Percy, who, incumbered with his shoes, had the child in charge; fortunately, in particular, for myself, who had the greatest difficulty, being a poor swimmer, in sustaining the senseless form of the brother. Indeed, it would have gone hard with me had not Frank bravely come to my assistance. The two of us made but little progress, and we were fain to be content with holding the boy's face above water till the yacht drifted upon us. In a trice we had fastened him securely to the boat.

"Well!" said Percy, when we were all clinging beside each other, "thank God we're safe; and if we can only hold out the wind will bring us to shore within an hour."

I had now an opportunity of observing Tom, and my heart sank at the sight. His polo shirt was in shreds, little else but the sleeves remaining upon him. His undershirt was torn just below the armpits, and there, standing out on each side upon his naked flesh, was the bleeding print of five fingernails. The poor boy's face was ghastly, his mouth was open, and he was panting from the terrible ordeal. Next him was little Frank, who of all the party was the least spent. Beside Frank lay the strange boy tied to the lower part of the mast. Lastly, between myself and Frank, was Percy, still holding the little girl.

"Give me the girl, Percy," said Frank, "while you take off your shoes."

The transfer was made; and Percy was soon prepared for more ventures in the water if need should arise.

I had been watching Tom's face for some moments. How wan it was growing! Presently his eyes closed.

"Percy! Percy!" I cried, "look to Tom!"

With a single stroke Percy was beside him, and just as he was slipping away caught him by the arm.

"Poor boy! He's fainted!" said Percy. "Oh!" he continued in dismay, on seeing the cruel finger-prints on Tom's bosom, "what sufferings he must have borne in saving *that senseless boy!*"

I think this was the first time that I ever heard Percy speak harshly of any one.

Tom very shortly opened his eyes and found him-self pillowed on Percy's hand, with those kindly blue eyes bent down in grief upon his pallid face. He smiled feebly.

"Never say die," he whispered. "Where are we?"

"Drifting right in to shore, Tom; patience—don't move; I can hold you without the least trouble."

"Well," whispered Tom feebly, "if anything hap-pens you look out for yourselves· don't mind me. I'm not afraid to die. And be sure to save that little girl, whatever happens. What was that prayer of hers? Oh, yes—'Jesus, dear Jesus; save us, dear Jesus.' Wasn't it beautiful? I guess that God intended us to be His instruments in hearing that prayer. Oh! I'm awful tired!"

The slow, labored tones in which Tom spoke brought tears to my eyes. Tired!

"Yes," he went on, "it was the hardest, bitterest thing of my life, but I had to do it. I'd as soon have drowned—sooner, in fact—but then both of us would have drowned. O Percy! it seemed so cruel, yet I had to do it."

"What, Tom?"

"Did you see his frightened face, his eyes starting with terror? Oh! what a look of agony came over his face when I got loose from him. Yet I had to do it; I had to draw my arm back and beat, beat, beat that face, which was piteous enough to move a

heart of stone, till the poor boy was senseless. Oh!
it was terrible!"

Tom closed his eyes and shuddered.

Tom spoke again; but I shall not record his
words as they were uttered. He was no longer master of himself, and in those moments of delirium he
laid bare unconsciously some of the beautiful secrets
that were between himself and his Maker. His mind
was wandering—but into what beautiful fields! We
had loved Tom for his gay, happy ways, his abid-
ing cheerfulness, his noble qualities; but now, as we
listened to him taken thus off his guard, we discovered that the life within was as saintly as the life
without was noble.

Again and again he spoke of his struggle in the
water.

How reverently we listened to these confessions
of a noble soul! It brought vividly to our minds the
frightful mental struggle that had gone hand in
hand with that physical struggle for life. It un-
veiled to us in sharp outline Tom's indomitable
will-power, his ability to grasp a situation and to
employ the boldest means on the instant.

"What was that song she sang, Percy?" he inquired, opening his eyes a few moments later.

> " 'Jesus, Saviour of my soul,
>   Let me to Thy bosom fly.' "

"That's what I say," said Tom wearily. "Oh, if
I could go there now; I'm so tired."

What infinite pathos in his simple words, "I'm
so tired."

"Keep up your courage, dear Tom," said Percy.
"We're drifting on splendidly. The lake is getting
calmer, and I think there's little danger."

"Percy, if anything happens, you'll pray for me, and you too, Frank, and you too, Harry?"

"O Tom," sobbed Percy, "don't! I'll hold you till we drown together, if necessary."

"No, you won't," returned Tom, something of his old energy and strong voice returning; "there's work for you. Now, remember, you're not to drown on my account. And, Percy, give my love to all the fellows, and if I've treated any of 'em wrong, say that I've asked their forgiveness. Pray for me."

And Tom fainted again.

Now followed a period of sadness akin to despair. The boy whom each of us had, I think, loved with a love deeper, stronger, tenderer than a brother's love, seemed to be dying in our sight; dying exposed, unprotected; dying surrounded by friends who could not stretch forth a hand to help him, yet dying as he had lived. How changed he was from the gay, happy, sunny lad he had been but a short time before. His dark eyes were curtained, we feared, forever. His hair had fallen over his face —jet-black hair that fitted so well over the nut-brown face of old, that looked so startling upon the ghastly pallor which had now usurped the hue of health.

Little Frank broke into a cry of grief.

"Let me get near," he said. "I'll hold him, Percy, and you see what you can do. We *won't* let him die. We *won't.*"

And Frank, with a few strokes, had put himself beside the two.

"Tom, Tom," he called, and placed his hand upon the unresponsive face.

Percy had succeeded in pulling off his over-shirt,

and tearing it into strips deftly, tenderly bandaged the bleeding breast.

"Now," he exclaimed, "perhaps that will stop the flow of blood."

"His face is as cold as ice," said Frank.

"Yes; but I think the color is returning," answered Percy.

And while the two made shift to rub Tom's face we all fell into a silence that lasted until the real darkness of night had come down upon the scene. It was a half-hour of awful suspense. What a relief it was to us when the little girl, now under my care, opened her eyes.

"Oh! where am I?" she exclaimed.

"Just as safe as though you were on shore," I answered. "Your brother is safe, too; Frank and I tied him fast to that mast there."

"You needn't be afraid, ma'am," added Frank. "Jesus heard your prayer."

Suddenly there was a cry of joy from Percy.

"He's coming to, boys! His face is quite warm. I can't see well enough to be sure, but I think his color is returning."

"Is it the brave boy that jumped into the water after me?" inquired the little maid.

I was about to make answer, when Percy held up his finger.

"Hallo, little girl!"

This from Tom. His voice was stronger, more natural, and there was in it a slight touch of his merry self.

"Hallo, sir," replied the child.

"How de do, little girl?"

"How de do, sir?"

"What's your name, little girl?"

"Rose Scarborough, sir."

"Much obliged, little girl—how's your brother?"

"Gordon? I don't know, sir."

"Gordon is all right, Rose," I interposed; "he's hurt a little bit, but he'll be able to talk and laugh before long."

"Are you fond of bathing, little girl?" continued Tom.

"No, sir; not very."

"Well, try to get used to it, anyhow, little girl. I say, Percy, I feel quite fresh again, though a while ago I thought I was going to die. I never felt so worn out in all my life. But now you needn't support me any longer; I can take care of myself. Suppose you help out Gordon."

These words gave us fresh heart. Percy turned his attention to Gordon. Overhead the stars came out one by one and the wind softened into a light breeze.

"Hallo!" cried Percy suddenly. "Just look at the lights along shore."

We turned our eyes to the east. The fulness of the night had come on, and it was impossible to make out anything save a number of torches which were moving up and down the border of the lake, and suggested to our imaginations men running along shore in anxious search, and, saddest of all, weeping mothers.

"Oh, poor mamma!" exclaimed Percy. "How alarmed she must be."

"And my mamma, too," added Rose. "She told Gordon not to sail without having papa or one of the hired men along to manage the yacht. This afternoon Gordon sent the hired man up to our house, and just as soon as he got out of sight Gordon started off.   He said he knew all about sailing a boat.   He didn't do what he was told."

"Well, we can try to let them know we're alive," said Tom.   "Suppose we all shout.   You must join in the chorus, too, little girl.   You've an excellent scream for your age."

"What shall we say?" I inquired.

"Well, we'd better reassure them.   If we shout for help they'll be frightened.   'Hip—hip—hurrah' is the right thing.   They'll think that everything is lovely, and come out in a boat to meet us just the same as though we were bawling for help. Do you hear, little girl?   You're to shout 'hip—hip —hurrah,' just the same as though you were a little boy, which you aren't, you know."

"I understand," said Rose.

"Now, boys—ready?" continued Tom.   "One, two, three."

"Hip—hip—hurrah!"

"Again."

"Hip—hip—hurrah!"

We paused anxiously and glanced shoreward.

"Do you think they heard us?" inquired Rose.

"I'm afraid not, little girl, and it's a shame, too, because little girls shouldn't be out late at night."

"But I never did it before," answered Rose seriously.

"Well, don't do it again."

"Pshaw! they weren't listening, or they might have heard," growled Frank.

"There's something in what you say, Frank," said Tom.   "Now if we had a torpedo, or a pistol, or a cannon, or even a Gatling gun——"

"Oh!" cried Percy; "I've got it!"

"You don't mean to say you're running a Gatling gun along——"

Tom was interrupted by a piercing whistle which rang out startlingly upon the air. It came from the whistle which Mr. Middleton, on a memorable occasion, had given to Percy, and which Percy had ever since jealously guarded.

"Eureka!" cried Tom. "That fetches it. Now, quick—all together, little girl."

"Hip—hip—hurrah!"

We waited eagerly; the crack of a rifle came from the shore, followed by the fuller report of a shotgun, which, ere its echoes died away, was succeeded by a sky-rocket shooting up into the sky and leaving a golden furrow in its track.

"Thank God!" Percy exclaimed.

"That settles it, little girl," added Tom buoyantly. "Your mamma's happy now; she heard you yelling out 'hip—hip—hurrah,' and she thinks you're having a good time."

"But I'm not," said Rose ingenuously. "I'm awful wet, and it's dark, and everything's wrong, and I wish I was home in bed."

"So do I, little girl; I don't approve of late hours and I'm tired. 'Sh! Can't you hear the stroke of oars? They're coming."

Hereupon Gordon made his presence known.

"Ow—oh—ouch—help!"

"Dry up!" roared Tom, "or we'll pitch you into the lake; you'll scare everybody with your howlings. Take a lesson from your sister."

"Where am I?" he gasped in a lower tone.

"This side the middle of the lake," said Frank Burdock.

"Keep cool," I whispered; "there's a boat coming and we'll be safe in two minutes. See the lights drawing near—they're coming straight toward us." And as I spoke I freed Gordon from the mast.

"Oh, I hope they'll hurry up and save me," cried Gordon.

"Give 'em another cheer," cried Tom.

We gave it with a will.

An answering cheer came gratefully upon our ears.

"Boat ahoy!" cried one of the rescuing party.

"Ahoy!" answered Percy.

"Are you all safe?"

"We are," returned Percy.

"Yes, but we're awful damp," added Tom.

"Are the Scarborough children there?" came another voice.

"Yes, papa!" screamed Rose.

"That's right, little girl; always tell the truth," said Tom parenthetically.

"I do, sir."

Here Gordon made his presence felt.

"Papa! papa!" he bellowed, "I'm drowning."

"No, he isn't," cried Percy, and to my astonishment he went on, addressing himself to Master Gordon, "and it's my impression, sir, that you never will drown."

Even Percy was disgusted.

"Oh, if we only had an ice-chest," groaned Tom.

"Why—why—what for?' sputtered Gordon.

"We'd keep you cool in it."

A minute later we were all safe within a large boat, and Percy presently was in the arms of his

mother, and—but the hugging, and crying, and
kissing are too much for my pen, and this chapter
has been in all reason long enough.

CHAPTER XVI.

*IN WHICH WE ATTEND A RECEPTION AND SPEND A NIGHT
AT MR. SCARBOROUGH'S VILLA.*

MR. SCARBOROUGH was a wealthy gentleman
of English birth, who, shortly after attaining
his majority, had chosen America for his home.
During the preceding summer he had taken a week's
outing at "our lake," as we boys called it, and was
so charmed with the beautiful surroundings that
he purchased several acres fronting upon the eastern
shore, and commenced at once the erection of a villa,
which he had formally occupied on the very day we
made the acquaintance of his illustrious son and
heir.

Mr. Scarborough had no words to express his
gratitude toward our party, and his admiration cost
us many a blush. Had we not been resolute in re-
fusing, he would have encumbered us with an ex-
travagance of gifts. Even as it was, he succeeded
in forcing upon each of us a complete summer outfit.
Vainly did he endeavor to induce Tom to accept
the *Aurora*, and it was only owing to our friend's
eloquent expostulations that the yacht's name was
not changed to *Tom Playfair*.

But his attentions did not end here.

A few days after our perilous adventure we received a warm invitation to take supper and spend
a night at his villa.

"I won't go," protested Tom; "I don't care about being lionized."

But for all that Tom did go, as did the rest of us. Imagine Tom's consternation when he discovered on our arrival that the supper was a formal party.

As we walked into the sitting-room, and found ourselves in the presence of a bevy of girls and boys, Tom caught me by the arm.

"Pshaw!" he grumbled. "Harry, honestly, I wish that this was your uncle's haunted house, and that everybody in this room was a ghost. I can stand ghosts, I believe, but a party makes me tired!"

Nevertheless, Tom endured the ordeal of introduction with great apparent composure. Frank Burdock was quite at his ease, while Percy was clearly the most finished little gentleman in the room. Doubtless Tom would have been somewhat embarrassed had it not been for Rose. She sprang forward eagerly to greet him.

"Hallo, little girl."

"Hallo, Mr. Playfair."

"Don't, or I'll faint, little girl."

"Don't what, Mr. Playfair?"

"Don't Mr. Playfair me, or I'll quit the country. I'm Tom, little girl."

I contrived to save myself from attention by keeping beside Percy. He was the bright particular star of the evening, and my little light was but a reflection from him. He was soon surrounded by a listening group, who drank in eagerly his account of our adventure on the lake. Aside from his ease and fluency of speech, I could not but admire the delicacy with which he kept himself in the background, and the judgment he displayed in the omission of such details as would have reflected on the courage of Gordon.

In due course a young lady seated herself at the piano, and running her fingers lightly over the keys by way of prelude—young ladies always run their fingers lightly over the keys, if I may credit the books—composed herself for a quadrille.

I wondered whether Tom would dance, and fixed my eyes on that young gentleman, who was still busy chaffing the little girl.

"Mr. Playfair," said Mr. Scarborough, advancing upon Tom with a smiling young miss leaning upon his arm. "Permit me to introduce you to my niece, Miss Carruthers."

Tom arose and bowed. He didn't murmur, "Happy to see you," or any such formula, for conscientious reasons.

"A dance," continued Mr. Scarborough, "is about to begin. Could you take Miss Carruthers for a partner, Mr. Playfair?"

"I'm afraid," answered Tom, "that I must decline. That storm came rather hard on me, and I'm still very stiff and sore. In fact, I feel like a cripple. However, Miss Carruthers, you'll lose nothing; if I'm particularly awkward at anything, it's dancing. You see, we're rather a solemn crowd in our family. I have no sisters at home to help me in the matter of parlor amusements; and I suppose that's the reason I have given most of my time to such solemn tasks as kite-flying and baseball."

"You don't look so awfully solemn," said Miss Carruthers, with a puzzled expression. She was not quite sure whether Tom was speaking seriously or not.

"Miss Carruthers," came the grave reply, "I labor to conceal my feelings."

There was no mistaking the twinkle in Tom's eyes this time, and the young miss, breaking into a giggle, was led away by Mr. Scarborough in quest of a more eligible partner.

Tom and myself were content to be "wall-flowers." We were not surprised on seeing Percy taking his place in the quadrille, but we certainly were when our infantine Frank, with Rose for his partner, went through all the figures and changes with the ease of a society young man.

Mr. Scarborough was a kindly old gentleman. Stealing up to us while the little figures were moving lightly about in what to me were literally the mazes of the dance, he invited us for a stroll about the premises.

"I'm half sorry," he said pleasantly, "that I got up this party. You boys are real boys, and would have enjoyed a game of baseball, or a foot-race, or any athletic amusement much better."

"We're all right, sir," said Tom. "I like to see people enjoying themselves. And I'm too stiff for games at present."

As we turned the corner of the house, we came upon Gordon, rather unexpectedly, it would seem; for he dropped a lighted cigarette and crushed it under his foot.

"There you are—smoking again," said the father sternly.

"Perhaps he was only holding it for another fellow," volunteered Tom, consciously or unconsciously borrowing his little witticism.

"I had to do something," growled Gordon. "You

know I can't dance; and I can't bear to see everybody enjoying things and myself out in the cold."

"Well, what can you do?" queried Mr. Scarborough.

"I can play billiards or cards," said the young
man plaintively.

"Euchre?" asked Tom.

"What! can you play euchre?" exclaimed Gordon,
in no little astonishment.

"Yes; anything wonderful in that?"

"Why, I thought you were pious. Pious people,
especially pious boys, don't play cards."

"Nonsense!" said Tom sturdily. "God doesn't
insist on our giving up amusements, unless they run
up against the commandments. Your idea of piety
is a long face. No wonder some boys give up trying to be good."

"Hear! hear!" said Mr. Scarborough; "you've
hit the nail on the head. Gordon has been associat-
ing with a queer lot of boys at the military academy
he attended last year. They consider piety to con-
sist in avoidance of laughter, of cards, baseball,
smoking, chewing—in fact, they mix up innocent
amusement and decorum with right and wrong, and
then go off and violate all the standards of piety
they have set up. They don't see how a boy can
be good and happy at the same time; consequently
they go to extremes and throw aside religion almost entirely."

Gordon took advantage of his father's monologue
to give us a familiar wink, and to put his finger to
his nose, signals which we ignored.

"Come on, let's play," he broke in. "There's
just four of us."

9

"All right," said Tom.

We were soon engaged at our "impious" amusement in an upper room. To do Gordon justice, he was quite skilful in handling the cards. He and I were partners, and succeeded in winning three games hand-running from Tom and Mr. Scarborough. The fourth game opened with Tom's deal. When Tom turned up the nine of hearts, it was noticeable that there were but *three* cards under the trump.

"Hallo!" I said, "some of the cards are missing."

"Yes," said Gordon, "some fellow's cheating."

"Suppose we turn our cards faces up on the table," said Tom affably.

"Just what I thought, the four Jacks are gone," snarled Gordon, looking over the faces of the cards.

"If only two had been missing," continued Tom suavely, "they might not have been noticed. The fact is," said Tom, with increasing serenity, as he picked the knave of hearts and the knave of diamonds out of his lap, "I've got two here, and I'll trouble you, Gordon, to hand over the other two."

"You're a cheat!" howled Gordon. "Keep away," he suddenly added in terror—"don't strike me. I take it back." For Tom had risen; not, however, to strike this ingenuous young gentleman. Taking him firmly by the collar, Tom assisted him from his chair.

"There!" said Tom sternly, pointing to the missing knaves upon which Gordon had been sitting. "I've been waiting for five deals to spot the man who's been keeping two cards out of the pack regularly. Pious boys don't play that kind of game."

"God bless me!" exclaimed Mr. Scarborough, "I didn't know my son was a blackleg."

Gordon was soon brought to his knees. He apologized, and promised to play above-board.

"I'll play fair, Playfair," he unconsciously punned; and it struck me for the first time that there was an accidental fitness in Tom's name. I may add that we won few games for the ensuing two hours.

After the game, there was a late supper, then— joyful announcement—bed.

As quite a number of young people were to stay over-night, the house was somewhat crowded in regard to accommodations. Feeling tired, I was shown to my room some little time before the others. The sleeping apartment had two double beds. One was alloted to Percy, Tom, and myself: the other, I was informed, to Gordon and two of his intimate friends from the military academy. There was, moreover, a cot for Frank.

Some minutes after I had gone to bed, my friends and Gordon with the two strangers entered.

The young gentlemen of the military academy at once set about exchanging confidences among themselves, while Tom took off his coat and Percy knelt down beside the bed and began his night prayers.

"Look," said a yellow-faced student of the military academy, as he pointed to the kneeling form.

The three of them engaged in an unmistakable stare of astonishment.

"Yah! the hypocrite," whispered the second stranger distinctly. "I hate hypocrites. Maybe I didn't see him dancing and laughing."

Tom was now staring, but they were too absorbed in Percy to notice this.

The bilious young man from the military academy

here struck his hand upon his thigh, and catching up a valise drew from it a pair of very prettily embroidered slippers. Selecting one, he turned toward Percy, poising the slipper in the air.

"Don't, Eugene, don't," interposed Gordon. (I must do this noble youth the justice of stating that he actually interposed.)   The yellow-faced one lowered his arm.

"Go on," interposed the other.   "I dare you."

Few boys of poor principle can take a "dare." He raised his arm and sent the slipper at Percy's head.

Tom caught it on the fly, walked over to the window, and threw it out into the night.

"That other slipper isn't worth much without its mate," he observed.   "Perhaps you'd like to throw that."

The yellow-faced individual took on a belligerent air, and, I judge, was about to offer to "fight" Tom, when a whispered word from Gordon changed his purpose.   Gordon's words were to this effect: "Look out, he can lick your whole family, you bilious fool."

So the challenge was changed into an apology.

"I only meant it in joke."

"Exactly," answered Tom.   "I understand: your style of joke is to throw slippers at the heads of people who don't want to be disturbed.   The best joke I know of is to throw slippers out of the windows. I do it regularly."

The young man of the coffee-and-cream complexion attempted a smile; while his companions took no pains to conceal their laughter at his expense.

When Percy rose from his knees, Tom turned to the military trio:

"Gentlemen," he began, "I hate to give offence; but I fear I shall have to hurt your feelings the same way as my friend Percy. In the mean time, if there are any little jokes in the way of flying slippers, Percy Wynn will show what a convenience a window is when a fellow wants to get rid of small objects."

And Tom knelt down and prayed with amazing composure.

The military students presently took to talking in a louder key. The tone of conversation, in form, at least, was not vulgar, but the matter was by no means innocent. As they went on, their converse became worse.

Percy was about to make a remonstrance, when Tom arose.

"Gordon," he said, "I'm sorry to say that we forgot to bring any more cotton along."

"I beg your pardon," said Gordon, who was an adept in the conventionalities of conversation, "but I don't exactly take your meaning."

"Well, the fact is," continued Tom, "we've nothing to stuff our ears with. So if you and your very nice friends want to continue that kind of rot, you'll please to go outside. Either do that or talk decently; otherwise, we'll leave this house right now."

Gordon turned to his companions, who were for the nonce thoroughly ashamed.

"I guess he's right, fellows. Let's get to bed."

They took the hint in all meekness; although the bilious-complexioned young gentleman as a parting salute made some confused remarks about milksops, little girls, and so on, till Gordon invited him to close his mouth.

I have reason to think that Master Eugene

changed his opinion the following morning. Mr. Scarborough brought us all upon the lawn, shortly after breakfast, and urged us to get up a game of baseball. On examination, it appeared that there was not a sufficient number to play.

Rose came to our relief.

"O papa, get up races; I want to see Tom and Percy run."

"Just the thing," said Mr. Scarborough, "who'll try a race. I'll give a fine jointed fishing-pole to the winner."

The bilious young man, who was blessed with long legs, stepped forth at once.

"Who'll run against Eugene?" asked Mr. Scarborough, looking around. "I'm afraid you're all too slow for him."

Eugene glanced disdainfully at Tom, Percy, and myself.

"Go on, Tom," whispered Percy.

"My legs are too short for him, and I'm too sore. Percy, if any of us can do it, you can. But you must make it a long run. Make it a question of holding out. I'll fix it. Mr. Scarborough, Percy Wynn will run him."

Eugene smiled, and glanced at the slim form of Percy with contempt that was not even ill-concealed.

"Hurrah for Percy!" put in Frank. "Make it a long race."

"Of course," continued Tom, "a hundred yards or so would be hardly fair, as Percy is younger and smaller. Give him a chance to show how he can hold out."

Mr. Scarborough glanced about him. There was a gravelled path opening from the gate on both sides, and leading up to his house. It formed almost a complete circle.

"Would an eighth of a mile be enough?" he asked.

"Pshaw! that's nothing," said Eugene.

"Very good; we will make it a quarter of a mile—that is, twice around this gravelled road. Now, you'll both start from this hitching post here, and the one who touches it first on his second round is the winner."

As these and other preliminaries were being arranged, Rose, who had stolen over to Tom, was begging him to take part.

"Oh, no, little girl. Percy's a better runner than I."

"Is he, sir? Ah, how I hope he'll win!"

"So do I, little girl."

"I like Percy very much."

"So do I, little girl."

"And there's another boy I like, too, and he's not far off, either." And Miss Rose glanced very archly at Tom.

Tom grinned.

"Much obliged, little girl."

"You're all so nice, and kind, and good; and you're not afraid to lose your lives. Oh! how brave you were, when you came to save me and Gordon!"

Tom should have blushed here and said that he had only done his duty. But he didn't.

"Little girl, when you sang 'Jesus, Saviour of my soul,' I felt perfectly happy out there on that ugly lake."

"Did you?" exclaimed Rose delightedly. "Oh, I meant it every word. Mamma taught me to sing it when I was little—that is, I mean," she added, as Tom broke into a smile, "when I was a baby. I didn't like to drown: but when I thought of Him, it was so nice. I'm not afraid to meet Him." As she gazed up into Tom's face with all the sweet innocence of childhood shining from her lovely eyes, Tom felt a lump rising in his throat.

"That's right, little one," he said, patting her golden hair, "and I hope and pray you never will fear to meet Him."

And the child and Tom turned away, each from the other, with such expressions as we see on the faces of those who have risen from fervent prayer.

The two runners, meantime, were standing on a line, while Mr. Scarborough was counting: "One—two—three—go!"

"God bless me!" ejaculated Mr. Scarborough a moment later, "but that little fellow can run."

"He's not even exerting himself," said Tom. "He's taking it easy; a little too easy, perhaps." For Percy had already in the first hundred yards given his rival a long lead. This lead Eugene continued to lengthen, as they both neared the gate.

"There's *one* quarter of the race over," said Frank anxiously, as Eugene passed the entrance to the drive, "and Percy's away behind."

"At least fifty feet," said Tom. "But look! Percy is putting on more speed. See! he's gaining a little, I think. I'll bet on him yet."

Eugene was now nearing the hitching post; he was breathing somewhat heavily, and the perspiration was rolling down his face. Percy, about forty-five or fifty feet behind him, was fetching his breath quite easily, while his face, just the least bit flushed, was serene and cheerful. Eugene had passed us with-

out moving his head one way or the other. Not so
Percy: as he passed, he turned his smiling face upon
us, bowed and doffed his cap, which he threw at
Tom's feet.

"That means a spurt," said Tom.

And he was quite right. As Percy passed the
post, he put on full speed; and then you should have
heard the "ohs" and "ahs" from the spectators.

With every step he seemed to gain upon his com-
petitor.

"That's the best base-runner at St. Maure's College," said Frank proudly. "And he can run better than that if he wants to, too."

I think Frank was exaggerating in this latter
statement; for Percy was now running at his best.
By the time Eugene had made his third quarter of
the race Percy was but fifteen or twenty feet behind
him.

"I'll bet he'll be up with him inside of one hundred yards," screamed Frank. "I'll put up my head
on it."

The words were scarce out of Frank's mouth when
Eugene stumbled and fell. And weren't we all
proud of Percy and of St. Maure's, when Percy
stopped himself almost at once, then went back some
twenty feet, and awaited patiently for Eugene to
arise and resume his running.

"There's a gentleman for you," ejaculated Mr.
Scarborough; "I consider it an honor to know him."

Percy in his generosity goes further than even we
who knew him so well had counted upon; he stands
still till Eugene had made a start. Then, with a
great spurt, he comes pattering closer and closer
upon his rival. Now they are neck and neck, and

the goal is scarce twenty-five yards from them. On they come, breast to breast, Percy full flushed but composed, Eugene with swollen veins and panting breath. Now Percy breaks away from him: one foot, two——

"Come on, Percy, run away from him," cried Frank.

With another spurt, Percy comes on, graceful and swift—a second later he is at the post with his companion some ten feet behind.

There were more races and other contests of skill, which I omit for the reason that graver matters are coming.

The quiet tenor of school-life is to be broken upon by a certain train of adventures which are so strange and improbable that, in looking back upon them, I sometimes fancy that they are such things as dreams are made of, not realities of life. The shadow cast upon my early years by my uncle's murder had not yet wholly lifted, as I was very shortly to find. The reader will see that the mystery is to give some hope—whether true or false, later events will show —of being solved; and so, leaving the pretty lake, and innocent Rose, and kind Mr. Scarborough, and all the natural beauties of our vacation resort, I invite the reader to a change of scene.

CHAPTER XVII.

IN WHICH TOM AND I SPEND A NIGHT IN THE "HAUNTED HOUSE," AND IN WHICH I MEET WITH AN EXTRAOR- DINARY ADVENTURE.

"YES, Tom, that's Tower Hill Mansion," and I pointed to the gloomy abode which had been my uncle's.

It was the twilight of August 16th. Tom and I were seated in a barouche, hired for the occasion, and rapidly nearing the house whose horrid memories had so important an influence on my life.

"It doesn't look any too cheerful in the gloaming," Tom observed. "What an awful racket those crows are making!" There was a number of these ugly black birds hovering in mid-air, uttering their raucous cries above the house, and very strange and eery they looked in the dying of the day. To my excited imagination they seemed to be incorporate spirits from another world—spirits of bloodshed and robbery and murder, gloating over a mansion conse- crated to their darling rites.

We dismissed the driver at the gate, bidding him return for us at six the next morning.

On reaching the massive, gloomy door I put down my valise, and opening it produced a heavy bunch of keys. They were quite rusty.

"Those keys look worse haunted than the house," observed Tom.

"They haven't been used in years, Tom," and I proceeded to fit the heaviest of the keys in the lock. In inserting it, not without difficulty, I shook the door in its frame. Forthwith there came a series of flapping noises within that sent my heart thumping against my ribs. I drew back with a start and would have fallen down the steps had not Tom caught me.

The noises continued within, and it was on my lips to beg Tom to give up what I considered his romantic idea.

"Cheer up, old boy," said Tom, in his heartiest tones. "Ghosts don't shake themselves in that style. I've got some holy water along; it's a good thing to have in a house whether it's haunted or not, you know, and then we've both got canes. Are you ready to unlock the door?"

"Yes; but I'm a little afraid."

"All right. Just wait till I get a good hold on my cane."

Tom grasped his cane at the lighter end, and raised it in such a position that he could strike at once.

"Now, old boy, make the sign of the cross and open that door."

I crossed myself and turned the key in the lock; whereupon the noises within, which had subsided while we were talking, were again renewed.

"Don't mind the racket, Harry; when you shove the door open, jump aside."

As I sent the door swinging ajar the hinges growled and grated, sounds not entirely dissimilar to the voice of him who had been their owner, while the flapping noises grew louder and quicker. You may be sure that I did not neglect to follow Tom's advice.

Tom, however, moved neither to one side nor the other; but, standing full in the doorway, strained

his eyes in an endeavor to read the secret of the
noises within the dark hall. For some moments he
stood listening intently; then an expression of relief
came upon his features.

"Bats!" he said. "There's been a window or
something left open, and they've taken charge of
the hall. Now get out your lamp and we'll go in,
this side up with care."

We lighted our lamp and entered. I shivered as
I crossed the threshold. The air within had the
uncanny chillness of a deserted house upon it. The
bats fluttered over us and around us, and certainly
did not help to put me at my ease, although Tom
changed not a muscle.

"Let's give the bats a chance," said Tom, in his
usual tone, as he threw the door wide open and
raised the window. Presently he added: "Suppose
we take a look at the library. This is it, isn't it?"

And Tom laid his hand on the door. I remembered it well; and as I entered I almost expected
to see the grim figure of my uncle, seated at his desk,
and peering at me over his spectacles. It was the
same dark room; darker, gloomier, dustier. As we
entered, a rat scudded across the floor into its hole.
There was dust on everything; dust on the straight-
backed chairs, dust on the solemn lines of volumes,
dust upon the floor, which gave our every footfall
a muffled voice, warning us to leave unexplored this
horrid home of dark-brooding silence.

"Let's get out of here," I said faintly.

Tom did not seem to share my impression, for he
gave a very close imitation of a Tom-cat at his best
(for the benefit of the rats, I presume), and, before
leading the way into the hall, traced his name

with his finger upon the dust-covered table.   As we were passing by the door we noticed hanging over it a clock of medium size.   It had stopped at twelve.

"I wonder how long ago that clock stopped?" said Tom.   "And was it midnight or midday?" I asked myself.

"Look at that clock in the hall!" exclaimed Tom, as we made our way out.   "Well, if this doesn't beat the world!   It's stopped at twelve, too."

I felt as though some one had thrown a bucket of ice-water down my back.   The coincidence startled me.   Who of us has not heard the popular superstition to the effect that a clock stops at the moment its owner is murdered?   It came upon me very vividly that my uncle, for all we knew, had met his awful fate at midnight.

I was somewhat relieved, subsequently, by discovering that other clocks in the house had stopped with the register of quite a variety of hours and minutes.   The large hall-clock seemed to have a strange interest for my companion.   He peered into it, examined it on every side, and, as it was over six feet high, procured a chair to examine its top.

"There's dust here half an inch thick," he said, and he brought out his handkerchief and was about to remove the layer, when he changed his purpose.

"This is Aunt Jane's handkerchief, and she's awful particular about her dry-goods."

Instead of dusting the top, therefore, Tom contented himself with inscribing his name with his forefinger on top of the clock.

"Fools' names and fools' faces——" I began.

"Are always seen in public places, but never on

top of clocks," retorted Tom. "So," he continued,
after we had ascended the stairs and were looking
down the gloomy length of the gloomy, long corridor, veiled in the gathering gloom of night, "this
is the floor where you spent the night. Where's
your room? Let's take that in first."

I led him to the end of the corridor, and opened
the door of the corner room. How that fearful
awakening came back to me! My own scream of
agony again rang in my ears. As Tom placed the
lamp on the table I gave a slight cry.

"Look! look! the bed, just as I left it. There's
the coverlet and the sheet thrown back exactly as I
turned them when I awoke and sprang from the bed,
in dismay at finding that Mrs. Raynor had disappeared. Look!" I continued, pointing to a dark
stain on the floor.

"What's that, Harry?"

"The stain of blood! my uncle's blood! and
here's the same black mark upon the pillow-slip."

Even Tom showed signs of emotion. He quickly
mastered it, however, and said: "Let's clear out
of this room; we've seen enough. Now for your
uncle's bedchamber."

We proceeded thither, where, to my relief, there
was no striking sign of the tragedy. The bed was
made, the room clean, saving, of course, the covering of dust upon everything.

"Now," continued Tom, placing the lamp upon
a table, "here's where we're going to pass the
night." At that moment I wondered what madness
had seized me to consent to this foolhardy enterprise.

"If your uncle's ghost," pursued my dauntless

friend serenely, "is allowed to wander at all, he'll be very likely to come in here."

It is easy enough to talk about ghosts in broad daylight, but to discuss the probability of a murdered man's spirit coming or not coming at night, and in the room where the man had been murdered, is an exhibition of daring in a small boy as rare as it is remarkable.

Tom saw dismay upon my face. He laughed and added:

"Well, we've got to keep distracted for awhile, or maybe we'll find out that we've got nerves. Suppose, Harry, we say our beads to begin on; I haven't said mine to-day. I don't know how it is with you, but the beads make me brave every time."

"It's a good idea," I answered.

Together we recited the five decades and concluded with the litany of Loretto.

"Now," said Tom, looking at his watch, "it's in order to take lunch."

And Tom opened the valise and placed upon a table a flask of cider, sandwiches, cakes, fruits, cold chicken, and a number of such things as boys at our age are wont to favor.

The reader may be astonished, not so much at our volunteering to pass a night in a haunted house as at the fact that our elders should have allowed us to carry out so madcap a scheme. And, indeed, had it not been for an accident our plan would have been early nipped in the bud.

For on my first proposing the matter to my father he had shown marked disapproval. However, when I told him of all that Tom had said concerning the mystery he had become lost in thought.

"Now, father, won't you please let us go?" I asked.

"I'll go myself," was the answer. "It will be no harm to try the plan. Of course, there's no question of the house being haunted; that's a bit of superstition. But there are some things worth looking up there in regard to your uncle's death, and if one goes there one can hardly help staying all night. You ought to know now, my dear Harry," continued my father, "that it was chiefly on your account I gave up the pursuit of Mrs. Raynor."

"On my account, father?"

"Yes; for it seemed to me that were we to succeed in bringing to justice the woman whom you had loved as a mother your life would become somewhat embittered. But now that old feelings have been softened by time, and that you are a strong, healthy, cheerful boy, it might be good to stir up farther inquiries. Tom Playfair's suggestion, though romantic, may have something of good in it. Yes; I'll pass a night at Tower Hill Mansion myself."

"But won't you let Tom and me come along, father?"

"Boys are best in bed at night."

"But we can sleep there, you know, and if anything happens you can wake us up."

"Well, on that condition you may come along."

Whereupon I hastened off to indite a note to Tom, telling him of my father's decision and pressing him to come on at once.

But before the letter could have reached Tom my father had an ugly fall from his horse. His hip was injured, and the doctor declared that it would

10

be madness for him to think of moving about for
weeks. When Tom came upon the scene my father
easily gave in to our pleadings; and so it was that
two hours after my friend's arrival we had taken
the train *en route* for my uncle's former dwelling.

We dispatched our lunch very pleasantly, though
I noticed with concern that Tom was beginning to
yawn. The meal, all the same, gave me heart of
grace, and I entered into conversation with Tom in
really good spirits. But as mine rose Tom's seemed
to fall. As I became talkative he grew taciturn.
True, he opened his mouth frequently, but only to
gape or to excuse himself. His eyes, too, had become heavy.

"Are you sleepy, Tom?"

"Awful; what a dunce I was not to have taken a
nap while we were journeying here. You see, old
fellow, I can stand a lot, but two nights in succes-
sion without sleep is more than I can go through
decently."

"Two nights!" I repeated. "What was the matter last night? Didn't you take a Pullman sleeper?"

"Yes; but a baby took it too. The baby might
have taken the smoker and smoked. It would have
succeeded in smoking just as well as it did in sleeping, and it wouldn't have been so much of a nuisance.
It made night hideous."

For a few moments the conversation dragged.
On taking out my watch, I found that it wanted a
quarter to eleven. I was about to communicate the
fact to him, when I discovered that he was nodding.

"Tom," I said in all the bravery I had plucked
up, "you're worn out for want of a little sleep.
You've been travelling all day. It's now a quarter

to eleven. An hour's rest would make a new man of you."

"Will you call me before twelve?" murmured Tom, without opening his eyes.

"Yes. Here, come over to the bed. "

I helped him across the room and was about to assist him into the bed, when he threw himself on a chair standing at the head, and burying his face in his arms and his arms upon the pillow, fell asleep at once.

And now, before I proceed any further with my account, I desire to warn the reader that from the moment of Tom's falling asleep to his awakening I tell the events as I then honestly thought they occurred.

I returned to the table then, and looked around the room; everything was in perfect order. I listened; nothing but the quiet breathings of my sleeping friend broke upon the silence.

Then making the sign of the cross, I took out of my valise—the "Pickwick Papers." I had brought this book as a special counter-irritant to any feelings of depression. I regarded it as a book which would bring sunshine into a desert. I selected for my reading that very curious chapter where Mr. Samuel Weller writes a valentine. During a quarter of an hour's reading I felt no nervousness at all. A little after eleven it occurred to me in a dim way that my head was becoming heavy. Presently I discovered that I was nodding, and even in the act my imagination had wandered from "Samivel" and his father and was dwelling upon those two clocks which had stopped at twelve o'clock.

" *Why did they stop at twelve?* "

I stared about me, alarmed by the sound my own voice had made.

"This won't do," I muttered, and I arose and took a turn about the room. In doing so I passed quite near Tom and laid my hand gently upon his hair. He had not stirred from the position in which he had fallen asleep—face buried in his hands, his hands pressed upon the pillow.

Feeling more wakeful, I again composed myself to read; and for ten or twelve minutes got on quite nicely. But once more I began to grow heavy. Shaking off the feeling, I took a glance at my watch, which was lying before me on the table. It was twenty minutes to twelve.

"In five minutes I'll call Tom," was my reflection as I resumed my volume.

It seems to me that after reading two pages and a half I caught myself nodding again; and I think that I half formed a resolution to jump to my feet and take a turn about the room. After this there was a blank.

Suddenly I started to my feet with a gasp and listened intently.

There was a loud whirring noise and my hair seemed to stand on end as I listened. Even in this state of alarmed expectancy I took up my watch and glanced at it. It marked twelve to the minute. As I was still gazing upon its face, the watch fell from my nerveless grasp to the floor, when upon a sudden every clock in the house began to strike.

One, two, three—

I could clearly distinguish the deep tone of the hall clock.

Four, five, six—

I wondered whether they would go to twelve.

Seven, eight, nine.

Ten, eleven, twelve.

Then there succeeded a deathly silence, and on the moment a cold shivering came upon me. I turned to wake Tom. I made for the bed calling "Tom!"

What was it that froze the word upon my lips? I could not see Tom. Between him and myself there stood a sort of veil, a mist.

I stood rooted to the spot, and as I paused, chainbound in an agony of fright, the lamp at my side began to grow dimmer and dimmer while the mist became more and more luminous, more and more defined, more and more clear-cut, till, as the lamp sputtered out its life, the mist was no longer a mist but a luminous shadow—yet far more than a shadow. There was no doubt to my mind that I was standing before the ghost of James Dee.

"Uncle!" I gasped.

"Nephew," came a hollow, sepulchral voice from that weird form, yet carrying in its hollow, sepulchral tones a hint of the old harshness. His face was still gloomy and heavy, stern and unrelenting—as it had been when I met him for the first time in the library —but it wore also the look of terror and agony which had fastened upon it in his last moments. I could now clearly see Tom behind, and through this strange apparition. He was still motionless. Was he alive? I called to him with all my force.

"Tom! Tom!"

But though my lips went through all the motions of speech, no sound followed. It was as though I had not spoken. My uncle, meanwhile, stood gazing

at me with his harsh frown and his stern eyes. I
could stand the suspense no longer.

"Uncle," I cried, "why do you appear to me thus?"

"Nephew! when did you see me last?"

"Here, uncle—on that sad Christmas eve."

"What did I do for you that night?"

"You made a will leaving me all your property."

"What happened to me that night?"

"You were murdered in your bed."

"Has the murder been avenged?"

"Not yet, uncle."

"Are you taking any measures to have it avenged?"

"No, uncle."

Oh! how I trembled beneath his searching glance.

"Nephew, listen: swear that you will take *reasonable* measures to have my murder avenged—*reasonable* measures. You are not bound to anything extraordinary. Do you understand?"

"Yes, uncle."

"Then lift up your right hand and say 'I swear.'"

I complied, and even as I spoke the lamp sputtered
again, the light rose higher and higher; my uncle's
figure became ill-defined and featureless, then resolved itself into a mist, till, as the lamp gave
forth its normal light, I was alone. I sank back
into my chair and my eyes closed. In a moment
I was again on my feet, and with two strides was
beside my friend.

Clutching him by the shoulder—

"Tom! Tom!" I cried.

CHAPTER XVIII.

IN WHICH THE HALL CLOCK TELLS A STORY.

"HALLO! What's the matter?" cried Tom, jumping to his feet and rubbing his eyes. "Is it twelve?"

"O Tom!"

I could say no more, but clinging to him, sobbed like a little child.

Tom glanced at me anxiously and took out his watch. "Four minutes past twelve," he exclaimed. "Tell me what's happened, Harry. You needn't be afraid. If you've seen a ghost you're better. off than most people."

"Tom, I've seen my uncle!"

"You did? Tell me everything from the time I went to sleep till now."

With no little incoherence I gave him a full account of my adventure. Tom was certainly astonished. At several points he was surprised, and was very particular in inquiring into the exact words my uncle used. These words and my answers he insisted on my repeating over and over again, and he seemed to find an import in them beyond what was on the surface.

"Hallo! What's this, Harry?" he exclaimed suddenly as he stooped to the floor and picked up my watch. "Why, here's more mystery. Your watch has stopped at twelve to the minute. There's a coincidence."

"Yes; but it can be explained," I answered. "I dropped my watch at twelve, and most probably the shock of the fall stopped it."

"Suppose we take a look at those clocks." Lamp in hand, Tom led the way through the hall and went from room to room. But the clocks were as we had seen them at first.

"Well, Tom," I said, when we had completed this investigation, "what have you to say—what's your advice?"

"Mrs. Raynor has to be found. Your uncle's appearance to you has thrown no light upon the matter; and what's more, I doubt whether he appeared to you at all. Ghosts that are anxious to have their murders avenged are good enough for story-books, but I don't believe in them. If they were so anxious to have their murders avenged, all they'd need to do would be to appear to the fellow that murdered them and make faces at him."

"But, Tom, I'm sure I saw my uncle."

"If he had come to ask your prayers for his soul, I could believe it; but the 'avenge-his-foul-and-most-unnatural-murder' sort of a ghost is a fraud. The fact is, Harry, I didn't believe this house was haunted from the first; and now I'm sorry I talked about it seriously to you. I'm afraid it wound up your imagination: it would have been better had I wound up the clock. As it was, it was your imagination that struck twelve."

Tom talked in the same strain at some length, but he failed to convince me.

The hours passed wearily, draggingly. What a cry of joy broke from me as the first faint streaks of day lined the eastern rim of the horizon.

"Cock-a-doodle-doo!" cried Tom. "Just wait till the sun takes his first peep at us. Then we'll

settle whether we think this house is haunted.
Then, lunch."

Brighter and brighter grew the eastern sky: the
birds broke into song without in my uncle's garden,
and their singing sank into my heart like a healing
balm.

"Whoop-la! The sun!" exclaimed my companion. "Now, Harry, give me your honest verdict.
Do you think this house is haunted?"

"I do: what do you say, Tom? Do you think it
is haunted? Don't be afraid to tell me the truth."

Tom put his feet apart, his hands behind his back,
and reflected. Suddenly his face lighted up and he
clapped his hands together. .

"Harry," he said, "I've got it. Come along."
And catching me by the hand, he hurried down the
stairs.

"Now," he continued, "look at that clock."

Much puzzled, I fixed a steady gaze upon the hall
clock, expecting from Tom's animation that I was
about to read the solution of my midnight adventure upon its face.

"Well," I said at length, "I see nothing striking
about that clock."

"If you don't see anything striking about it, perhaps you hear something striking?"

"Look here, Tom, if you've hustled me down here
to work off a vile pun like——"

"Oh, hold on; there's sense in my pun. You
didn't——"

Here Tom suspended his sentence as he jumped
upon a chair and examined the top of the clock.
As he looked, his face brightened; he exclaimed
under his breath, "I knew it," and added aloud:

"You didn't hear that clock strike last night, and I'll bet I can prove it. Here—hop up on this chair and take a good look at the top."

I got up beside him on the chair.

"What do you see?" he pursued.

"I see lots of dust, varied by the name 'Tom Playfair.'"

"Now, Harry, take a good look at that name; look at it letter by letter. Try to photograph it on your memory."

I was now deeply impressed, for I saw that Tom was both earnest and excited, so I gazed at the letters one by one till I was perfectly satisfied that examination could no farther go.

"Harry," resumed my companion when we had stepped down from the chair, "have you read many ghost-stories?"

"Yes. The two years before coming to St. Maure's I read every ghost-story I could get my hands on till our doctor found me out and told my father I was ruining myself. The doctor said that an occasional ghost-story might not harm a healthy boy, but that for one in my state of health nothing could be worse."

"Oh, bother the doctor! But didn't you come across a good many ghosts appearing at midnight and just on the stroke of twelve?"

"Yes; but, look here, Tom Playfair," I began, somewhat nettled, "you needn't try to make me be-lieve that I'm a born fool. I——"

"There's no use in getting excited, Harry, and it's no sign of foolishness to have a vivid imagina-tion. But even your doctor is against you. Why in the world should a ghost wait till it strikes twelve? That's a bit out of story-books. But just wait till I prove you're wrong."

Tom opened the clock-door, and after peering about for a few moments discovered the key.

"Now, Harry, I'm going to put the hand of this clock back to one half minute to twelve. There! that's done. Now I'm going to wind it—so! and now that it's wound we'll both wait for results."

"Tick, tick," went the clock solemnly and slowly. The sound of it sent a shiver through me. Tom, quick to divine my feelings, caught my hand and held it in his warm clasp. I gave his hand a hearty squeeze, and as I gave it I could see that Tom understood the squeeze to be an apology for my touch of temper in the conversation just set down. Tom answered the apology by a grin, which I interpreted as meaning "that's all right, Harry."

It is thus that the small boy saves time and many words.

Presently there was a whirr—whirr—whirr—a rasping convulsion that seemed to set the clock-case into a tremble and certainly sent me into that undesirable state; then the clock began to strike.

Tom's arm came around my neck at the first whirr; and I was indeed grateful, for I had as lief face a wild beast of the forest just then as this striking clock.

With much groaning and wheezing and internal agitation the clock gave forth its twelve strokes. Had it not been for Tom's protecting arm I fear me I should have run away. The reader may laugh; but such is the fact. Tom seemed to be highly pleased with the clock's performance.

"Look here, Harry, did the clock strike just that way last night?"

"Exactly," I answered promptly; "only, of course, I make allowances for the difference in dis-. tance."

Tom was not pleased with this answer, and knit his brow in thought.

"Oh!" he exclaimed presently, "didn't you hear that clock strike the night you were here before?"

"Yes, indeed."

"And did you notice it particularly?"

"It scared me. I thought it sounded like my poor uncle and Caggett growling and groaning together."

"Whoo! what an imagination you had, Harry. No wonder you dreamed of it last night."

I was about to lose my temper, when Tom jumped upon the chair, gave one look, and uttered a cry of triumph.

"*Quod erat demonstrandum*, Harry. Hop up here quick and tell me what you think about it."

I took my former place beside him on the chair.

"Your name is a little blurred by the dust," I said.

"Precisely: the clock, when it struck, set the dust a-flying, and that's the result—see?"

"Pshaw! what else could you expect?"

"Harry Dee," exclaimed Tom in his highest tones, "where are your brains? If that clock struck at twelve o'clock last night my name would have been blurred then. It wasn't. The dust upon the top wasn't disturbed one bit last night; now do you see?"

"Tom, I take it back; I *am* a born fool; that clock did not strike last night."

"Consequently——" suggested Tom.

"Consequently I dreamed that it struck; and— and—Tom. you're right; it was a vivid dream."

"Now you're talking sense. I'm mighty glad I put my name up there last night; it spoiled a ghost. This house, Harry, is no more haunted than I am. The fact is I never thought it was; but I thought it wouldn't hurt to spend a night here, especially as it's the best kind of fun."

"Yes—that's all right, Tom; but we're as far off now from the mystery as we were before."

"Not at all," retorted Tom, "at least you are not. And now, Harry, you go to work and hunt up Mrs. Raynor, and you'll find out something more."

CHAPTER XIX.

IN WHICH THE CHAPTER PROCEEDS FROM GAY TO GRAVE, FROM LIVELY TO SEVERE.

"*THOMA, quænam est hujus vocis significatio?*"

"Tom, what's the meaning of this word?"

I asked, pointing him to the word "*naviculariis*" in the "Manilian Law."

"*Revera, nescio: nunquam antea vidi.*"

"I'm sure I don't know: never met it before."

"*Nonne derivatur a voce 'navis' quæ anglice significat* 'ship'?"

"Isn't it from '*navis*,' a ship?" inquired Harry Quip.

"*Utique, Henrice: jamjam magistrum hac de re rogavi, qui me certiorem fecit vocabulum istud significare* 'ship-owner.'"

"Yes, Harry; I've already asked our professor, and he tells me that the word in question means a ship-owner," came from Percy.

"*Si quis me rogaret, quomodo anglice redderem istam*

partem 'mercatoribus et naviculariis injuriosius tracta-tis,' ita redderem: 'Our counter-jumpers and ship-owners having been severely sat upon.' "

" Were I asked to translate *'mercatoribus et navicu-lariis injuriosius tractatis,'* " put in Tom, " I'd render it this way: 'Our counter-jumpers,' " etc.

" *O gratiæ decentes, quæ, si credendum sit Horatio, tempore veris terram alterno quatitis pede ubi gentium estis !* "

" Ye comely Graces, who, if we may credit Horace, strike the vernal earth with changing feet—where are ye?"

No one but Percy could have delivered such an apostrophe. He alone of our band had dipped into Horace.

It was an afternoon in October. We were in the blue grass—Quip, Ruthers, Tom, Percy, Whyte, Richards, and myself—each with Cicero's "*Pro Lege Manilia*" in his hand. Percy was seated with his back against a tree; the rest of us were lying about in various easy postures. Here we were in the class of Humanities and talking Latin twice a week.

Not one of us had laid aside our Latin during the vacation months. Before leaving school we had agreed, "for the honor of the class, for the honor of the school," to give a certain number of hours each week to the reading of Cicero's " *De Amicitia.*" To make this more binding, we had furthermore agreed to submit ourselves to an examination in it (in trans-lation only) from Mr. Middleton on our return. In addition to this, we had kept up a correspondence with one another in Latin. Whence came all this energy? The answer presents itself to every reader. From none other than Tom Playfair. That vigor-

ous little man had made up his mind that our class
was to secure the intercollegiate medal if human
exertion could bring it about. On our return to
college he had at once organized this Latin academy. Every Tuesday and Thursday afternoon we
came together in the blue grass, and for an hour
studied and read and discussed that supreme work
of elegant Latinity, Cicero's "Manilian Law."
This speech belonged to the matter of rhetoric class,
but we took it up all the same. During this hour
all the talking was in Latin. Strange as it may
seem, these hours were among the pleasantest of the
week. We had become really interested in Latin,
and took as much pleasure in a new idiom or turn
of expression as a botanist in a strange specimen.
All of us had our note-books and made memoranda
of every phrase that struck our fancy.

On this bright October afternoon we looked much
the same as during the preceding year.

Percy had grown somewhat taller, but he was
for all that a small boy. He was still clad in his
sober black coat and black knickerbockers, for
though taller than boys are wont to be who wear
these latter, Percy still retained them; and indeed,
his natural grace and fine figure, so different from
the "hobble-de-hoy" form, manner, and emotion of
the ordinary boy of sixteen, gave a peculiar fitness
to his costume. Tom, stout as ever, but two inches
below Percy in height, was outwardly and inwardly
the same noble fellow. Harry Quip had developed
into a bookworm.

Keenan and Donnel were no longer with us. They
had been promoted to the senior division, leaving
the leadership of the small yard to Percy and Tom.

On the occasion of this present meeting Tom was bubbling over with good-humor, but he found Latin a poor vehicle for his witticisms, and so grew very reckless about moods, tenses, and idioms.

"*Habeo aliquid novi communicare.   Sed nescio quomodo*—hang it!—*nescio quomodo—nescio—nescio——*"

"I have some news, boys," he said, "but I don't know—a—hang it!—I can't—can't——"

"*Non potes, quæ tua est paupertas verborum—rem Latine exprimere.*"

"You can't with your narrow vocabulary put it into Latin," said Percy, smiling.

"*Rem acu tetigisti.   Oh quomodo volo* (shade of Cicero!) *hora esset supra!*"

"You've hit the nail on the head," was his answer. "Oh, how I wish the hour was *up*" [*supra*].

It was some time before we came at Tom's meaning of "*supra.*" Percy announced the discovery with a musical laugh, in which we all joined.

"*Tempus est; licet anglice loqui.*"

"Time's up—you can talk English," said Percy in due course; whereupon Tom began:

"Boys, the best news in the world! Mr. Middleton thinks we're losing too much of our play-time at this Latin business——"

"Oh! that's great news," interpolated Quip sarcastically.

"Let me have my inning out, will you? He's been thinking about the matter, and he's gone to the president and obtained permission for all the Humanities boys in the small yard to stay up half an hour longer than the other small boys every night!"

"Hurrah!" With what unanimity that cheer issued from six pairs of vigorous lungs!

"And that's not all. He's going to superintend our work himself. His plan is simply gorgeous. Listen, will you?"

"We're all ears," said Quip.

"Every night he will assign us fifteen or sixteen lines from Cicero—a passage that we have never seen. The crowd of us are to spend ten minutes in making out the translation. Then the next night we are to take an idiomatic English translation, which he himself will make out, and put it back into Latin, trying to reproduce, as nearly as we can, the idiom and turns of expression which Cicero employed. For this we are allowed twenty minutes."

"Splendid!" interjected Percy.

"But that's not all. We are to hand in our themes to him when we go up to the dormitory. He will examine every one of them before he goes to bed, and he'll pencil-mark them wherever we're particularly bad in blue, and where we're particularly good in red, and occasionally, when he thinks it suitable, he will jot down a few words of criticism on our Latin style."

"Isn't it great!" exclaimed Ruthers.

"We'll get a better course of training than the boys in day colleges," Joe Whyte observed.

"There are not three out yet," observed Tom dryly. "Allow me to finish my inning. During this half-hour we can talk as much as we please."

"Oh!" came the chorus.

"But only in Latin."

"Ah!"

"And I've given my word of honor that that condition will be observed faithfully. Now, in return for this favor, Mr. Middleton wants us to give up

11

this hour on Tuesday and Thursday and put it in
at good, solid physical exercise."

And then we gave Mr. Middleton such a cheer.

"I wish I was Pope," Quip observed solemnly.
"I'd canonize our teacher the first thing."

"No, you wouldn't," contradicted Richards with a
smile.   "You'd have to kill him first, and you'd be
slow about that."

"Methinks," exclaimed Tom, throwing himself
into a dramatic attitude, "I see a golden medal."

Then he spoils the attitude by leaping into the
air, knocking his heels together, and adding: "'In
my mind's eye, Horatio.'"

"Just think of the six rhetoric and poetry classes
that are to contend against us," said Ruthers.
"They're older and they've been studying longer."

"Age hasn't very much to do with it," I put in.

"Very little, indeed," supplemented Percy.   "We
read of prominent men in England who were skilled
in the classics at the age of ten or eleven.   I knew
a lawyer in Cincinnati who had been taught in childhood by his father. He could read any Latin author,
almost, when he was eleven."

"And there's the Opium Eater," added Richards,
our great reader.   "When he was seventeen he used
to read Greek tragedies, not to speak of Latin, with
as much pleasure as we read a novel."

"The difference between them and us, I should
think, aside from the talent," added Percy, "is that
they go at the study in earnest.   They take hold of
things with a strong grasp and don't let loose
easily.   They don't shirk difficulties."

"I reckon that's what makes the difference between
a great man and a small potato," said Harry Quip.

"But now let's look at our chances calmly," and Tom became very thoughtful as he spoke. "Carlyle says that our—what was that quotation you made from Carlyle the other day, Percy?"

"'Our wishes are presentiments of our capabilities.'"

"Precisely. Tally one for Carlyle. Now, we wish to get that medal just a little bit—don't we?"

"Oh! don't we!" ejaculated Quip with a solemn roll of his eyes.

"Very well. In the next place, we've had a great advantage in keeping the same teacher. He's followed us, and knows just where we are weak and where we are strong. He doesn't have to spend a week or two each year in finding out what we don't know. Best of all, he's *such* a teacher. The boy who can't learn from him must be made entirely of mud. In the third place, we're in a boarding-college, where it's easier to study than in a day college. Now, the six other competing colleges are day schools."

"Yes," said Ruthers. "But what about the poets and rhetoricians of St. Maure's?"

"Well, that's the great point. But if you come to look at things, I don't see why we should be afraid of them. It's this way. As a matter of fact, though we are only in Humanities, we've actually studied as much Latin *already* as boys have ordinarily studied when leaving poetry. Look at this! Last year we did double work in Latin; that is, we saw as much as we ought to see in two years. This year we're going to do double work in Latin again; and our double work doesn't run on versification, prosody, and the erudition of Latin, but is all bent to the one single purpose of making ourselves good theme-writers."

"That's a solid reason," said Percy, as indeed it was. There was another argument which Tom did not bring forward and which, in fact, could never have occurred to him. It was this. His little Ciceronian society was made up of members extraordinary not only in their energy, but also in their mental ability. Percy I consider to be the most gifted lad I have ever met. Very close to him came Tom. Richards was a boy of wondrous memory and a maturity beyond his years. The others were bright, quick, energetic. Taking it all in all, these little boys in their knickerbockers were as intellectual a set for their age as one could wish to meet with.

Week after week passed away. October glided into December. January raged, February stormed, March wept—but change the seasons as they might, the Ciceronian club was hard at it night after night. The progress we made was something remarkable. At first I led all in command of idiom, while Tom was the authority as an off-hand translator. Insensibly Percy came to take rank with me, and long before spring he was my superior, not only in idiom but in facility. At Christmas we made one change in our programme. We shortened the time of translation from ten to five minutes. This we did for two reasons. First, we found that as the weeks went on it became quite easy for us to read Cicero; secondly, we wished to give more time and finish to our theme.

So wrapped was I in my studies that in looking back into that year I remember but few incidents of any note.

The only matter which distracted me from my books were the steps taken with regard to discovering the whereabouts of Mrs. Raynor. My father had placed the affair in the hands of a detective agency. The chief detective had assured us that although the search would be difficult we need entertain no doubts as to the final result.

"Yes, sir," he said emphatically, "we'll find her —dead or alive. Our agency commands well-nigh every district in the United States, sir. Why, sir, a case like this is child's play to us. Only two years ago one of our men yanked a defaulter out of a boat on the Zambesi River—followed him up, sir, from America to Europe, and then right smack into the heart of Africa. We never sleep, sir."

It occurred to me as I looked up into his blood-shot eyes that it would be a good thing for this vigilant detective were he to take a sound nap.

I had not been two weeks back at St. Maure's, when a telegram reached my father to this effect:

We've got a clew. Mrs. R. known to have been in St. Louis two nights after the tragedy. Further news in a week.
HORACE TINKER, Chief Detective Bureau.

One week later there came this letter which my father kindly sent me:

It's a mistake. It was not a *Mrs.* Raynor, but a *Mr.* Raynor at St. Louis two nights after the tragedy. Detective Green (one of the best men on our force) says that he thinks he's got another clew. He will not mention it till he has discovered a few missing links.

Probably Detective Green never came upon the missing link, for that was the last I heard of him.

There was a long silence on the part of these sleepless officials.

In January the indefatigable Tinker announced that Mrs. Raynor was at length found. A week later he was compelled to acknowledge that this lady's name was not Ada, but Gertrude, that she was over seventy years of age, and though old enough to be Mrs. Ada Raynor's grandmother, no relation to my former nurse at all. Then Mr. Tinker relapsed into vigilant silence.

CHAPTER XX.

IN WHICH WILLIE TIPP CHANGES HIS NAME AND BECOMES THE LEADER OF A MISCHIEVOUS ORGANIZATION.

IT was in the course of this year that Percy and Tom were instrumental in bringing about a great change for the better among the small boys. In order to make the incident intelligible, it is necessary to say a word about the " Artful Dodgers."

During my first year at St. Maure's a boy of twelve, with light hair, sharp blue eyes, a nose that turned up slightly, and a fine mouth, which betrayed, in conjunction with the eyes, a strong sense of humor, entered the college. His sense of humor seemed to develop with the passing months, in so far that in the spring he was already recognized as the wag of the small yard.

Willie Tipp was as good-hearted a boy as ever came to St. Maure's; but he was as thoughtless as he was good-hearted.

When he returned at the beginning of September he became a leader at once. All the fun-lovers, all the harum-scarum boys, quite a number of the

worst boys, and quite a number of the best, enlisted
under his standard.

At this time "Oliver Twist" was being read to
us during meals. Tipp's sense of fun and lively
imagination were taken by the character of the "Artful Dodger." He procured, one fine evening in September, a set of garments, such as Dickens bestowed
upon his too-fascinating thief, and taking the pose
and mannerisms of his prototype, Master Tipp con-
vulsed us all with laughter. From that evening he
answered to the name " Artful Dodger," or " Dodger,"
as the case might be; Tipp was discarded.

Next day Tipp persuaded Frank Burdock to start
a pawnshop as the Jew, Fagin. Then the inventive
young gentleman sent five or six of his companions
right and left through the yard for the purpose of
stealing handkerchiefs, pencils, and whatever they
could discover worth taking out of their fellow-
students' pockets.

"You see, Fagin," he said to Frank, "whatever
we get we fetch to you; then you write out a ticket
with a number and stick it on. After awhile I'll
send one of our 'pals' to the fellow whose goods
are in your hands to let him know where they are;
then he'll come to you——"

"Yes," broke in Frank. "He'll come along and
hit me over the head or throw me over a fence or
something. No, you don't, Dodger; I don't want
to play pawnbroker."

"But look! I'll have a lot of our fellows around
to stand by you. When he comes up, you will tell
him that you're a poor old man named Fagin, and
that you can't give him back his goods unless he
pays one chocolate caramel for each piece."

" He won't do it."

"Yes, he will. Now go down in that corner of the yard, get your tickets ready, and I'll have a bench fetched over for a counter."

Master Tipp had his will, and very soon Frank was standing behind a bench, gay with six handkerchiefs, three lead-pencils, two bean-shooters, and one memorandum-book.

Tipp was right. The victims of this desperate gang of pickpockets took their losses very pleasantly, and willingly redeemed their possessions with the ever-popular caramel.

In this way thirty caramels passed into Frank's hands up to the ringing of the first bell for studies. Then in a body came the elated band of pickpockets, five in number, to their pawnbroker.

"Frank," said Tipp, "you did splendidly."

"Didn't I?" exclaimed Frank.

"Now, boys," continued Tipp, addressing the happy pickpockets, "we'll have a square division. Frank, bring out the candy."

Frank was astonished.

"Candy! Why I ate it just as soon as I got it."

Then Frank had to run, as it were, for dear life.

The experiment, in consequence, was not repeated; but the reformed thieves still clung to the name of the "Artful Dodgers." Gradually, by common usage, everybody found ordinarily in the company of Tipp was set down as a member of the " gang," and thus Tipp became notorious. In many ways Tipp had the qualities that go to the making of a leader of boys. He was good-natured, energetic, and truth-loving. This latter was a very necessary qualification. As a rule, boys hold a liar in contempt, howsoever various and estimable be his other qualities. But what most of all secured Tipp his leadership was his power of invention. He was ever devising something new. One day it might be a game; another day a practical joke. Whatever it was, his followers counted on having some fun in the issue and they were rarely disappointed.

The study-hall was his chosen field for quips and pranks. We had not passed a week at college when Tipp created his first diversion in that place of almost sacred silence.

Broadhead, a neighbor of his, commonly known as the "Anarchist," owing to his bristling hair and his disregard for law and order, taking out a bean-shooter, had aimed a dried pea at Tipp's face. The pea struck Tipp on the cheek. What was the amazement and horror of Broadhead when Tipp gave a scream which rang through the study-hall, jumped from his seat, and, with much agony upon his countenance, hurried toward the study-keeper's desk, exclaiming aloud as he advanced:

"O Mr. Middleton, some fellow's hit me on the cheek with a piece of shot."

Mr. Middleton made a sharp gesture, which arrested the young wag's steps; then he said deliberately, but in so low a voice that only those near him could catch the remark:

"Tipp, if you'll be kind enough to show me the exact spot on your face where you were struck, I'll kiss it for you."

Tipp never tried a practical joke on Mr. Middleton again; and the Anarchist lost his bean-shooter.

In nowise discouraged, Tipp changed his base of operations, or rather his time. The second hour of studies was kept by Mr. Middleton's assistant prefect, Mr. Auber.

The night after his encounter with Mr. Middleton Tipp, anxious to make up for his lost prestige, took out his bottle of red ink, and, to the intense interest of some of his admirers, stained the tip of his nose red. Covering his mouth and lips with his handkerchief, he rushed up to the study-keeper's desk and madly waved his hat.

It looked like a serious case of nose-bleed.

The assistant prefect, who thus far had refused Tipp permission to go out every night, nodded assent, and Tipp, with a solemn face, despite the wink he bestowed upon his chums, left the study-hall in triumph.

The joke was unanimously voted a capital one; so good, indeed, that it was resolved to repeat it night after night with a different boy as chief actor each time. The plan worked nicely for a week till it came to Broadhead's turn. This young man lost courage when, on entering the hall, he found that the prefect of studies, Father Tieman, had Mr. Auber's place. Indeed, he contemplated abandoning his part, when a note from Tipp put him on his mettle.

He daubed his nose, therefore, and advanced. Every boy in the study-hall watched the proceeding.

"Stand here with your nose to the wall," said Father Tieman; "and if you show so much as the tip of it to a single boy during this hour, I'll attend to you privately in my room."

There were no further cases of nose-bleeding after that.

Tipp next turned his attention to the yard. Some

of his jokes were good; many of them, I am bound
to say, subversive of order. Tipp was a good boy
in the main, and frequently felt remorse when, as
the event showed, he had gone too far. On such
occasions he invariably consulted Tom; and it was
owing to the latter's influence upon the leader that
the "Artful Dodgers" did not go to extremes. Even
as it was, they worried and annoyed poor Mr. Auber
in season and out.

One evening a number of us were seated on a
bench at the end of the yard, some fifty feet west of
the old church building, when Anarchist produced a
cigarette.

"I'm dying for a smoke," he observed.

Tipp glanced about the yard; it was twilight, and
Mr. Auber was presiding prefect.

"I'll tell you what, Anarchist," he said, "you can
smoke right along without the least danger of being
caught. You sit where you are, and ten or eleven
of us will stand around you. Mr. Auber can tell
that somebody's smoking, but he won't know who
it is."

The crowd thought this an excellent plan, and
forthwith a number jumped up and surrounded Broadhead, who at once lighted his cigarette and puffed
away with great satisfaction. To make matters
pleasanter, he passed the cigarette round to a few
of his special friends, after the manner of a pipe of
peace.

Mr. Auber very soon noticed the smell of the
burning cigarette, and moved slowly down toward
where we were stationed. Of course the cigarette
disappeared long before he got near us.

"Good-evening, boys."

We all lifted our caps and tried to look cheerful, but no one ventured upon uttering a word.

Poor Mr. Auber became nervous.

"I thought——" he began: then he paused, looked irresolute, removed his hat, passed his hands through his hair, and walked away, leaving Broadhead to resume his smoke undisturbed.

On the following evening I took care not to go near the bench, where, as usual, a number of the Dodgers had assembled. As I afterward learned, cigarettes were in abundance, Tipp, Broadhead, and several others having made provision, and the air soon became heavy with cigarette-smoke.

To every one's surprise, Mr. Middleton (who seldom entered the yard after supper before the sound of the first bell) suddenly appeared.

The crowd was about to disperse.

Mr. Middleton made a gesture which plainly signified, "Stay where you are."

"Now we're in for it," said Tipp as the prefect walked rapidly toward them.

"He can't find out who was smoking, anyhow," suggested Richards.

"Maybe he can't," answered Tipp; "but he'll fix us some way or other."

"Shoo!" exclaimed Broadhead in a raised voice, "he can't punish a fellow if he doesn't catch him. You can just bet I'm not going to take any punishment."

"Suppose you all sit down, boys," said Mr. Middleton, giving no sign to show that he had heard the words that Bob Broadhead had evidently intended for his ears.

All obeyed and vainly tried to look comfortable.

"Now," continued the prefect, "I'm going to give you fellows a lesson in catechism. Suppose a thief wanted to rob a man's house, but couldn't do it without the help of three other men. He explains his difficulties to three of his friends; they come to his help and assist him to rob. He clears one hundred dollars. You understand?"

"Yes, sir," answered Tipp.

"Very good. Now, who is bound to make restitution?"

"Why, the thief, of course."

"But suppose the thief died, leaving no effects: who in that case would have to make the robbery good?"

"All three of them, I reckon," volunteered Richards.

"And suppose all four were proven in court to have had a hand in the stealing, how many of them would be punished?"

"All of 'em would, sir," answered Tip.

"Now, apply all this to smoking on the sly; it's against the college law and all concerned in it are liable to punishment. Next time you boys combine to help a smoker you shall all perform the penance. This time I'll let you off. Broadhead, I'd like to have a word with you."

The Anarchist went about with his history under his arm for the next few days.

The irrepressible Tipp now devoted himself to the wash-room, and Mr. Auber was put to his wits' end at times to prevent serious disorder there. He was a timid man, rather retiring, and one could see that he was at a loss as to how he should deal with his troublesome charges. He generally confined himself to running his hands through his hair and looking annoyed.

The Dodgers used to feel sorry for him, for he was very gentle and they really liked him. But their sorrow was not sufficient to induce a lasting amendment.

One morning in December matters went worse than usual. A quantity of red pepper placed on the stove set all the boys sneezing; the water-pipes were stuffed so that the boys had to go outside to the pump with their basins, and when they returned prefect and boys found themselves locked out. The locking-out had not been set down in the original programme; it was a happy thought, at the last moment, of the Anarchist.

Mr. Auber was thoroughly discouraged; so discouraged, in fact, that he could not conceal his feelings, though most of the boys were too excited and too intent on mischief to notice it.

There is a certain class of students who, when once they make a fair and successful start in disorder, know not where to stop. During this day it became evident that the spirit of mischief was abroad. After supper the leading members of the Dodger crowd took their places in a far corner of the yard and engaged in an earnest consultation. Tom, Percy, Harry Quip, and myself were standing by the wash-room.

"I say, boys," said Tom, "Tipp is losing control of his crowd."

"Is that so?" said Percy; "why, I thought he could turn them round his finger."

"So he could, but they're getting the start on him of late; and now Anarchist is beginning to get

the run of things. Tipp feels pretty blue, not so
much because he is no longer leader, but because
the Dodgers are going too far and he feels that he's
to blame for it. He was talking to me to-day and
I advised him to draw out."

"Is he going to?" asked Harry.

"He'd like to, he says, but he thinks that by
staying with them he can keep them from following Anarchist blindly."

"I tell you what," pursued Quip, "those fellows
are hatching something now, or I'm badly mistaken.
Tipp is there, but the Anarchist is doing most of
the talking. His hair is standing up worse than
ever, and if he keeps on getting excited it will raise
his hat off his head."

"Tom," suggested Percy, "suppose we go over
and join them; you can do more with them than Tipp
and the Anarchist put together."

I should note here that both Tom and Percy were,
owing to their popularity, honorary members of the
Dodger gang; while myself, Harry, and Joe were
always treated as welcome guests.

"I've a notion to go down," said Tom. "In fact,
Tipp wants me to help him out. He feels blue
about the way Mr. Auber's been treated, though he's
responsible for nearly everything that's happened
himself, and now he's afraid that they're going to
give Mr. Auber just pecks and bushels of trouble
straight ahead. I've been thinking about the matter all day, and can't see how to start them in
some other direction. Somehow the idea won't
come."

"Suppose we go down anyhow," urged Percy,
"and once we get the fellows talking, you might

strike upon a plan right on the spur of the moment."

"Well," answered Tom, "we can't do much harm and we may do some good. 'Come on."

CHAPTER XXI.

IN WHICH TOM PLAYFAIR AND PERCY WYNN COME TO TIPP'S RESCUE.

TIPP received us with enthusiasm and made a place for Tom and Percy beside himself.

"What are you fellows up to now?" asked Tom.

"We were just talking about the way we worked Auber this morning," volunteered Broadhead.

"It was a pretty good joke, Anarchist—all except the locking-out business," commented Tom, "and of course you did that. It's like you to think that standing out in the cold is funny."

"I am told," said Harry Quip, "that when the Anarchist was at home his father, in order to make him laugh, used to read him all the explosions, murders, and railroad collisions out of the papers; and it seems that the more killed there were the more Anarchist laughed."

"That's a fact," said Tipp. "And when other boys were taken to a pantomime, Anarchist's papa used to take him off to see the pigs killed. One day, after seeing a thousand pigs done up, Anarchist got to laughing so hard that he nearly died of it."

"Oh, look here now; if you fellows get to poking fun at me like that I'll go away."

"Heavens!" ejaculated Quip. "He calls this fun."

"Yes; and I'll end the joke by throwing you over the fence," snarled Broadhead.

"Wouldn't it be nicer if you were to make his nose bleed, Anarchist?" said the suave Percy. "The blood might remind you of old times."

Broadhead made a dash at Percy and aimed a blow which would have considerably marred my friend's beauty had not Percy, by a quick movement, escaped it. The fence-paling awaited Broadhead's fist; and the next thing we knew Percy was bandaging Broadhead's hand as though they were inseparable friends, at the same time apologizing profusely for the words he had just uttered.

"You needn't be so mad, anyhow, Anarchist," added Tipp. "You ought to know how to take a roasting just the same as the rest of us."

"That's so," said the chorus.

By a happy accident Quip had taken a good step in making fun of Broadhead. Tom saw there was a point to be gained and followed it up. And even Percy, who studied to offend no one, had deliberately continued the teasing for the one purpose of lessening Broadhead's influence with the crowd.

Broadhead, by losing his temper, had helped them in their purpose; in a few moments he had lost the prestige gained by three or four weeks' hard endeavor.

"So," continued Tom, "you were talking about the surprise-party you gave Mr. Auber this morning. Is that all?"

"No; we're getting up another surprise-party for to-morrow. He'll run his hands through his hair till there won't be any hair left to run 'em through."

12

"What's the scheme, Dodger?" asked our spokesman.

"It's not completely hatched out yet, but it's going to begin this way. To-morrow afternoon's a half-holiday, and there's the privilege for all to go out walking if they get permission. Of course most of us can't go, because the prefects won't allow fellows out who are not on the conduct list. Well, we're going to get permission anyhow."

"How'll you do that, Artful?" queried Quip.

"Why, this way: we'll wait till Mr. Middleton goes to dinner at a quarter to one. Then the whole crowd of us will get together by the pump and begin whispering and monkeying, as though we were up to some mischief. Of course Mr. Auber will get rattled right off, and he'll come over to see what's going on. Now, just as soon as he's very near us, two of our fellows, who are on the good conduct list, will go up to him and say, 'Mr. Auber, will you please let us go out?' Of course he'll say 'yes,' or something of the sort. Then those two will give a whoop and say to all of us, 'Hurrah! fellows, Mr. Auber says we can go out.' Then the whole crowd of us will give a lot of whoops and scoot out of that yard as hard as we can put; and before Mr. Auber can tell a single one of us that he didn't mean the permission for any except the two who asked, we'll be clear out of sight."

"That's about as cheeky a thing as I've heard in a long time," observed Quip.

"Is it?" exclaimed Tipp in delight.

"And it's clever, too," added Tom.

"Do you think it will work, Tom?"

"Yes—on one condition."

"What's that?"

"On condition that you fellows all back each other up by the tallest kind of lying."

Tipp's jaw dropped.

"I don't like that. We Dodgers have kept out of straight lying so far."

"And, of course, you're not going to begin now," added Percy. "Then there's another thing, too. Aren't you boys imposing on Mr. Auber too much? He lets you off so easily. I've heard it said that he can't bear to punish a boy."

"That's a fact," put in Tipp promptly. "He gave me fifty lines for talking in ranks, and we were at it for a week and then he let me off. But as sure as you're born, when I got to thinking about it, it looked as if *he* had been punished and I had all the fun."

"There's another thing," put in Tom. "Mr. Auber doesn't believe in punishing if he can avoid it. But if you fellows keep on he might start in wholesale. He's a timid man and very kind; but if he gets on the war-path the Anarchist will have a chance to snuff blood."

"You just leave me out of this Sunday-school meeting," growled Broadhead, rising from his seat and walking off. Whereupon the boys, following time to his footsteps, whistled, with zeal and propriety, the "Rogue's March."

"The fact is, fellows," said a boy whose face was noticeable for its good-nature and decided squint, "we've been a heap too hard on Mr. Auber."

"That's so," assented several.

"In fact," said another, "we've been mean; he's always been very kind to us."

"The boys of Rhetoric class," put in Percy, "say that he's the most wonderful man they ever met. They say that when he gets started in class he talks like a book, and when he warms up to a subject he becomes really eloquent. His timidity all goes, his eyes flash, and he talks like an orator. He's a poet, too; and the leader of the class said that Mr. Auber was the nearest thing to a genius that he ever met."

"All the same," pursued Harry Quip, "we treat him as if he were nobody."

The conversation soon became very general, and quite a number who had feared to express their sentiments in the presence of Broadhead now came out strongly in favor of Mr. Auber. There were several close observers among the Dodgers, and it was astonishing to hear all the little traits of kindness and consideration they had noticed in their prefect during the preceding three months.

"And yet," said Percy, "Mr. Auber thinks you're all down on him; and one of his class told me to-day that he felt he'd have to give up prefecting as a bad job."

"Talking about giving him a surprise-party," said Tom with great animation, "it just now occurs to me that we can kill two birds with one stone—we can give him a surprise and at the same time show him that we like him."

"What's your scheme?" asked Tipp.

"Why, suppose we club together and get him a present, and you in the name of the Dodgers make the speech."

For a moment there was silence. Tom's move was certainly bold.

"Here's two dollars, Tipp; it's every cent I've got," continued Tom; "and if I had more I'd give it."

"Immense!" cried Tipp; "I've only got fifty cents and I owe fifty-five, but in it goes." And Tipp put his money with Tom's into his cap, and when he had made the rounds there wasn't a boy there who had a cent left.

"By the way," said Quip, "there's a rule in the college forbidding the boys to give presents to any of the professors."

"The Dodgers don't mind a rule more or less," observed Tipp with a grin.

"Yes, but Mr. Auber does; he won't take your present."

"Suppose we get permission from the president," suggested Percy.

"Yes, Percy," said Tom, who was helping Quip count the money, "you and Tipp and Harry Dee go up and ask him while I count these nickels."

We were off at once.

The president was seated at his table poring over a bit of paper; he started on seeing who we were and with an effort smiled. I could see at once that he was disturbed about something.

"Father," began Percy, "we'd like to make a present to one of the teachers."

"It's not allowed, Percy. I thank you, in his name, for your good-will."

"But, Father, it is not exactly to a professor but to a prefect we want to make it."

"Oh, indeed. Mr. Middleton is already assured of your good-will, and I——"

"Excuse me, Father; we're talking about Mr. Auber."

The president sat bolt upright.

"What's that?"

"The Artful Dodgers, Father, want to give Mr. Auber a present."

The smile upon the president's face was no longer forced. He took the paper over which he had been poring and tore it into small bits.

"The Artful Dodgers?" he repeated.

"Yes, sir," put in Tipp. "It'll do us good, sir, if you give us permission."

"The Artful Dodgers," answered the president, "may give anything they like to Mr. Auber."

"I wonder what that paper was?" exclaimed Tipp as we started for the yard.

"So do I," said Percy.

I never forgot that paper; and seven years later I learned from the president himself that it contained reasons pro and con for expelling Tipp. Just as we knocked at his door he had determined to expel Tipp on the morrow as being a promoter of disorder.

"Well," said Tom, when we had announced the result of our petition, "we've got just nineteen dollars and seventy-five cents."

"Pity we can't make it twenty," sighed Tipp.

"Of course we can," said Quip; "what's the matter with Anarchist?"

"That's a fact," cried Tipp. "Boys, we'll make the Anarchist fork over or we'll kick him out of the gang—eh?"

There was a unanimous chorus of assenting voices.

Five minutes later Broadhead had resigned, and twenty-five cents were still wanting.

Then Tipp went to the wash-room and brought out his baseball bat, which was the envy of every boy in the small yard. Tom had offered him a dollar for it, Percy a dollar and a quarter; but Tipp loved that bat and had said that money could not buy it.

And now he got permission to go to the large yard. He returned presently without the bat and handed Tom a quarter.

"There's the twenty dollars, Tom."

And when the boys heard of Tipp's most epic sacrifice they were dumb with admiration.

Tipp was the hero of the hour, and he retired to bed that night the most popular boy, for the time being, in St. Maure's, and, I verily believe, the happiest that ever laid head upon a pillow.

Tipp had a good heart.

\

CHAPTER XXII.

IN WHICH PERCY WYNN GOES BAREFOOT FOR THE FIRST AND ONLY TIME IN HIS LIFE.

"HARRY," said Percy to me just before night-prayers, "I want you to keep your eyes on Broadhead."

"Why, what's Anarchist up to?"

"That's just what I'd like to find out. During first recess, while Tom and Tipp and myself were walking up and down talking about the silver watch we're going to buy Mr. Auber, Broadhead came up and called Tom an awful name."

"And what did Tom do?"

"He asked the Anarchist whether he wouldn't take some candy. Then the Anarchist became furious and offered to fight. Tom only laughed. Broadhead rushed on him, but Tipp and I got hold of his arms and held him. The Anarchist really seemed to foam at the mouth and said: 'Never mind; I'll get even with you fellows, pretty quick, too.' And he walked off swearing in an awful way."

"The Anarchist is a pretty hard nut," I said. "But is Tom nervous?"

"Nervous? I should say not; and there's just the trouble. It's my opinion that Broadhead means mischief. He's a bad boy, and from all I've seen of him this year of a very revengeful disposition. We'd better look out for him."

I now follow Percy's account.

That night he tossed restlessly upon his bed, unable to sleep for thinking of Broadhead's words and conduct. It was hard upon midnight when he fell into a troubled sleep. His visions centred about Tom. Tom was standing upon the edge of a precipice; stealthily creeping upon him was Broadhead. Percy essayed to shout out a warning, but his tongue seemed to be tied; again and again he tried to shout, but to no purpose. Nearer and nearer crept Broadhead; nearer and nearer, and still Tom was unconscious of his imminent danger. Percy tried to pray, but words of prayer came not. Suddenly the Anarchist made a spring upon Tom, and Percy's best friend, with a loud cry, disappeared over the edge.

The cry seemed to awaken Percy; he found himself sitting up in bed with drops of perspiration rolling down his face. How eagerly he thanked God that it was but a dream! He jumped from his bed and ran over to Tom. His friend was sleeping soundly, his face, tranquil and composed, pillowed upon his arm,

Percy ·then looked toward Broadhead's bed and gave a start. Broadhead was not there.

Not stopping to think, but acting by a sort of intuition, Percy pulled on his knee-breeches and, bareheaded and barefooted, hastened to the dormitory door. It was locked.

Broadhead, therefore, must have made his way out through one of the two windows giving upon the shed at the eastern end of the dormitory. To get out of either of these windows it was necessary to pass over a sleeping form: Mr. Middleton was in one bed, Harry Quip in the other.

On first thought Percy determined to go out through Mr. Middleton's window; he knew that his teacher, like many hard, energetic workers, was an extremely sound sleeper, and he felt certain that he could thus escape unobserved. But even then Percy's strong sense of reverence and respect asserted itself, and he chose the other window.

Harry Quip, as Percy's foot pressed upon his bed, gave a light start; but before he had opened his eyes our midnight adventurer was upon the sloping roof of the shed. The ground, twelve feet below him, was rough and stony; ordinarily Percy would not have thought of jumping down even in his shoes. But on this occasion he gave himself no time, but dropped at once. A sharp pain ran through his foot as he touched ground — a pain to which he gave no attention. Off he dashed, this barefooted boy, for dear life toward the study-hall. And it was well he had done so; for as he came near he saw plainly, by the light of the moon in its third quarter, Broadhead jumping out of the window.

Broadhead, on the instant, saw him too, and at once took to his heels, making toward the college gate with a start of at least four hundred feet.

"Now for a long run," thought Percy, and he fell into a slower but steady, long-distance pace.

To understand what follows it should be stated that Broadhead was supposed to be, with the exception of Tom, the strongest boy in the small yard. He was thick-set, with very strong legs and arms, and if his own account could be believed, the hero of many a fight. He had begun his career in St. Maure's by thrashing some five or six of the Dodgers; consequently he was highly esteemed by a large number. He was an athlete, too. On the turning-pole he was second to none, and in baseball he succeeded Donnel as the heavy hitter. Such was the boy that Percy the gentle, who had never yet engaged in a fight, was now pursuing. Percy was slightly taller, but he was lighter by at least fifteen pounds.

Broadhead, on passing through the gate, turned eastward toward Pawnee Creek. Whether he knew who was his pursuer or not it is impossible to say. Probably he suspected that a man, perhaps even a college official, was after him. Whatever was the case he ran at full speed, and for the first five minutes he continued to increase the distance between himself and his pursuer. Percy, meanwhile, held an even pace, breathing quite easily. Very soon Broadhead lost his wind: he was forced to go slower, and saw himself that unless something be done his capture would be a question of time. Percy saw it, too, and wondered what he should do upon their coming together.

His deliberations were cut short, for Broadhead, who had reached a part on the track just opposite a spot on the highway where repairs were being made, suddenly dashed aside to a pile of stones, and before Percy was aware of his purpose, sent one of these missiles at Percy's head.

Percy paused, while another and another and another stone flew past him. To go nearer would inevitably lead to his being knocked senseless. Broadhead was throwing with all his force. Suddenly a light flashed upon him. Just three days before Frank Burdock had received from his father a toy pistol. Now, Frank happened to have at that time no room for it among the curiosities that swelled his pockets; so partly as a matter of convenience, partly to show favor to the boy whom he delighted to honor, he had intrusted it to Percy's care. Drawing this from his pocket, Percy covered Broadhead.

"If you don't drop those stones, Broadhead, I'll shoot."

There was prompt obedience.

"Is that you, Percy Wynn?"

Percy never answered, but moved on steadily, still covering his antagonist.

"Say, put down that pistol."

Percy paused.

"I won't hurt you if you don't move. Promise to stand perfectly quiet and I'll put it down."

"I promise."

Still holding the pistol in his hand, but pointed toward the ground, Percy walked forward till he stood face to face with Broadhead.

"Hallo!" cried Broadhead. "You've fooled me; that's a toy pistol."

"Just so," answered Percy, "but it has served its purpose."

"What do you want, anyhow? Is it any of your business if I choose to run away from school?"

Percy paused to nerve himself.

"Bob Broadhead, I want to examine you."

"To examine me?"

"Yes. I want to go through your pockets and see what you're carrying away. There were twenty dollars in Tipp's box in the study-hall last night——"

"Do you mean to say I stole 'em?"

"No; but I mean to find out."

"I'll tell you what, Wynn, I'm going to give you the worst thrashing you ever heard about."

"Maybe; but you're not going to get away till I know what you're taking with you."

Percy had restored the pistol to its place and was watching every move of his adversary.

"Oh, you want to fight, do you?"

"No, indeed; I'd prefer not to, but I've got to find out at any cost what you're taking away."

Broadhead laughed; he knew that there wasn't a milder boy in Kansas than Percy.

"If you don't clear off," he said contemptuously, "I'll smash in your face."

"Once more," said Percy, "will you show me what you've got?"

Broadhead folded his arms and laughed again.

"Tom Playfair isn't around to back you up, Wynn."

"Well, I'm going to go through your pockets anyhow, Broadhead."

He took one step forward; Broadhead met him half-way and would have closed with him, but Percy, who had come to the conclusion that he had a right to search Broadhead now that he was certain that he had to do with a thief, and who was resolved to use every lawful means to attain his end, at once drew back. He feared that in a wrestling-bout he would be no match for his heavy, muscular opponent. Several quick blows were parried on both sides, when Percy succeeded in striking Broadhead a blow under the chin that sent him staggering. Before Broadhead could recover himself Percy delivered two very telling blows which sent the thief to the earth.

On the instant Percy was astride him, pinioning his legs by the position he took, and holding him down in such a manner that Broadhead could scarcely move hand or foot.

"Now, Broadhead, you see how I've got you," Percy began when he felt sure of his position. "Unless you want to get thrashed, hand over that money."

"I won't."

"Very well; I'll give you a half-hour or so to think about it."

And there Percy sat for several minutes.

It was a cold night. The stars, calm and soft, gazed down upon the bareheaded, barefooted, delicate, gentle-faced small boy, who, though he shivered at times, did not seem to realize that a light undershirt and a pair of knee-breeches were very inadequate garments for such a vigil. The stars, too, must have seen a trail of blood upon this strange boy's right leg. Ah! but the soles of his

feet! Percy had never gone barefooted in the
course of all his summerings, and the many lines
and gashes that marked his soles could not be seen
for the blood that was flowing from them. There
was a time when Percy would have fainted at the
sight of blood; now he gave it but a passing thought
as he stared straight into the eyes of his prostrate
foe.

But though he seemed to be intent on staring
Broadhead out of countenance, he was feeling his
way for the money. By moving his legs, now one
way, now another, he satisfied himself that there
was nothing in Broadhead's trousers pockets but a
pocket-knife and one or two small articles. As
Percy knew that the money had been tied up in a
handkerchief, he could infer that there was no ne-
cessity of taking Broadhead's vest into account. It
followed, then, that the money must be in the boy's
coat pocket. But which pocket? In order to carry
out his plan Percy must make no mistake. He
must know the right pocket or his whole plan would
fail and the struggle would have to begin again.

Broadhead had neglected to take his overcoat with
him. The coat he wore had two outside pockets, one
on the right and one on the left.

With these data before him Percy reasoned thus:

"Broadhead hurries out of the dormitory and
makes straight for the study-hall; when he gets to
the study-hall he is in a great hurry, for he doesn't
even take time to get his coat, which I saw him
hang up just before he went to bed. He is nervous
and afraid of being caught, otherwise he'd have
taken that coat, as it wouldn't have taken him two
seconds of time. Now, when he opens the box he

turned the key with his right hand, because he's right-handed; he opens the lid with his left, takes out the handkerchief of money with his left, and drops it into his left-hand pocket and hurries away. If he didn't do that he ought to have done it, anyhow. Therefore it's probable that the money is still there."

Here Percy, before acting upon this hypothesis, breathes a short prayer. He is beginning to suffer from the cold night air and sharp pains are shooting through his bare feet.

Then suddenly he gives Broadhead a jerk that throws him on his right side, dives into his left-hand pocket, and with a cry of joy brings out the handkerchief just as he saw it last night in Tom Playfair's hands. He makes no pause to examine it, but springing to his feet dashes at full speed back toward the college. He has cleared twenty yards before Broadhead arises; as he patters on a few stones pass by him, for Broadhead, satisfied that he is no match for Percy in speed, is contented to throw stones. The robber has been robbed.

When Percy got to a safe distance he fell into a walk and then noticed that his feet were covered with blood.

Before he reached the college he was hardly able to walk at all. With pain and exceeding difficulty he made his way to the infirmary, and there he was kept for a week.

He had Tom by his side next morning, and there, under strict secrecy, related his adventure and restored his astonished friend the money. None of the Dodgers, save Tipp, knew till long afterward what a strange midnight adventure had been brought

about by their twenty dollars. The story leaked
out gradually, though Percy absolutely and constantly refused to talk of it in public.

Broadhead never returned.

CHAPTER XXIII.

IN WHICH TIPP MAKES A SPEECH.

IT is hardly necessary to state that Mr. Middleton was let into the secret that swelled the
breasts of the Artful Dodgers. He was delighted
with their purpose and abetted the benevolent con-
spirators to the full of his power.

Before supper on a Monday evening Tipp approached Mr. Auber:

"Mr. Auber," he said, touching his cap very respectfully, "I wish you'd kindly let me have the
keys of the wash-room. Myself and the rest of the
Dodgers want to fix up in style."

A vision of flying shoe-brushes, knotted towels,
missing shoe-blacking, much raising of dust, and
general confusion shot before the prefect's fancy.
He was familiar with such occurrences and he looked
at Tipp very seriously.

"Oh, we're not going to cut up—honor bright, Mr.
Auber. If there's a single thing out of place you
can punish me."

Mr. Auber, much as he had suffered from Tipp,
knew that the boy before him could be depended
upon. Out of the wreck of Tipp's reputation truth
had been saved; and it is hard to despise a boy so
long as his word is sacred.

So the prefect tendered Tipp the keys; more, he

refrained from going near the wash-room, though for
the next twenty minutes it was occupied by fifty
boys who in the matter of scrapes were makers of
history.

And his trust was well placed; never was there a
more sober set of students than the fifty now in the
wash-room. They spoke quietly and pursued their
work steadily. One would think they were preparing for a funeral.

"There's one thing I notice, boys," said Tipp,
when nearly all were ready to go out, "and it's
worth thinking about. We've been in here nearly
twenty minutes; I reckon, and Mr. Auber hasn't
come near us."

"What did you tell him, Tipp?" queried Tom.

"I told him I'd be responsibe and that our fellows didn't intend to cut up. Yes, sir," cried Tipp,
his eyes dancing and his face flushing, "and he
takes my word and he trusts us Dodgers just the
same as if we had acted like gentlemen all the time.
There he is now, down at the other end of the yard,
looking on at a game of 'nigger baby' just as if we
were all in San Francisco."

"And I guess if most of us were in his place," put
in Harry Quip, "we wouldn't trust the Dodgers half
as far as we could see 'em."

I really believe the Dodgers as they left the wash-
room were in love with Mr. Auber. They were a
wild set of fellows, but owing partly to their naturally good dispositions and their religious training
partly to Tipp's control and Playfair's influence,
they were roughly honest. Show a set of boys such
as these that you value their honor, that you take
their word as something serious and sacred, and you

13

can count on them infallibly. I am speaking here of the small boy.

The Dodgers created a sensation when they entered the yard. There were no "dudes" in that notorious association, the popular taste among them tending rather to slouchiness. But now! Tipp led the procession, wearing a stiff hat, and upon his spotless white shirt rested a jewelled neck-tie. He wore his "Sunday" clothes and his boots were blacked. Nor was it the perfunctory style of blacking which generally characterized his efforts in that direction; even the back of the heels (where the lively small boy finds it difficult to reach) shone as perfectly as the shining toes. Tipp's splendors were emulated, though not surpassed, by those of several others. In a word, and to bring the picture vividly before all, there were fifteen stiff hats in the crowd. Now, the Dodgers were known to be prejudiced in the matter of stiff hats, each member ordinarily feeling it to be his duty to smash in every one he could reach with his hand. Clearly, then, something great was at hand.

The bell rang for supper and the boys, with a promptness and order that were commendable, fell into ranks. So prompt were they that Mr. Middleton gave the signal to march before the large boys had fairly gotten together.

The large boys, still waiting the signal to start, at once noticed that there was something strange about the advancing line, and Mr. Cavanne, who with his back to the approaching procession was eying his charges, suddenly saw one hundred solemn faces break into luxuriant grins, like a transformation scene in a pantomime.

He turned; he saw the solemn-faced Tipp, the serious line of small boys, the fifteen stiff hats variegating the procession like so many banners; and then Mr. Cavanne, the strict, the exact tamer of boys and trainer of men, burst into a roar of laughter.

The small boys passed on unmoved, though their every step was accompanied by bursts of hilarity.

"Supper went off with a snap," Harry Quip remarked as we pushed out of the refectory, which being interpreted means that we ate a good quantity of food in the smallest compass of time.

"Mr. Auber," said Tom, "it's a pretty cool night, and if you please the fellows would like it if you'd open up the wash-room."

As not a boy remained in the yard, Mr. Auber was compelled to enter with the crowd.

On his entrance there was a dead silence. Tom moved over quietly to the door and shut it; every boy rose and removed his hat; and Tipp, nervous but eager-eyed, stepped forward.

"Mr. Auber," he said, "we Dodgers have permission to make you a present. Here it is."

Frank Burdock advanced and presented a silver watch. Mr. Auber took it mechanically with one hand while he began passing the other through his hair very rapidly.

It was difficult to judge which of the two was the more frightened, which blushed the more violently, Tipp or Mr. Auber.

"Ten to one they both faint," whispered the irreverent Quip in my ear.

"Go on, Tipp, you're doing immensely," said Tom in the voice that so often carried encouragement.

"Mr. Auber," continued the orator, shuffling his feet and getting one shoulder hopelessly higher than the other, "we've been a blamed hard lot."

One of Tipp's arms seemed to get out of joint at the escape of the word "blamed."

"Go on," growled Tom; "'blamed' is all right."

"And, sir, we've acted in such a way that I guess you wish we were all dead."

He paused.

"And buried, too," he added in a burst of inspiration. "But we didn't mean any harm, and we're sorry, and we like you, and we're going to do better—ain't we, fellows?"

Every variety of affirmation came mumbling forth from the chorus.

Then Tipp made a bow and limped away. He looked like a person suffering from almost total paralysis.

"Boys," said Mr. Auber, taking his hand out of his hair, "I'm astonished; I'm gratified; I'm touched. I wasn't prepared for this. I'm afraid I don't understand you at all. If things have gone wrong it must have been my own fault."

His lips quivered and his eyes grew moist.

"I'm not able to say what I'd like to say, but I'm deeply, deeply grateful."

With these words he ran the *watch* through his hair, but not a boy laughed.

"There's going to be a dead-lock," whispered Joe Whyte to Tom.

"I'll bet there won't. Boys," he added aloud, " three cheers for Mr. Auber."

All shrieked three times.

"And three cheers for the Dodgers."

The hurly-burly was renewed.

"Now, Mr. Auber," continued Tom, "there's half an hour left. Won't you please tell us a story?"

Mr. Auber's face put on new terror.

"I can't tell a story. I'd be delighted to oblige you all, but I never told a story in all my life."

"Perhaps you never tried, sir."

"Go on, Mr. Auber," implored Quip; "if you get stuck we'll help you out."

Mr. Auber put the watch in his pocket, to the great relief of many of us, who feared he would destroy it, ran his hands through his hair, and said:

"Once upon a time——"

He never finished that first sentence, but began bravely on another. It was the first step that cost. Presently Mr. Auber was transformed. His eyes flashed and his hands moved in easy, striking gestures; and in a flow of English, strong, pure, simple, the like of which we had never heard, he poured forth a tale of heroism and adventure that set our eyes blazing, riveted us to our seats, brought the tears to our eyes, and convinced us that we were listening to the most eloquent story-teller we could hope to meet with.

In the course of the narrative Mr. Middleton came in; but not six of the spell-bound audience, I dare say, observed his entrance. On he went, this wonderful Mr. Auber, till he had almost mesmerized his hearers. We suffered and loved and laughed with the hero, and when Mr. Auber came to an end none of us dared break the silence. Mr. Auber was gone before Tipp remarked:

"Well, that was stunning."

"It's the story of the 'Hidden Gem' all over,"

said Tom; "and the only thing that I feel bad about is that Percy missed it. Mr. Auber was the hidden gem."

Mr. Auber's trials were over. If any boy wished to give him trouble, he knew that he would have to answer to the Dodger crowd. Twice a week after supper during the winter did we assemble in the wash-room to hear our prefect's narratives. He carried us away with him—and up. His stories were elevating; they filled us with longings to be noble, to be heroic, and it is no exaggeration to say that the ideals of many were revolutionized.

For example:

Tipp came to Tom one day and said: "Tom, will you do me a favor?"

"If I can, certainly."

"Well, I want you to stop calling me 'Dodger.' Get Percy and all your chums to do the same. You see, I used to be proud of that name; but now— eh—you understand?"

And Tipp became Tipp again and went home to help his father at the end of the year, as honest, as gay, and as good as though he had done all the noble things which Mr. Auber had narrated of his choicest heroes.

CHAPTER XXIV.

*IN WHICH IS GIVEN SOME ACCOUNT OF THE INTERCOL-
LEGIATE CONTEST AND IN WHICH WE BID OUR KIND
PROFESSOR A LONG FAREWELL.*

"SAY, I went to Holy Communion this morning," said Frank as he came upon me in the yard after breakfast on a certain beautiful spring morning.

" Why, Frank ?"

" For the Ciceronians. Other fellows went too, and there were lots of prayers said for you."

" Thank you, Frank."

" I prayed for you to get second place of honor."

" Indeed ?"

" Yes. You see, Percy's first on my list. He's the best boy alive. Then Tom comes next. He's to get first place of honor. Of course all the fellows thought in the beginning of the year that you'd come out ahead. But you've been so bothered about Mrs. Raynor that you've given Percy and Tom a chance to catch up. Of course you don't expect me to like you as much as I do Percy and Tom!"

Frank gazed at me in anxiety.

I laughed.

" I'm glad that you like me at all, Frank."

" I believe you are," said our honest little man. " I've known them longer than I've known you. But you and Harry Quip are third and equal, and you can bet on me for a friend, and I do hope you'll get second place on the list of honor. You begin working at it at nine o'clock this morning, don't you ?"

" Yes, Frank."

" Well, I hope you'll all do your best. You look heavy round the eyes, Harry. Didn't you sleep well last night ?"

" Not as well as usual."

Indeed, I fear that few of our Ciceronian Society had slept well that night. We had been in a feverish state the preceding morning, and could not even take part in the sports of early spring with any relish. For my own part, my sleep was disturbed by unpleasant dreams. I held several interviews

with my ghostly uncle, at one of which he informed
me that there would be no intercollegiate medal
given out if I neglected to bring the murderer to
justice.

Well, the day had come.   How we bent ourselves
to our work!   The theme, though not extremely
difficult, was quite long.   I don't think that a single
one of us Ciceronians so much as looked at each
other during the four hours allowed us for our effort.
What a groan of dismay went forth when Mr. Middleton announced that but fifteen minutes were left!
Then, indeed, was there much scurrying and scratch-
ing of pens.

Time was called at length, and each boy handed
in his paper, signed, not with his own name, but with
a *nom de plume.*   His own name, with the correspond-
ing *nom de plume*, he put into an envelope and delivered to the vice-president of the college.   The
papers themselves were to be sent on to the donor of
the medal, who was to put them in the hands of
three competent and unprejudiced Latin scholars.
These were to select ten papers in the order of
their merit—the first in merit gaining the prize and
the others taking the nine places of honor.   The
judges themselves, according to this plan, could
have no more idea as to who were the leaders than
the boys most interested.

"Boys," said Mr. Middleton when we were about
to leave the class-room, "one remark.   You all
know how heartily I wish you success in this contest.   But permit me to congratulate you now for
what is far better.   I congratulate you, my dear
boys, on what, as Johnson truly says, is more than
success—on your deserving it.   You have done your

duty. That is the essential; success is the accident."

Calm and logical as these words may appear in type, they were spoken with such feeling that when Mr. Middleton came to the words, "You have done your duty," there was a quiver in his voice, and we felt more than repaid for all our endeavors.

"Much as I'd like to get the medal," said Tom, "I'd rather get words like that from Mr. Middleton than any prize they can put up. What names did you take, boys?"

"I took '*Sic itur ad astra,*'" said Percy.

"And I '*Gaudeamus igitur juvenes dum sumus,*'" said Quip.

"Mine was '*Parturiunt montes,*'" laughed Ruthers.

"'*Miserere mei, Deus,*'" said I.

"That's near mine," Richards exclaimed. "I took '*In te Domine speravi.*'"

"And I went to Horace for mine," said Tom— "'*Nil ardui mortalibus; cælum ipsum petimus,*' and then I left out a word because I thought the examiners might find it between the lines of the whole theme."

"Oh," said Percy, "I remember it: '*Cælum ipsum petimus stultitia.*'"

"Young gentlemen," cried Tom, "the Ciceronian Society is adjourned *sine die.* We'll now go to bed early and get ready to play those Juniors of the large yard another game, and see whether we can't do them up as we did last year."

We got ready accordingly, played the Juniors, and were defeated pretty badly. Keenan and Donnel were against us.

June came, and with it a renewal of that sweetest

of devotions, devotion to the Sacred Heart. We
Ciceronians were all members of the league. Indeed, with the exception of myself, all of us were
promoters. During the month I learned more fully
the secret of Tom's meekness and Percy's sweetness
of disposition.

It was the night of closing exercises. We Ciceronians were huddled together in the hall, and how
we did growl at the music and speech-making and
singing. When these things had come to an end
we breathed a hearty thanks.

"There's the president going up. Why doesn't
he hustle?" growled Tom. "Oh, gracious! he's got
to dispose of those graduates first. Then we'll get
our innings."

Not one of us attended to the conferring of
degrees or listened with the least bit of interest to
the able lawyer who addressed the graduates for
something over an hour. At length our "innings"
came.

"The gold medal in the intercollegiate contest
between six competing colleges has been awarded
to a student of St. Maure's—winner, Percy Wynn."

The applause which we Ciceronians broke into,
ably supplemented as it was by the entire audience,
would have startled the echoes of a muffled hall.
Harry Quip and myself were necessitated to hold
Tom Playfair down by main force, for he had
jumped to his feet at the name and was about to
disgrace us by dancing, a feat, by the way, which
Frank Burdock, who, with his father, was in
another part of the hall, did actually perform, to the
smiling amusement of the astonished audience.

"Places of honor," continued the vice-president

when the applause, under which Percy was blushing
violently, had subsided. "First—Thomas Playfair
and Harry Dee, equal. Both of St. Maure's."

Tom and myself came very near blushing, and
were happier than if we had won the medal. After
all, we knew Percy was our superior, and had either
of us outstripped him we would have felt that we
were the favored children of luck. You may be
sure that our fellow-members, as the applause continued, shook our hands and pulled us about in an
ecstasy of happiness.

"Third place—John Ray, of a competing college."
There was a silence.

"Hurrah for John Ray, boys," whispered Tom.
"Let's applaud him."

The people followed where we led.

"Fourth place—Harry Quip, of St. Maure's."

"Cæsar!" ejaculated Harry, his merry face taking
on the hue of an angry sunset and retaining its color
long after the clapping of hands had subsided.

"Fifth place—John Cynic, of a competing college.

"Sixth place—John Robertson, of a competing
college.

"Seventh—Joseph Whyte, of St. Maure's.

"Eighth—Charles Seebert, of a competing college.

"Ninth—Charles Richards, of St. Maure's."

Each of us named for a place of honor was presented by the president with a book, and as the audience realized that we, the successful competitors,
were, with the exception of Richards, small boys
in knickerbockers, they fairly went wild. Some
among them must have got a hint of this magnificent victory for St. Maure's, for bouquets came flying
upon the stage. Nothing could be seen of Percy

presently but his high shoes, his silk stockings, and his eyes and forehead. Percy's ten sisters were in attendance, and I have a strong suspicion that each one sent him a bouquet. Our hero of the hour, as the flowers still came, was in quite a predicament, when, to his relief, Master Frank Burdock came bounding upon the stage, his eyes flashing with excitement.

"I'll help you, Percy," he piped; "let them come on with their baskets. The biggest is the one I sent." And amid fresh applause Master Frank relieved Percy of a few of his bouquets and escorted his friend off the stage. Tom also was laden with flowers, for which I'm quite certain Percy's sisters were largely responsible. Nor were the rest of us forgotten. We could have combined that night and set up a fine florist's establishment.

None of us took interest in what followed. We soon stole out of the hall and shook each other's hands over and over. Willie Ruthers had received no mention, but, as he naïvely remarked, "We Humanities boys don't want the earth. Some of us had to fall through. But next year see if I'm not on."

Next day we went in a body to bid Mr. Middleton farewell. Our beloved professor was to leave us. His college work, for some years at least, was over.

"Aha!" he exclaimed gayly as we entered his room, "here are my little Ciceronians. But what's the use of my congratulating you on your success? The great thing is that you've deserved it."

He shook each of us warmly by the hand, nevertheless, and how sweetly, kindly did those gentle eyes of his shine upon us.

"Mr. Middleton," said Percy, "you're going away ?'

"Yes; but after what happened last night I can leave the field of my college labors saying with holy Simeon, '*Nunc dimittis servum tuum, Domine in pace.*'"

"Well, Mr. Middleton," continued Percy gravely, "we've come to bid you good-by. All of us have been under you for several years, all of us long enough to love you. You have taught us to love our books, to love our religion, to love one another, and in teaching us all this to love you. Should we never meet again, Mr. Middleton," here Percy's voice almost broke and all of us cleared our throats, "you may be sure that we shall not forget you. Day and night our prayers shall rise to God that He may bless you and prosper you in all your ways; and should any of us go wrong for a time, should we forget your kind words, should we give up the pious practices you have taught us by example more than word, should we become such that we would not wish to meet you—O Mr. Middleton! I can't go on!"

And we all broke down with Percy. That last artless touch, more powerful than his prepared speech, overmastered all of us. And the brave, strong, earnest man we all loved so well turned his face from us, bent his head, and placed his hand upon his brow.

"God bless you, my dear boys. Good-by."

With that benediction upon us we left him, and none of us spoke till we had reached our yard.

There we found Donnel and Keenan awaiting us and looking unusually grave. "Good-by, boys," they said; "we're going for good."

"What! where?" General astonishment.

"John's going off to the seminary at Baltimore, and I'm going to the Novitiate to try and become a Jesuit."

There was a great deal of hand-shaking, though we spoke softly—parting is ever a sorrow, no matter how sweet. We had always looked up to George and John as model boys and leaders. None of us was surprised at the step they were about to take; some of us envied them. For all this, our parting was sad.

And so we broke up for the vacation. Changes were marking the inexorable flight of time. When we returned we missed three whom we had loved from their accustomed places, and we realized then that these changes, sad as they are, must go on year after year, till upon each of us comes the great change beyond which there is no shadow of vicissitude, no parting, but everlasting peace and deathless reunion.

CHAPTER XXV.

IN WHICH ROSE SCARBOROUGH RENEWS OUR ACQUAINT-ANCE AND SINGS US SEVERAL ASTONISHING SONGS.

HARRY QUIP, Percy, Frank, Tom, and myself took our outing beside the pretty lake in Wisconsin, where we renewed our acquaintance with Mr. Scarborough and his graceless son. Rose renewed our acquaintance herself. She met us at the depot, all smiles and courtesies.

"Hallo, little girl!" called Tom.

"Hallo, sir."

"Can you sing 'Jesus, Saviour of my soul' yet, little girl?"

"Oh, yes, sir; and I know ten, eleven, twelve new tunes. How do you do, Frank Burdock? You didn't write to me, after all your promises."

Poor Frank blushed scarlet, Harry Quip grinned, while Tom choked and coughed and laughed till the tears ran down his face. Frank scowled on each of us in turn, but relented on catching Percy's eye.

The *enfante terrible* did not exactly perceive in what she had been witty, but taking it for granted that there were sufficient reasons for laughing, she joined us in our merriment. She continued:

"Say, Percy, I know two of your sisters. They go to the Sacred Heart Convent at Clifton, near Cincinnati. That's where I go to school now; and I'm going to be a Catholic next year; and that's where I learned to sing twelve new tunes, and I'm going to sing them all for Tom Playfair, because he likes my singing and I like him. [Here she gave Tom an ingenuous look, this *enfante terrible*, which sent Percy into a musical laugh and a flush of color upon Mr. Tom's cheek.] Oh, yes! I was talking about your sisters. They're the sweetest, nicest girls! Oh! how I love them. They're nicer than any girls I ever met—as nice and kind and gentle as you are, Percy."

Thereupon we all departed incontinently, leaving the artless miss not a little astonished at our strange conduct.

She bore us no ill-will, however, for she came over of set purpose that evening to sing, for Tom's special behoof, "Jesus, Lover of my soul." Very vividly as her sweet treble broke so gently upon our

ears did we recall the scene upon the lake. I turned
my head aside till the little one had finished, and
thought I heard a sob from Percy, but could not trust
myself to look around.

"Your voice is nicer than ever, little girl."

"Is it? I'll sing you another song, Tom." Thereupon the delighted vocalist gave us a very pretty
"*Ave Maris Stella.*"

We all applauded.

"Did you like that?" she asked, her eyes dancing.

"We did, little girl."

"Then here's another for you, Percy," and to our
amazement and Percy's total discomfiture she sang
a very tuneful German song, beginning "How can I
leave thee?" but when she came to the words, "I
would sooner life than thee resign," Tom held up
his hand.

"Desist, little girl, desist!"

"I beg your pardon, sir."

"You see, little girl," went on Tom gravely,
"we've got to draw the line somewhere."

"What do you want to draw a line for?" said
this very ingenuous little one.

"All the way around that song, little girl. It's
too personal. This isn't leap-year."

"Isn't it?" Rose was very much puzzled.

"No—you'll have to wait two years more at least
before you can sing that song for Percy."

"Oh! but I've got another song for Frank Burdock."

"What's it about, little girl?"

"It begins, 'Believe me, of all these endearing
young charms.'"

Even Tom could keep his countenance no longer.

"You don't mean to say, little girl, that the nuns coached you up in these songs?"

"Oh, no, sir. I learned them all by myself."

"You did! But they're love-songs."

Rose looked at him very composedly.

"I don't care! I'm not going to be a nun."

Whereupon Tom gave up.

From that day Miss Rose became a frequent visitor. She had a supreme disregard for conventionalities and conducted herself in a way that was certainly unique.

Vacation passed all too quickly. During these summer months I received, through my father, letters from the detective bureau, each and every one of them announcing a fresh clew. My father got weary of this at last and wrote:

DEAR MR. TINKER:—I am completely discouraged. If you announce any more clews I shall resign all hope of ever meeting Mrs. Raynor in this world. Tell your sleepless detectives to take a little needful repose.

Yours sincerely,

JOHN DEE.

In answer to which he received very promptly a heavy bill for services rendered. Each announcement of a clew cost a good round sum of money.

My father inclosed the full amount by return mail, and took occasion to inform the indefatigable Tinker that he would try to worry along without the services of his insomnia-ridden bureau, and that, were it necessary, he would be willing to pay him a certain yearly allowance to induce him and his men not to unsteady their intellects on the looking up of labyrinthine clews.

14

So it seemed to us we were done with clews. As the sequel, to which I now hasten, will show, we were mistaken.

CHAPTER XXVI.

IN WHICH A STRANGE REVELATION THROWS NEW LIGHT ON THE MYSTERY OF MY UNCLE'S DEATH.

SOME of the happiest periods in our lives become insufferably dull when we undertake to render an account of them. The following year at St. Maure's was for us poets a golden year. Much as we had loved our studies in the lower classes, we now threw ourselves into them with renewed ardor. For we were at an age when sentiment, with its vernal freshness, awakes in the youthful heart, and in a class where all the studies—be it of Latin, Greek, or English—are directed toward stimulating sentiment, developing it in some directions, pruning it in others, rendering it, in short, a noble instrument for appreciating all that is highest and holiest in human life, thought, and endeavor.

It is hardly necessary to state that all of us poets had exchanged our knickerbockers for trousers, and walked about with the certain step of man—so, at least, we thought.

Percy was the real poet of our class. His delicate imagination was a storehouse of fancies, sweet, pure, charming—he had but to touch a seemingly dry idea and it burst into blossoms of beauty.

Tom was not so successful in poetry proper, but in English prose, for strong, vigorous thought and expression he led all. In Latin, too, he advanced rapidly and soon took the lead of Percy, who, it must be confessed, relaxed a trifle in the pursuit of the classics that he might give more time to the muse. Frank Burdock remained in the small yard, not a little to his disgust. He was growing fast, however, and gave promise of joining us the following year. Whenever he met me he invariably asked in a whisper:

"Say, Harry, don't you think I'm growing?" and he would draw himself up and look me fixedly in the eye.

It was a bright, cool Thursday morning toward the end of May. Percy, Tom, and myself were out for a long walk. We had obtained permission from the president of the college to visit the village of Sykesville, six miles to the east of us. Our plan was to make it by half-past nine, procure lunch there, depart at ten, and reach the college by noon-time.

"Harry," remarked Tom, after a pause which had succeeded a desultory conversation, "it's strange that you've got no news lately about what your lawyer is doing."

"That reminds me," I answered; "my father sent me a letter of his yesterday. The lawyer holds out little hope. He says that our finding Mrs. Raynor is almost a matter dependent upon chance. He thinks that in all probability she is going under an alias. Then he adds: 'From the fact that she lived with you on intimate terms for several years without giving any clew to her former life up to the very night of the murder, I infer that she is a very extraordinary woman. A woman or even a man of such reticence is a hard subject to overreach.'"

"He's quite a different character from the invaluable Tinker," said Tom. "I think he's quite right. Chance is your hope, and yet I'll wager my last poem that you'll meet her yet."

"Isn't it sad," said Percy, in his sweet, winning way, "to think that this woman, whom you looked upon in the sacred relation of mother, should turn out to be a criminal. It's cruel! I don't want to believe it."

"Nor I, Percy; but I fear I must. God knows I loved her as a mother, and she loved me. I'm certain of it. She'd have laid down her life for me, I once thought."

"It looks strongly against her," said Tom. "But the great mystery is to reconcile her love and affection for Harry with the cruel way in which she took her revenge. Children don't love people like that. Innocence is the greatest detective in the world."

"Well, for the present it is a mystery," said Percy. "Who knows when it may be cleared up? 'It is the unexpected that always happens.'"

We entered Sykesville presently, soon found a bakery and confectionery, where, taking seats in a back room, screened from the front part of the store by heavy curtains, we ordered our lunch of a smiling young man with heavy eyes, who looked as though he had gone to bed very late and hadn't succeeded in sleeping well even then.

"Bring in your shop," said Tom.

"Shop! shop!" echoed the heavy-eyed. "Do you mean Scotch cakes?"

"Exactly. Scotch cakes for three and cream cakes and baker's toast and——"

"Yes, sir."

"And lemonade."

"All right, sir." And the young man hastened off.

If the three of us had put off the small boy we had not put off his appetite. We kept the young man busy, while Tom worried him into the lowest depths of stupidity by his absurd remarks.

In the midst of an amusing story Tom stopped short.

"What in the world's the matter, Harry?" he exclaimed as I sprang from my seat and peered through the curtain; for a strangely familiar voice had stirred the roots of my hair. I looked through the curtain and a dizziness came upon me.

"Catch him, Percy—he's falling."

For I staggered, the wheels of life stood still, and I would have fallen to the floor had not Percy caught me and restored me to my chair.

"Here, drink this," said Tom, putting a glass of water to my lips. "Hallo, there!" he added in a louder voice. "Bring in some wine, quick!"

Startled by his tone, the shopman came hastening in with a bottle of wine. Tom very calmly knocked the neck off the bottle and filled me a glass. As this was a prohibition town, the intelligent reader will understand how it was that wine was on sale in a bakery.

"What is it, Harry?" inquired Tom as I showed signs of coming to.

"I just saw Mrs. Raynor. She's in this shop now."

Tom bounded to the curtain and peeped cautiously through the opening. He saw standing at the coun- ter a woman of middle age, poor but neat in dress, with a refined face, on which lines of suffering and, it may be, of privation had written the pathos of many years. She had just bought a loaf of bread and was turning to go out.

"Harry," he said, "you just stay where you are. I'll not speak to her at all. But leave everything to me." Saying which, he drew the curtains aside and hurried away.

Percy and I were very sober. We knew that a great crisis in my life was come. Terrible fancies stared me in the face and conflicting emotions fought strong within me. At sight of that familiar countenance all my former filial affection returned. Oh, it was cruel! She had been a mother to me, and now it might become my duty to hand her over to the law. Percy perceived my distress.

"God help you, my dear friend," he said, his blue eyes swimming. "Be brave and strong; trust in Him."

I bowed my head upon the table and wept and prayed.

Tom came in at length, his face softened with pity.

"I've got her house, Harry. Of course you'll see her alone first?"

"Of course."

"Well, we'll be near, so as if anything happens to help you."

"O Tom! if what we dread most proves to be true, what shall I do? It is my certain duty to have her put in custody."

"Go and see her," said Tom. "If the worst does come, old boy, Percy and I will see to the unpleasant parts."

We left the bakery together, quite different from

the merry, laughing, happy-eyed boys who had entered.

Walking down the length of the street and turning to our left, we presently found ourselves before a tiny cottage overgrown with creeping plants and standing back in a small, tastily-arranged garden.

"That's the house," said Tom. "Go in, Harry, and be a man."

"God bless you!" added Percy.

Summoning all my courage, I walked up to the cottage. A small window gave me a view of the interior before I reached the door. I paused and looked in. Oh! what a trial it was to me—what an agony even to think of going one step farther. At a sewing-machine sat Mrs. Raynor, her face, furrowed though it was, calm and serene. Beside her was a boy of ten or eleven, dark-eyed, black-haired, neatly but poorly clad, working at a lathe. His beautiful face was lighted with an expression of joy. Near them and playing upon the floor was a bright little girl of six or seven. As I stood looking in upon the scene, the boy turned proudly and held up his work to Mrs. Raynor. She smiled approvingly, then bent over and kissed his cheek. Whereupon the little girl, with the socialistic spirit common to children, came running over to claim her share, too.

"I'm learning fast, mamma," said the boy. "In a few weeks I'll be able to do two hours' good work every day—you've promised me, you know—and then you're going to get a rest, mamma. And then you'll get strong and well—and sis and I will be so happy!"

When Enoch Arden gazed upon the happy household whereof his own lawful wife was the light, he crept away like a guilty thing, dug his hands into the earth, and prayed! Not unlike his position was my own. Should I enter and destroy this sacred home-life? God knows I would have departed on the moment had I but felt certain that I knew all, had I felt certain that Mrs. Raynor had done the deed. Yes, I would have departed even should I be haunted from that day to the day of my death by my uncle's ghost. But the one element of uncertainty—the mystery; Tom's words so often repeated urging me to see Mrs. Raynor; the sense of duty— all conspired to move me on.

And so, with the merry laugh of the children ringing in my ears, " like sweet bells jangled out of tune," I knocked.

" Come in!"

I threw the door open and stood gazing at my former attendant, who on the instant had arisen, putting aside her sewing as she did so.

The eyes I knew so well—had they not met mine a thousand times in love and tenderness?—looked at me inquiringly, then there was a sudden start, then a cry, and she was weeping with joy upon my bosom.

" My own dear Harry!" she sobbed.

I was unmanned for a moment. But with a wrench at my heart I drew myself away and looked meaningly at the children.

She took my thought at once. Her face was very pale as she turned to the little ones and said:

" My dears, go out. I shall call you in a few minutes."

How hateful I appeared in my own eyes as they each kissed their mamma an affectionate farewell.

When they had left the room I cleared my throat and began my story. I told my nurse of my terrible awakening on Christmas morning, of the scene in my uncle's room, of my visit with Tom Playfair to the haunted house, and of the dream ghost that had seemed so real.

"And oh! Mrs. Raynor," I concluded, "black as stands the evidence against you, for God's sake give me your word that you are innocent! I will believe you now as I did when, a little child, I called you mother."

"Harry, my own dear boy, in God's name I assure you that I am innocent."

I gave a gasp of joy. A great gloom lifted from my heart, and I would have thrown my arms about my nurse's neck had not a peculiar quivering of her lips, a growing paleness in her face, warned me that she had left something untold.

"Who was it?" I cried. "You know more!"

"Harry—God help you, my dear boy—you killed your uncle yourself!"

The room swam; my brain reeled; Mrs. Raynor in a moment helped me to a chair.

"Listen!" she said. "Let us recall together what went before that dreadful night. I knew when we took the train that sad Christmas eve that I was to face the only man I had ever had reason to hate. I had never seen him nor he me. I counted on saying nothing when in his presence, but the very moment we stood before him all my pent-up wrongs came thronging upon my memory. I failed to restrain myself, and you remember well the scene that ensued between me and your uncle. Then you remember how, when at eight o'clock we went to your bedroom, I told you all the sad story of my life—of my noble husband, of his death of a broken heart. You in your sweet love mingled your tears with mine. You were angry at your uncle, and at ten o'clock, when you fell asleep, you left me meditating on the terrible wrongs James Dee had done my baby children. I had not told you of them, Harry. You saw them just now. I had left them in charge of an aunt under their real name, for Raynor was not my married, but my family name. Now, please to remember that when you went to sleep at ten you left me sitting beside you, worn out with a day's journey—as you know I did not sleep on the cars—and still more worn from the terrible emotions that had shaken my soul. For an hour or more my thoughts were busy with the past—vividly busy. Then came a sort of heavy feeling; sleep was coming upon me. I arose and paced the room; but walk as I might, sleep was struggling with me and I detected myself staggering as I moved up and down. But notwithstanding all that, I would have fought it off, I think, had not a sudden weakness come upon me. I felt that I was about to faint; I made over to the bed and tried to call you, but fell to the floor, midway in the room, unconscious. It was some time before I recovered at all, and even then I continued to lie half-conscious upon the floor. During this period, which lasted, I imagine, fifteen or twenty minutes, I remembered, in a sort of horrid nightmare, that I was in the house of an enemy. Then I heard, or thought I heard, the sound of some one walking on tiptoe, and it occurred to me that perhaps your uncle was coming to kill me. I tried to move and failed; the nightmare became more and more vivid;

the footfalls, slow, stealthy, came nearer. Oh, the horror of that dream!"

Mrs. Raynor paused and wiped her brow.

"At last I burst the spell upon me and rose to my feet in a state of terror you can hardly imagine. I stood for a moment listening to catch those ominous footfalls. But I heard nothing. Then I turned to your bed. It was empty. Oh! my dear Harry, you were gone. For a moment I stood paralyzed with fright! Here you were alone, in a strange house, walking in your sleep. I shivered as it occurred to me that you might have fallen out of some window! Even as I stood I heard without the sound of a light footstep—not like the heavy footstep I had heard or thought I heard in my nightmare. That was the sound of a man or woman's tread on tiptoe; this was the sound of a child's bare feet. As I caught your tread, Harry, I took up the lamp and hastened to the hallway. How I thanked God as I saw you coming along quietly, easily, from the further end of the hall. I hastened to meet you. But as I got near, imagine my feelings when I saw that your night-shirt was dabbled with blood. It was an awful sight! You with your innocent face and eyes wide open—yet seeing nothing—walking along unconscious of those awful stains. I kept beside you and followed you to your room, where you walked straight to your bed and got into it. Then, lamp in hand, I hurried down the corridor to the very end, where I saw an open door. I entered trembling, and holding the lamp up gazed around. Then, my dear boy, I saw what you saw the next morning—your uncle cold in death."

CHAPTER XXVII.

MRS. RAYNOR paused for a moment and wiped her eyes.

"Then," she resumed, "it flashed upon me that I, and I alone, was to blame for this frightful tragedy, since I had sent you to sleep with sentiments of horror and disgust toward your uncle. Oh, how I blamed myself for my harsh words against that poor dead form! I came near and examined your uncle more closely. The knife had reached his heart. He was dead. Then I formed my plans in an instant. If any one were guilty of his blood it was I. I remembered, my dear child, that you were delicate and sensitive. I feared that should you learn how you had killed your uncle you would be made miserable for life. And then I thought of all the qualities in you which had won my love. I imagined the future of happiness which should be yours by right, and I knew it would all be blighted did you come to know at that tender age what you had so innocently done. As for sacrificing my own reputation, that weighed little. I was a stranger among strangers and had little to gain, nothing to lose. But when I thought of you, my dear boy, I felt the sacrifice I was making. If I could have let you know that I was not guilty of the crime, my course would have cost me nothing. But that was out of the question. The only feasible way for me to throw a mystery about the murder which would make it fairly impossible for any one to find out that you had done it was to throw all the suspicion on myself. I bathed one of my gloves—my right-hand glove—in your uncle's blood; then hurried back to your room. I threw the glove on the floor after first drawing it across my chair by your bed-side. Then I turned to take my last look upon you. Your little arm was stretched over the coverlet, your hand red with blood. You were sleeping calmly, and even as I gazed down upon your face your lips quivered into a smile, and then, Harry, though I had promised myself not to bid you farewell, I bent down and kissed you and threw my arms about you in all the fond agony of a last embrace. And—O my God! shall I ever forget it?—without opening your eyes you threw your little arms about me and softly whispered 'mamma.' Then I tore myself away, as I thought, forever."

As the noble woman stopped, overcome by her emotions, I arose and softly kissed her.

"But I did not make the sacrifice a perfect one, my own dear boy. I was resolved that when my body lay in the ground you, at least, should have tender memories of your nurse. So after making good my escape I wrote out a full account of what had happened. It was to be delivered to you at my death, and you, you alone were to know the secret. You were to read it and destroy it, and it has been the one comfort of my life that when I was dead and gone you would think kindly and tenderly of your unhappy nurse."

She paused for a moment.

"Of course I foresaw that, acting as I did, I would throw a shadow on your life. I knew that you loved me and I knew that the shock to your sweet confidence in me would be terrible. But what else could I do? I had little time to think. It was narrowed down to a question between two evils. Often and often have I since pondered over the matter. Sometimes it has seemed to me that my conduct was wrong. But God knows that I tried to do what seemed to be for the best. My judgment may have been wrong, but at the time I thought it was the best I could form. I acted, perhaps, on impulse, but if I sinned I trust God has long since forgiven me. And indeed I feel quite sure that had I let you know what you had done when you were so weak and sickly, you would not be the strong, manly boy, dear Harry, that you now are."

I pass over in silence the ensuing few minutes. My brain was in a whirl. Love, gratitude, the shock of this revelation, all conspired to unnerve me. I heard the light prattle of the children as they drew near the door and then I burst into a fit of weeping.

Mrs. Raynor hurried to the door and sent them away and devoted herself to soothing me. Slowly I became calmer, until, after the lapse of an hour, I was exteriorly, at least, something like my old self. Then Mrs. Raynor called in the little ones.

At the sound of her voice the dark, handsome boy —a little prince in patches—and the bright little girl—a fairy princess who had escaped not only from the dragon-guarded castle, but even out of the pages of the story-book into real life—came dancing in.

"Harold and Louise, this is your mamma's best friend, Harry Dee."

"Your brother, your true brother, my little ones," I added. "Remember, Mrs. Dorne," I continued as I caught the willing hands of brother and sister and drew them both to my side, "you have promised to regard me as your son. Harold and Louise are to be my brother and my sister."

As I spoke the children gazed up earnestly into my face, and I am glad to say that their pretty eyes expressed at once full confidence in their new friend.

"Brother Harry," began the boy, "why are your eyes so red, and what makes your lip tremble so? And you are so pale. Did you hear mamma call me Harold? That's my real name, but I don't remember that she ever called me Harold before. She used to call me Harry."

"Mamma always calls me Louise," said the little princess, who had climbed upon my knee and was playing with my watch-guard. "Poor mamma! she doesn't have a bit of fun; mamma's working all the time with big needles. I hate needles."

"I know how to use needles," put in Harold. "I just kept on teasing mamma till she let me try them now and then. I'm not ashamed to sew, even if girls do it mostly. You see, brother Harry, I'm the man of the family; and it isn't right for mamma to do all the work, and Louise is too young to do anything yet."

"I'm five," said Louise, "and I'll be six in free months; and I want a doll, a new doll for my birfday. Oh, brother Harry, don't you know any nice fairy-stories?"

"Not nice enough to tell to you and Harold," I answered with a smile.

"I know a beautiful one."

Mrs. Dorne had gone over to the window and was

looking out. She was still under the influence of strong feelings. Ah! how little had I dreamed, during those years of separation, of the strength and intensity of the love which had nerved on that noble woman in her lonely path of sacrifice.

"Let's hear it, Louise."

"It's a real fairy-story, too."

"So much the better," I answered absently, for my thoughts were absorbed in memories despite the bright little faces turned so eagerly up to mine.

"Yes," Harold broke in, "but it hasn't any fairy in it."

"Now, Harold," said Louise, raising an admonitory finger, "that isn't fair; you mustn't let brother Harry know what's going to happen till it's all happened."

"All right," said Harold, laughing. "Go ahead, Louise."

"Once upon a time," began the little one, "there was a beautiful prince; and he didn't have any sister. And he was the nicest prince—oh! he was so good and pleasant and kind—nicer than Harold!"

"Oh! a heap nicer," said Harold enthusiastically.

"And all the people loved him, but he didn't have no mamma either."

"No?" I said, for Louise had looked at me very earnestly and paused in her story.

"No. He was all alone 'cept his father, who was awful rich and had gold and silver and fine horses. Now, this nice prince used to have beautiful pitchers."

"Visions," put in Harold.

"Yes; beautiful visions after dark; and then he'd get up and walk in his sleep."

"With his eyes wide open," broke in Harold.

"Like this," said Louise, jumping to the floor, opening her eyes very wide, and walking about. "And so," she continued, "his father put out a notice——"

"Issued a proclamation," interrupted the brother.

"Yes; issued a pockermation that he wanted a lady to play mamma to the beautiful prince. What's the matter, brother Harry? Your face is red all over."

"Go on. I'm interested." Indeed, this fairy-story had at length succeeded in riveting my attention.

"And the king said that the lady should always watch by the side of the beautiful prince and never go to sleep."

"Not even for a minute," added the boy.

"And the king had heard from a magician that if ever the lady went to sleep somefin terrible would happen to Prince Harry. And so the king said that if ever the lady went asleep he would cut her head off with an axe. Now, there was one lady who offered to take care of the little prince, and she loved him ever so much because he was so beautiful and so good. And she watched over Prince Harry for many years wivout going to sleep. Now, the young prince had an uncle who was very rich, and the uncle asked the young prince to come and see him. He and the lady went. The lady was always sad, because she had two beautiful children that she loved and she never saw them. Wasn't that too bad?"

"That was very hard," I said softly. Mrs. Dorne was still standing at the window with her face against the pane.

15

"And the very night that Prince Harry arrived at his uncle's castle—it was such a gloomy castle—the lady fell asleep in a faint."

"The first time it ever happened," said Harold.

"And when she woke up the little prince's bed was empty. Somefin awful had happened. Guess, brother Harry."

"Maybe the prince fell from a window," I suggested.

"Guess again," cried Louise in delight.

"Or maybe he was killed by his uncle."

"You're getting hotter," put in Harold.

"Harold, don't tell. Do you give it up?"

"I do."

"Well," here Louise became very solemn, "the little prince killed his uncle wivout knowing it."

"Yes," said Harold; "he stabbed his uncle with a dagger."

"Oh!" said I, "how bad he must have felt when he found out what he had done."

"Ah! but he didn't find out. The lady made it look as if she had killed the uncle and ran away."

"She was a good lady, wasn't she?" I said.

"Ah! mamma—there!" cried Harold, while Louise clapped her hands. "Didn't I say she was good? She wanted the prince to live happy, and how could he live happy if he knew he had killed his uncle?"

"And since then," continued Louise, "the prince has been very happy and the lady has been very poor."

"Is that all?" I inquired, for Louise looked at me in such a way as to force this question.

"No," cried Louise, "the story isn't over yet. Some day there's going to come a pretty fairy to tell

the prince that the lady didn't kill his uncle; and
then the prince will come and see the lady, and he'll
take the lady's little girl for his sister and the lady's
little boy for his brother, and then they'll all live
happily together. There; that's all."

"Could we play that story?" I inquired.

"Oh, yes; let's play it."

"Very good. Louise, you be the little girl, and
Harold, you be the little boy, and your mamma will
be the lady."

"Oh, how nice!" cried Louise. "And you'll be
the prince."

"But I don't look like a prince."

"Yes, you do," said Louise.

"He *is* the prince, my darlings," said Mrs. Raynor,
"and you are now his brother and sister. The story
has all come true except the fairy part. Instead
of a fairy, some beauteous angel of the great God
has sent him hither."

"It's nicer than a fairy-story," cried Louise.
"Angels are nicer than fairies."

And the two little ones grew very happy, though
they did not realize till long afterward that their
pretty story had actually come true.

"But gracious me!" I suddenly exclaimed. "Here
I've been sitting nearly two hours, and two of the
best boys in the world waiting for me down the
street."

Harold jumped to his feet.

"I'll get 'em," he exclaimed, rushing to the door.
There he paused. "But how'll I know who they
are, brother Harry?"

"In the first place both are handsome and look
like college boys. In the second place, the larger

who has blue eyes and golden hair, will smile at you if you catch his eye, and the other, who is darker and jolly-looking, will be pretty sure to say something."

Very shortly in danced Harold, pulling Tom Playfair by the hand and evidently upon very intimate terms with that young man.

"Oh, brother Harry," he said, "it was just the way you told me. The tall one smiled and this one winked at me this way——"

Here Harold put up his hand, shut one eye with it, and continued:

"Then he said, 'How de do, little boy?' and I knew him."

"Thank God! it's all right," I whispered to Tom and Percy as I led them over and introduced them to that good mother.

"Say, little boy," said Tom, "do you like candy?"

"Oh, don't I!"

"I do, too," cried Louise with much interest.

"Well, here, go and buy up the baker shop; and save a piece for me, won't you—you and Louise?"

"Thank you. Yes, sir."

"I'll save you all I don't want to eat—and more, a great deal more," said Louise impressively.

Then there was a scampering of little feet; and as they left the feeling of bewilderment and exhaustion again came upon me. I could not trust myself to speak and, by a sign which Mrs. Dorne interpreted aright, begged her to tell the story to my friends.

Tom and Percy listened very attentively. Percy was shocked on hearing that I myself murdered my uncle. Tom's face gave no signs of emotion during the whole course of the recital, but he seemed buried in thought throughout and in the end un-satisfied.

"Mrs. Dorne," he said at the conclusion, "you have been very brave and noble, but there is one circumstance connected with the murder which was the strongest circumstance, I am sorry to say, in throwing the suspicion upon you, and which I am sure Harry has forgotten all about in his excite-ment."

"What was that?" she asked.

"On the night of the murder, fifty thousand dol-lars disappeared and have not been accounted for."

Mrs. Dorne started to her feet, ashen pale.

"So they thought me a thief, too. Oh! why didn't I know this before? It wasn't mentioned in the papers at the time. So strange! It is possible that Harry may have taken the money in his sleep. We read of that in books. People in their sleep hide money and remember nothing of it when they awake."

"Another thing, Harry," continued Tom, turning to me with a broad grin: "that ghost you saw was the greatest numskull of a ghost on record. Think of a ghost coming to the murderer and persuading him to swear that he'll bring himself to justice. Worse than that, think of a ghost wanting justice to be inflicted on one who wasn't responsible for what he did. God and the law are at one on this point, that what a person does in his sleep cannot be im-puted to him as a crime. And just the same, your uncle is as unreasonable in the other world as he was in this. Even if the clock hadn't made it plain that your ghost-story was a dream, this story would."

I nodded assent.

"The next thing is," continued Tom, "to find out something about that money."

"I'll go there this summer, Tom, and look it up all over the premises. If I hid it, it is doubtless there yet. As everybody who knew that the money had disappeared suspected the murderer, no search was made for it, so it's all but certain that the money's on the premises."

"Could I trouble you, Mrs. Dorne, to repeat that part of your adventures where you fell senseless up to the time when you sprang to your feet?" asked Tom.

Mrs. Dorne repeated that episode in substantially the same words which she had used in telling it to me.

"Oh!" exclaimed Tom suddenly.

"What's the matter, Tom?" I asked.

"We'll talk about it on the road back; I want time to think. It seems to me that I've got a new light."

Further comment on the mystery was cut short by the arrival of the little ones.

"Harold," I said, "how would you like to go to St. Maure's College?"

"What! The big boarding-school?" cried Harold.

"Yes. Percy, Tom, and I go there."

His eyes sparkled with joy, but his face fell as he looked at his mother.

"Who'll take care of mamma?"

"She won't need your help after this, Harold. The fairy prince owes her a big lot of money on his uncle's account, and your mamma won't have to work hard any more."

It was a touching scene when the little lad with a

cry of joy ran to his mother, caught her in his arms, and pressed his cheek against hers. Louise, of course, could not stand idly by and allow Harold to do all the loving. She added herself to the group in no little haste, and a very sweet domestic tableau it was.

"Is it all right, mamma? Can I go?"

"You don't want to go at once, Harold. It is now near the end of the school year. Perhaps it would be better to wait until next September."

"Don't you think it would be well for him to spend the month of June with us, Mrs. Dorne? June is a great month at our college," said Percy.

"Yes, Mrs. Dorne," put in Tom, "the boys have very nice practices in regard to devotion to the Sacred Heart, and Harold will be all the better for what he will learn on that point alone."

It was settled, then, that Harold should join us at, St. Maure's on the following Monday, which was June 1st.

A little before twelve we bade our friends a cordial farewell and set out smartly for St. Maure's.

"It's strange," I began as we passed out of the village, "that I should have hidden that money. Just think of fifty thousand dollars lying unused for all these years."

"I don't believe you did it," said Tom.

"What? Surely you can't suspect Mrs. Dorne after what you have seen and heard?"

"No, Harry; and what's more, since the night we spent in your uncle's house, it's been my suspicion that Mrs. Dorne ran away to save you. I'd have told you my opinion, only I didn't see any way of accounting for the money. But there's no doubt to me, or to Percy either, that you were right in your feelings of love toward Mrs. Dorne, and her story has given us what it is now stylish to call a 'clew.' Harry and Percy, mark this——"

Tom stood still and caught me by the arm.

"She had a sort of nightmare. She heard heavy steps as of your uncle coming to kill her—the steps of a grown person stealing along. When she sprang to her feet she could not hear them any more. Now, it's my strong belief that she actually did hear the real steps of a man or woman—remember, she was half-conscious—and if you can find out who that man or woman was you'll find the thief who took the fifty thousand dollars."

CHAPTER XXVIII.

IN WHICH TOM PLAYFAIR SURPRISES US.

"TOM," I exclaimed, when I had recovered from the surprise which this view of the case gave me, "do you really think that the money was taken by some one else after I had caused my uncle's death?"

"More than that! I think—otherwise I don't see how everything squares—that the person who stole the money saw you kill your uncle; that that person was in the hall when your nurse came out to meet you; and that that person stole away while your nurse was examining your uncle's body."

"Tom!" exclaimed Percy, "you'd make an excellent detective."

"I hope to make something better," said Tom gravely; "and that brings me to the very subject I

intended talking about when we started. This murder business threw it clear out of my head. You've
both heard me speak of James Aldine? Pretty often,
too. Oh, you should have known him! He was
more of an angel than a boy. He was too gentle to
live, in fact. Well, before he died he told me a
great many things about himself—he had offered up
his life for my recovery, a life, too, he had intended
to consecrate to God. James died the very morning
I made my First Communion; and as I knelt over his
body I promised God that with His blessing I'd
take James Aldine's place."

"And you have taken it, Tom," put in Percy fer-
vently; "you've taken the place of any possible boy."

" 'Am I never to be permitted to soliloquize?' "
said Tom, quoting from "The Mikado." "Evidently
you don't understand what I meant by my promise.
James intended to give his life to God by working
for God; since the death of James I've prayed and
prayed every day that I might be deemed worthy to
take his place. And last Christmas, as I was praying before the Tabernacle, I got a distinct call, as I
thought, to follow Christ. Boys, this summer I'm
going to join Keenan."

I caught Tom's hand and shook it cordially, and
was warmly congratulating him, when we were both
silenced by Percy's strange manner of receiving this
news. For Percy, instead of joining me in congratulating our dear friend, of whom we were both
so proud, had put his hands before his eyes.

"Surely you're not sorry, Percy," I exclaimed,
"that Tom is choosing the more perfect life?"

"Of course he's not," whispered Tom. "He's
too saintly for any such view as that."

"Sorry!" exclaimed Percy, taking down his hands from his tearful eyes and catching Tom's hands.

"Of course you're not," said Tom, gazing earnestly into Percy's face. "But there's something or other troubling you."

"There is," answered Percy. "Up to this present year it had been my darling wish to take the course you're going to take, Tom. But this year it's all changed. Oh! if you only could know how I've suffered. Tom and Harry, pray for me. I need your prayers very much."

I do not think that even Tom had ever before heard Percy complain. And now there flashed upon me, for the first time, one of the awful mysteries of life. Here we were three boys on the most familiar footing with one another. I had thought that I knew my two friends thoroughly, and yet for years the one idea of Tom, the mainspring of all his actions, had been to take the place of a departed friend. And Percy, the gentle, the good, he, the prefect of the sodality, whose days had been made up of noble thoughts—he had been suffering silently. I saw between his words the desolations and temptations which God so often sends upon those who are dearest to Him. And in that one moment of insight I remembered how often during the course of the year Percy had been closeted with his confessor. Yes, this saintly young man had gone on treading the wine-press of doubt and difficulty alone, and in this solemn moment had shown us that for all his happy, lovable ways he had tasted the bitterness of temptation and trial. Truly "we myriad mortals live alone."

"Boys, let's change the subject," said Tom after

a few moments of silence. "These are things to think about. They are songs without words. Harry, I doubt whether it will be worth your while to examine your uncle's house till your lawyer has ascertained a few little facts."

I looked at Tom inquiringly.

"To begin with—who took the fifty thousand dollars? That's a great point. Besides the advantage of getting the money back, the thief will be able, perhaps, to tell you where you got that knife and give you some details about the way in which you dispatched your uncle. Your lawyer should collect data to account for all the servants in the house, their whereabouts, their way of life—if any of them took the money the way they have since lived will make it clear. A servant with fifty thousand dollars——"

"O Tom!" exclaimed Percy. "Is it quite certain that there were fifty thousand dollars stolen?"

"That's a fact! Caggett said so, but was he lying? It's certain there was some money taken, because it's certain that Mr. Dee always kept a large sum in his room. But fifty thousand dollars, now we begin to think about it, is putting it rather high."

"Perhaps," said I, "it was even a larger sum. Whose footsteps were they? How about Caggett?"

"Hardly Caggett's," said Tom. "If we assume for the sake of argument that he stole the money, we must also assume as extremely probable that he saw you kill your uncle. Now, it strikes me that Caggett, in that case, unless he's a genius in cunning, would be the last man to accuse you of the murder. And yet he was the very one who did. Again, Caggett was the man who made the biggest fuss

about the stolen money.   I think, Harry, that there's
more to be found out yet.   It's a problem.   And
I've no doubt that before very long you'll succeed
in making it out."

CHAPTER XXIX.

*IN WHICH MR. LANG OBTAINS FURTHER DATA CONCERN-
ING THE MISSING MONEY AND TOM BIDS US FARE-
WELL.*

THAT very night I dispatched two long letters,
one to my father, the other to Mr. Lang,
our lawyer, giving them a full account of the interview between Mrs. Dorne and myself, and asking
Mr. Lang to study up the records of the servants
who were in my uncle's house at the time of my visit.
I insisted particularly on his finding out, if possible,
whether my uncle actually had fifty thousand dollars
in his possession.   The following day I wrote again
to my father, who, during my minority, had charge
of the property and moneys accruing to me, and submitted a plan for putting out a certain sum of money
in Mrs. Dorne's favor and for giving her children
an education.

My father's letter came very promptly.   He
assented to all that I had proposed, and sent a
bank check to Mrs. Dorne on his own account.

But it was some weeks before I heard from Mr.
Lang.   His letter contained news of importance.

DEAR SIR :—Have traced up Caggett's record.   He became a
coachman in St. Louis—spent little—then a car-driver, which
position he retained for a year, when he was discharged for
drunkenness.   Got another position as carriage-driver and spent
all his money on liquor.   The last year and a half he's had odd

jobs off and on, but nothing steady. Has become very seedy. Tramps occasionally. One of my clerks managed to meet him ; treated him several times. He got this much out of him : that your uncle deposited his money in the bank every three weeks. I think out of this we can trace up the exact amount in his possession that night. If you have anything further to communicate in the matter of Caggett let me know at once.

Yours respectfully,

WALTER LANG.

P. S.—If your father has no objections I will now put an expert at examining your uncle's books and papers. Your uncle seems to have been a methodical man, and I think we'll have no difficulty in tracing up all the money he took in subsequent to his last visit to the bank. I shall write Mr. Dee at once for permission.

On the very last day of school I received the following:

DEAR SIR :—After an examination of five days expert reports that your uncle had at least forty-three thousand five hundred and seventy-odd dollars in his room on the night of December 23d, 18—. It was nearly three weeks since his last deposit. The detectives who took the affair in hand first seem to have taken everything for granted. It now transpires that three men— James Nagle, a stock-broker; Howard Wilmott, a farmer; and Cyrus Smith, a wholesale grocer—were each aware that your uncle had a large sum of money about him. Nagle, on December 23d, accompanied by Cyrus Smith, paid your uncle twenty thousand dollars on account in a stock transaction. Wilmott, who was in the library at the time, waiting for a receipt for six thousand dollars paid for a piece of farm-land, tells me that your uncle casually remarked that he'd keep all the money three days longer.

" In this house ? " exclaimed Nagle. "That's risky."

Whereupon Mr. Dee gave a growl.

" It'll be riskier for the man who comes near me. I sleep light, gentlemen; and besides the money under my pillow there's a knife on the chair beside my bed. Besides, the house is locked pretty tight."

While the presence of the dagger on your uncle's chair accounts for your using it, the fact that these two men—I exclude the farmer—knew that your uncle had money under his pillow makes it necessary for me to study up their record. The stock-broker will give me most difficulty. That kind of business is so queer. I have already looked up the case of the cook and housemaid; they have not taken the money. There remains to be investigated, then, the cases of the stock-broker, wholesale grocer, and coachman. The latter two I can dispose of in two weeks, but for the first I shall need at least two months.

> Yours respectfully,
> WALTER LANG.

It was midsummer when his next communication reached me at our lake in Wisconsin. Harry Quip and I were engaged in a wrestling contest, when Tom, who was dressed in a travelling suit, came out with a letter.

"Mr. Harry Dee," cried Tom.

Harry did not enjoy the pleasure of throwing me just then, for I broke away at once, hastily took the letter from Tom, and broke open the envelope. I ran my eyes down the lines.

"Listen, boys."

> DEAR SIR:—Coachman and grocer are O. K. It now only re-mains to trace up stock-broker. If he be innocent, things are about as dark as they were before.
>
> Yours,
> WALTER LANG.

"The detective is wrong there," said Tom quickly. "If your broker and servants and your grocer are all innocent, it follows, Harry, that you not only killed your uncle, but also stole over forty-three thousand dollars from yourself."

"So you're wrestling, are you?" continued Tom. "I've just weighed myself—one hundred and forty-five pounds. You see I want to know how much I change in the Novitiate. I'm five feet seven and one-half inches high, and, if I can believe my looking-glass, the best-looking fellow in the crowd."

"Take a walk," said Harry. "I suppose you think you can throw the whole crowd of us."

"That's what," said Tom.

"Come on—catch as catch can," said Harry.

"I'm in my best clothes," said Tom apologetically, while taking off his coat, "but I'm willing to ruin the whole suit rather than stand that."

The next moment he and Harry were pulling each other about in the approved style. The contest was brief.

"If you had six shoulders instead of two," Tom remarked over Harry, "I'd make every one of 'em touch."

Tom arose, gazing ruefully at his cuffs.

"They'll think I'm a tramp when I arrive home to-morrow to bid 'em all good-by."

"Come on; try me," said Percy, "and I'll fix you up so that they'll think you're an exiled prince."

"*Et tu, Brute,*" said Tom, and flew at Percy.

The struggle began forthwith; presto, Tom went down, but sprang up like a bit of India rubber, and the spinning, and swelling of muscles, and quick changes of position were resumed. Percy came to the ground next, but was up on the instant. Of the two Tom was the stronger, but Percy the more supple. After seven or eight minutes, both were glad to call the contest a draw.

There they stood, two panting, blushing young men, looking, one would think, as though their whole lives were bound up in athletics. Yet these two friends were about to part, each under the noblest of aspirations. Even as they were wrestling, the carriage which was to take Tom to the depot was being drawn out from the coach-house.

Percy now took off Tom's hat (which Tom had just picked up and put on), and producing a pocket-comb proceeded to give Tom's hair a presentable appearance.

In the midst of these operations a happy thought struck me.

"Tom!" I exclaimed, "if I ever recover that money——"

"Which you stole yourself," interrupted Tom.

"I'll put it out at interest, and if you should need it for any particular purpose just let me know."

Tom thought for a few moments.

"I'll tell you an idea I've had for years," he then said. "What we want just now is a good Catholic magazine for boys and girls. Instead of having Catholic writers growl at the books boys read, we must get them to write something that they will read instead. American boys don't care for translated French stories, and I don't blame them. They want stories about themselves, and that's why they go to Oliver Optic and Harry Castlemon. Instead of running these writers down, our writers ought to go to work and give us the American Catholic boy: he is the best boy in the world. In ten years or so who knows but we might use that money to bring out just such stories? One good Catholic story will do more than a dozen volumes of snarling against books that boys ought not to read."

"'It is better to fight for the good than to rail at the ill,'" said Percy, employing one of his favorite quotations.

"Precisely. But as I'm going to take a vow of poverty, it wouldn't be just the thing for me to count upon having a big sum in the bank at my disposition. Percy is just the boy to take such an enterprise in hand along with you, Harry."

"Tom! you've given me my vocation," cried Percy, his face illumined with a smile I shall never forget. "It has come upon me like a flash. Oh! you've no idea how I have prayed and prayed for light. My confessor told me not to think of taking the religious state till my mind should clear. It has not cleared till now. But now I think that God wants me for just such a work. I have plenty of money, and if my father has no objections, I shall invest fifteen or twenty thousand dollars and let it accumulate till I'm ready to start your magazine, Tom."

"I'm with you, Percy," I cried. "No matter whether that money is recovered or not, I'll put in twenty thousand dollars out of my uncle's estate."

This was no boy talk. Percy's father was a man of immense wealth. As for myself, my uncle had left me a fortune of some three hundred thousand dollars.

How quickly the time passed as we discussed, in all the glow of roseate youthful hope, the prospects for our magazine.

But alas! the hour of parting came. I still see our dear Tom standing upon the rear platform as the train moved away, waving his hand and smiling till a curve shuts off from our view one of the noblest, bravest boys——

We were all on the verge of tears. Harry Quip changed our emotions in his peculiar way. Taking

16

an ancient slipper from beneath his coat, he threw it after the train and burst into sobs.

The slipper was too much for us! We all relaxed into a smile, tear-stained it may be, yet a smile.

Quip was indignant.

"You're a set of fools!" he sputtered. "I wouldn't give Tom Playfair for a car-load of fellows like you!"

CHAPTER XXX.

IN WHICH I HAVE THE DOUBTFUL PLEASURE OF RENEW-ING MR. JAMES CAGGETT'S ACQUAINTANCE.

FOR Percy and myself, our year in the rhetoric class did not run smoothly. We had an excellent teacher, it is true, and started in with a will. But early in November Percy was called home, owing to the serious sickness of his mother, and I too was called away later. We missed him sorely in the class-room and in the yard. Frank Burdock, who to his great joy had been promoted to the senior division, was inconsolable. Quip, Ruthers, Whyte, Richards, and myself formed the remnants of the Ciceronians. Harry took Tom's place as leader, and he performed his part well. Yet when we met together we missed our two friends, and felt that the "old order was changing, yielding place to new."

Late in November I received a letter from Mr. Lang which bears closely upon the strange adventures I have yet to relate. Let me put it before the reader in full:

DEAR SIR:—After long and careful study am certain that stock-broker had nothing to do with making away with that forty-three thousand-odd dollars. We must conclude, then, that you yourself secreted the money before or after stabbing your uncle. This is the only possible solution, as far as I can see. My idea, then, is that all of said money is on the premises. If there it can be found. However, before taking any steps in the matter, I would like to have a personal interview with you—for I wish to make you thoroughly satisfied that I have used all human prudence in studying up this very complicated case. Will call on you at St. Maure's, if you wish : but, as am busy with other cases, would prefer it could you contrive to come here.

Yours sincerely,

LANG.

After reading this letter I fell into a brown-study. As matters now seemed to look, the facts in the case were all phenomenal. First of all, it was improbable that I should kill my uncle with one blow of a dagger, even in waking hours. And still in my sleep I had struck him with the nicest precision. Again, it was improbable that I should have examined his bed and made away with and secreted all his money. Were I to tell a stranger these details he would laugh at me or brand me as a falsifier.

There were other difficulties. Did Mrs. Dorne really hear an adult's foot-fall in addition to my light patter, or was it a part of her dream?

The evidence gathered by the detective would seem to negative the former. But despite all evidence these doubts still lingered in my mind. The desire to solve the mystery of my uncle's death had now become the leading thought of my life. There was no risk I would not encounter, no danger I would not dare, to arrive at the truth. If necessary I was resolved to give not only my money, but also to venture my life for the unravelling of this tangle. I should state here that for some months past the entire management of the case had been intrusted to

me by my father, who, confined to the house by an
attack of bronchitis, had been compelled to put
aside all business affairs. My good father had the
utmost confidence in me. Of course I consulted
him on every step; and I must say that he rarely, if
ever, gave me any advice.

"Think it out for yourself, Harry," he would say.
"You have shown your obedience by asking my advice, and I am grateful. Now show your self-
reliance by choosing your own course."

That boy is blessed whose father can teach him
docility and independence in one lesson.

As I read and reread this letter I remembered
the few words which Tom had whispered me as we
shook hands at the depot. "Harry, old boy, you're
not out of the woods yet with regard to this muddle.
The time will come when you'll feel it your duty to
yourself to go to that house again, and who knows but
the second visit will bring out more than our first?
I can't be with you next time. But you can get a
better companion; take Percy Wynn. Percy's as
gentle as a girl; but he's as bold as a lion. He's not
afraid of anything in this world or the next, except
sin. As for ghosts—why, Percy would as soon talk
to a ghost as to a peanut-seller. You can rely on
Percy." It struck me now that Tom's prediction
was coming true, and I determined, if I could bring
it about, that in case I should make another visit to
the haunted house Percy should be my companion.

Two days after the receipt of this letter I was
closeted for six hours with Mr. Lang. His statements were luminous; not a loophole seemed to be
allowed for error. I was staggered, and before
leaving him I was convinced that I had slain my

uncle, and made away with a large sum of money belonging to myself.

I was too troubled in mind to return to St. Maure's, and besides my father was very low. I felt that my place was by his side. As the days went by in the pleasant companionship with my father, the conviction borne in upon me by the data of Mr. Lang softened into doubt. The old difficulties presented themselves.

"Father," I said one evening in mid-December, "I'm not satisfied with Mr. Lang's statements."

"Don't you believe him?"

"Yes, father; that is, I believe that he believes his own conclusions. But I'm not satisfied."

"Well, what do you propose to do?"

"I propose to spend another night at Tower Hill Mansion."

"Alone?"

"No, father; with Percy Wynn."

"When?"

"As soon as Percy Wynn can join me, father. I'll send him a dispatch at once."

It was now Dec. 20th, and Percy was in St. Louis. Without delay I wired him the following message:

Will you accompany me to the Tower Hill Mansion at earliest convenience?

The prompt reply came:

Certainly : we can start on the morning of Dec. 24th.
                                                    PERCY WYNN.

The following morning I received this letter:

MY DEAR HARRY:—My mother is now out of danger, and it will be a great pleasure, my dear friend, for me to clasp your honest hand after so long a separation. I'll be delighted to have

your company even for a single night, and even in a haunted
house. What's a haunted house, after all? We're in God's
hands there just the same as anywhere else. "Isn't God upon
the ocean just the same as on the land?" asks the little girl
in the poem. Do what we may, we can't get away from Him,
nor lose a hair of our heads without His permission. And so,
dear friend, we'll spend Christmas together.

Were it not for that I'd wish you a million pleasant things in
this letter. But how much better than cold writing will it be to
speak to you from my heart and face to face!

I have seen Tom. They call him "*Carissime* Playfair"
(*Carissime* is short for the vocative "*Carissime frater*"). He
is well, and oh, so happy! He's more of a wag than ever—but
when he does stop laughing — which happens seldom — there's
such an expression of sanctity upon his features! When he lived
with us, much as we thought of him, we were entertaining an angel
unawares. He sends you his dearest love. I have just now written
him a few lines to let him know where we are to be at midnight
of Christmas. He will be at a midnight mass; and I've given him
strict injunctions to batter the gates of heaven with storms of
prayer all during that midnight mass for our intention. You,
my dear Harry, value Tom's prayers as I do. He's an American
saint. Well, good-by, my dear friend—you have no idea with
what pleasure I look forward to meeting you. I have examined
the time-table and find that I'll reach Sessionsville at seven A.M.
Your train for Tower Hill Mansion leaves at nine; so there'll
be no difficulty in my calling at your house and making the
connection. Good-by once more, dear Harry.

Yours most affectionately,

PERCY WYNN.

P. S.—Am delighted to hear that your father is so much better, and that the doctor pronounces him to be on the road to
recovery. Give him my sincere regards. Pray for me as I pray
for you.   P. W.

On Dec. 22d I was walking homeward toward
nightfall, when a man came shambling up to me
asking for an alms. I was struck, for some inex-
plicable reason, with his appearance. Clad in rags,
a battered old hat upon his head, a thick brushwood

of beard upon his roughened countenance, he was every inch a tramp. His hair, long neglected, was iron-gray. But what impressed me most was his rugged, forbidding forehead fixed in gloom, and bordered below by heavy, forbidding eyebrows. I gazed at him for a moment, while he continued his entreaties. The air of gloominess about him, by a natural transition in my present state of mind, brought back the memories of Tower Hill Mansion; then in an instant it flashed upon me that no less a person was standing before me than my uncle's old butler, Mr. James Caggett.

My plans were formed on the instant. Here before me was the very man who, of all men living, was best acquainted with the interior of my uncle's mansion. In case a protracted search were necessary, who could be a more useful assistant? On the other hand, I knew full well that, of all the places in the world, Tower Hill Mansion would be the last place where Caggett would go of his own free choice. In common with the other servants of that ill-fated mansion, as I had learned from Mr. Lang, he held it was a house of haunted horrors. All the same I was determined that Caggett should accompany me, if anything short of downright physical force could bring it about.

"If I'm not mistaken," I began, "I am talking to an old friend of my family, James Caggett."

The bloodshot eyes glanced at me very sharply from under their rugged brows, while the forehead wrinkled into a hideous frown.

"Who are you?" he said, with the rasping voice which he appeared to have caught the trick of from my deceased uncle.

"Don't you remember the little boy who came to spend Christmas night with his uncle six years ago?"

Again he looked at me keenly, and I saw, as the blood deserted his cheeks, that he recognized me.

"Yes, I know you—ha, ha, ha!" (what a blood-curdling laugh it was!)—"I thought you were the murderer once—didn't I? But I meant you no harm. Honestly I thought you did it in your sleep. But I was glad when I heard that that she-devil had done it and not you."

My anger at his allusion to Mrs. Dorne almost got the better of me. But I held myself in check.

"So you're in need of help?" I said.

"I haven't had a square meal in three days, sir. Things have gone awful hard with me. An honest man can't make a living in these hard times. Yes, sir; I've been obliged to beg. Couldn't you get me something to do, sir?"

"Yes," I answered quickly. "You come to my father's house at eight sharp on the morning of December the twenty-fourth, and I'll give you a job that will pay you well, and if you satisfy me, I'll try to help you along."

"I'll be there, sir. Will it be ready money?"

"You'll get a good sum from me on Christmas morning. Here are two dollars and a half for your present needs. I'd give you more, only I count on making it up when we meet again."

"Thank you, sir. [How eagerly he clutched the money!] You may be sure that I'll call on the morning of December 24th."

His rasping voice still rasped in my ears as I

made my way home; and into the disordered dreams
of that night floated this gloomy-browed, hideous
tramp, moving about in all the fantastic shapes born
of unpleasant memories.

CHAPTER XXXI.

*IN WHICH MR. CAGGETT ALLOWS HIMSELF TO BE PER-
SUADED TO SPEND A NIGHT IN MY UNCLE'S HOUSE.*

IF my dreams were unpleasant on the night of
the 22d, they were positively frightful during
the succeeding night. My uncle came and went in
various loathsomeness of shape. Caggett came and
went in all the bloated proportions of unhealthy
dreamland; both, by way of variety, invaded my
slumbers together, and their harsh, rasping voices
cut my agonized dream-self like a knife. These
hideous apparitions were succeeded by moments
of wakefulness, at which intervals I half repented
of my morrow's expedition, and devoutly wished
that my uncle and his money had never come within
the sphere of my life.

At three in the morning I arose in disgust, took
a cold shower-bath, and composed myself to read.
After an early breakfast I threw my things into my
valise, and was taxing my memory to find whether
anything had escaped me, when I heard a sharp ring
at the door-bell. Being on the tiptoe of expecta-
tion I hastened to the door myself and opened it
upon a boy, who delivered me the following telegram:

Train delayed six hours. Can't make it so as to meet you
at Sessionsville. Will see what I can do.

PERCY WYNN.

My heart sank on reading these lines; the disappointment was keen, and again I was tempted to abandon the extravagant project. What! spend that night of all nights, in that house of all houses, with that man of all men—Caggett? The fear and loathing with which the very thought of this fellow filled me is unspeakable. To the reader it may appear childish, and, indeed, in a certain way it was childish. There are impressions made on us in early days which many years efface not. In the presence of Caggett I was still, so to speak, the small, nervous, sickly boy not yet in his teens. Yet why should I fear him now? I was strong, healthy, well developed, his superior in intellectual training, nearly his equal in strength. Thus I reasoned; but feeling and memory were not to be carried by syllogisms. I was afraid of Caggett—that was clear. I was resolved that he should be my companion—that too was certain. But I could not bring myself to think of spending a single night alone with him. Accordingly, within three minutes of receiving the telegram I sent a note to Mr. Lang, telling him I needed him at once, and unfolding the circumstances that made me request his attendance. I sent this note by a special messenger, and after an interval which, short as it was, seemed an age to me, I received this answer:

DEAR SIR:—I regret exceedingly that business of most pressing moment, and to which I have pledged myself, will not allow me to accompany you on your visit to your uncle's house. Am very sorry, indeed, for am most interested in the case. The best thing I can do—the only thing—is to send you the only available man I can command—Mr. John Nugent. He is a good man, very acute, but young, inexperienced, and as yet much

wanting in physical bravery. Hope he will do. It will be a
good novitiate for him in our line of life to spend a night in
what is popularly supposed to be a haunted house. With re-
grets, I am yours sincerely, LANG.

P. S.—Nugent has given me trouble; doesn't want to go at
all. But I've put the screws on him. He'll be at your house
within a few minutes of this letter.

L.

This missive did not raise my already depressed
spirits. Everything seemed to be going awry, even
the weather, which had grown ugly.

A few minutes before eight a young gentleman
with nondescript clothes, straw-colored hair and
mustache, and a washed-out complexion, presented
himself to me as Mr. John Nugent. I was struck
with his retreating chin, weak mouth, and general
air of irresolution.

"I'm afraid," I said, as I shook his hand, "that
I'm taking you upon a very uncongenial task."

"Oh dear no! not at all. You don't know how delighted I am," and he smiled as men smile when
they are lost for facial expression.

"My friend," I thought, as I gazed into the face
of the very weak man, "if unnecessary and injudicious lying be a passport to success in your pro-
fession, you'll stand at the top in a disgracefully
brief time."

Further reflections were cut short by the appearance of Mr. Caggett; every inch a tramp still, but
a tramp brushed up as to his shreds and patches for
a special occasion.

"Good-morning, Caggett," and as I spoke I felt
grateful for the encouraging presence of even the
insignificant Mr. Nugent; "you're on time for a
splendid job. I'll need your services to-day and

perhaps to-morrow, for which I'll give you twenty-five dollars."

"I'm your man," said Caggett promptly. "What do you want me to do? I'll begin right off."

"I want to examine my uncle's house."

What a living horror his face became as he took in these words!

"The haunted house?" he gasped.

"Pshaw! that's talk," I answered.

"No, it isn't," he protested. "You'll never come out alive."

"Nonsense; I spent a night there already, and I liked it so much that I'm not afraid to go again."

"But I am, and I'll not go. Lord! to think of staying there alone where my old boss was murdered."

"But you'll not be alone," I urged. "This gentleman and myself will keep you company."

The horror was still on his face as he repeated:

"I'll not go."

"Caggett, I need you. I want to search all the rooms for a large sum of money. You know the house better than any one alive. I'll make it worth your while to go. You'll get fifty dollars."

Was it the fifty dollars which changed Caggett's purpose? I thought so at the time. Perhaps the sequel will supply the reader with another and a stronger motive. At any rate, after due pause and consideration, Caggett asked:

"Will you give me one pint of brandy to-day, another to-night, and another to-morrow?"

"Yes," I answered, after reflection; "but mind, if you get drunk, you get no pay."

He laughed a laugh which was as the swinging

of multitudinous hinges, whereat the law-clerk changed color, and tugged nervously at his mustache.

"You needn't fear that I'll get drunk on that allowance. Well, I agree to go: but remember I'm not to be alone for a single second during this night."

"That you may rely upon," I said, "if you follow instructions."

Thus it came to pass that Caggett, Nugent, and myself, a most ill-assorted trio, took the nine o'clock train for Tower Hill Mansion, arrived there on a gloomy evening, and established ourselves in my uncle's house, to pass a night so full of strange occurrences, so remarkable in its turn of events that I shall give it the benefit of at least one chapter to itself.

CHAPTER XXXII.

IN WHICH I GET A LETTER AND MAKE A DISCOVERY.

"NOW," I began, when we had taken a general survey of the whole interior, "I want you both to understand what I'm after. I have reason to think that my uncle died with over forty thousand dollars by his side. That money, I have also reason to think, is still in the house. Probably it is in one of the three rooms——"

"I thought," interrupted Caggett, "that that Mrs. Raynor ran away with all the money."

"So did others," was my answer, "but later events have changed that opinion. As I was saying, I have reason to think that if this money is about at all, it is probably in my uncle's library or in his bedroom,

or in the room where I slept that night. We'll begin by making a thorough search of the library; then
we'll go on either to the room where I slept that
night or to my uncle's bedchamber, according to
the time it takes us to complete our search in the
library."

"I don't understand," said Caggett, with his
frown and rasp in the superlative.

"Well, you know enough for the present."

We entered the library and began the search.
At first I was amused by the nervous, terrified
glances of my two companions. Nugent was constantly looking over his shoulder, while his fingers
were flying up and twitching his mustache every
minute. Caggett was less nervous in his movements, but by no means less frightened. The peculiar look of horror to which I have already referred was his characteristic expression; his hand
was cold and clammy, his face pale and drawn.

All this, I repeat, was amusing at first. But the
amusement was short-lived. Nothing is more con-
tagious than fear; and very soon I discovered that
I too was yielding to fright. Unconsciously I be-
gan to take an occasional look over my shoulder.
In short, we were a trio of cowards. Frightened as
I was, however, I was determined to brave it out.
In comparison with my companions, I was a hero.

Despite our condition we effected a thorough
search of the library. Not a case, not a shelf,
scarcely a book remained unexamined. Then we
sounded the flooring and the walls. Here my weak
friend, the clerk, showed that he was not utterly an
ignoramus. So interested did he become in tapping
the walls and partitions that he lost sight of his ter-

for and actually put fresh spirit into me. The library was a large room, and I discovered when we had finished its examination that it wanted but five minutes to eleven.

"Now, gentlemen," I said, "we shall go to my uncle's room, and examine it in the same manner."

But here the wretched Caggett objected.

"No, no!" he exclaimed, his voice hoarse with emotion. "Not that room! Take your own first. We can go to your uncle's in the morning."

"My mind is made up. My uncle's first."

"No! or at least wait here till midnight passes."

There was a great fear upon his features.

"Come on," I said sternly, catching up the lamp.

"I'll not go," he growled.

"Very well," I said, "then I'm going to lock you up here alone without light, and besides——"

"Oh! I'll go! I wouldn't be alone here for all the money in the world."

As he spoke he took a mouthful of brandy.

How closely these two men clung to me as we ascended the stairs together! so closely that I could feel that they were trembling, and hear, as I thought, their heart-beats. As we were midway between the first and second floors, the woodwork upon which we trod gave a dismal creak; Caggett jumped with fright, and had it not been for the support of my free hand would have fallen down the stairs.

Soon we were hard at it examining my uncle's room. Nugent was now a trifle brave. There was something of the detective in him, for he was really earnest in the work of finding out every nook and cranny of the apartment. Within fifteen minutes we had explored my uncle's wardrobe, his table, and his desk. Then Nugent took the lead. Caggett was in a state of terror, which he kept within limits by frequent applications to the bottle of brandy. After we had examined the flooring he threw himself into a chair, and addressed the detective:

"It's no use; if I were you I would sit down. We'll put in our work in the other room. Hadn't we better try the other room now?" he inquired, turning to me.

Neither Nugent nor myself paid him the least attention. We were both busy sounding the walls. I had come within a few feet of my uncle's bed when Caggett jumped to his feet and ran over toward me.

"For God's sake!" he cried, "let us leave the house now. To-morrow will be the time—to-morrow."

"Sit down, you coward," I said sternly.

He complied, yielding rather to his own terror than to my words, and I continued tapping the wall.

"Have you ever made a close examination of the bedding," asked Nugent, turning to me.

"Tom Playfair and myself took a look at it when we were here," I replied. "But we didn't spend much time at it."

"There's nothing there," growled Caggett. "I made it up myself before I left this horrible house."

Nugent, taking no notice of the remark, proceeded to throw coverings, pillowcase, and mattress upon the floor.

Scarcely had he done so, when Caggett rose and advanced to his side.

"Let that bed alone,' he growled.

Caggett was an awful spectacle. His eyes were bloodshot, and his face was quivering with fear and rage. Nugent was daunted by the horrid sight. He stepped back, and stood gazing spell-bound upon this wretched figure.

"Here, Nugent!" I exclaimed. "You try your hand at this wainscoting. I'll examine the bed myself."

Caggett closed his hands tightly and made a few steps toward me, brandishing his fists as he advanced.

"Stand still!" I cried. "Nugent, I call upon you to look at this man."

Nugent, who had put himself beside me, lifted his head, and the two of us eyed the would-be aggressor in silence.

Caggett quailed before our stare. Muttering a curse, he returned to the chair and buried his face in his hands.

Suddenly an involuntary exclamation from my lips brought the detective to my side.

"What's this?" I exclaimed, pointing to a letter which was pinned to the under side of a bed-slat. The clerk, without answering, pulled away the pin, and the letter fell to the floor.

There was a muffled sound from Caggett.

"Why," I cried, as I picked it up, "just look at this address."

Nugent bent over and read:

MASTER HARRY DEE,

Present.

"Get the lamp, Nugent," I said. "This letter looks very old, and who knows but it may have come from my.uncle."

I tore open the envelope, and, as the clerk held

17

the lamp, I read with wonder and dismay such as no words can express:

Dec. 24th, 18—.

NEPHEW HARRY:—To-night at twelve o'clock I commit suicide. If you should enter this, my room, to-morrow, you will find me dead with my own knife in my heart.

JAMES DEE.

"Good God!" I cried, "am I awake or dreaming."

Nugent took the note from my palsied hand and read it with eagerness.

"What do you think of it?" I asked.

He handed me back the note, glancing as he did so toward Caggett. And again the terror of that sight seemed to penetrate Nugent's inmost being.

"Look! look!" he gasped.

Well might he be frightened. Seated beside the table Caggett was the personification of horror—his facial muscles were twitching madly, his eyes were fixed upon us with a glassy stare; his mouth was open, and he appeared to be struggling for breath. It appeared to me at once that the wretched man had been taken by a fit. Placing the lamp on the table, just at his elbow, I hastily took another pint of brandy from my valise and filled him a small glass.

"More! more!" he gasped, as he drank it down at a single draught.

I filled him another.

His terror moderated sensibly.

"Caggett," I said, when I was satisfied that he was calm enough to converse. "Look at this letter from my uncle."

He endeavored to hold the paper, but it fluttered from his hands to the floor.

Picking it up I read it aloud.

" Do you understand this, Caggett ?"

There was a fearful play of the muscles about his throat and a few deep gurgles as of a man choking to death, before he succeeded in forcing out the words:

" Yes, and it's true."

" What!" I cried, " all these years you have known that my uncle made away with himself, and you have allowed an innocent woman to be hunted ? But how did you come to know of my uncle's suicide ?"

The same struggling and play of his throat ensued before he labored forth the words:

" More brandy."

I administered him another glass. " That night," he began with an effort, " I was working in the cellar till after twelve o'clock. When I came upstairs I knocked at his room."

He paused to pass his hand over his brow.

" There was no answer, and I entered, and then I saw your uncle lying in the bed, dead—killed by his own knife. On the chair beside him was that letter addressed to you. I read it. I took the letter and hid it in that place where you found it."

" Why—why ?"

" I don't know."

" That's a lie; tell me the reason."

" I—I—I had overheard what your nurse had said to your uncle, and I wanted to throw his death on her."

I was not satisfied with this explanation, the more so as his halting way of delivering it gave me reason to suspect that he was holding something back.

" Now, Caggett, why should you want to throw the suspicion on Mrs. Raynor ?"

"Because I—I thought people might think I did it.'"

"Was that your only reason?"

Caggett seemed to have fallen into a stupor.

"Don't give that man any more brandy," whispered the frightened young man in my ear. "If you do, there's every chance that we'll have a madman on our hands. I was a fool to come here." With which Nugent, taking another shuddering look at the hideous tramp, turned his back to us and resumed his examination of the wainscoting.

"Caggett," I repeated, catching him by the shoulder and shaking him, "was there any other reason?"

He opened his lips to reply, but though his lips moved there came no sound.

"Do you understand, Caggett?"

"I intended to steal his money," he answered with an effort.

I glanced at the detective.

"Tom Playfair was right," I muttered. "Mrs. Dorne did hear real footfalls besides my own, and here is the thief."

"No," said Caggett. "When I got here the money was already stolen."

I looked at him earnestly; he seemed to be speaking the truth.

"Mrs. Raynor stole it," he added.

"You wretched villain," I broke forth, "if you ever speak of Mrs. Raynor in that way again——"

"Look! look," Nugent suddenly broke in. "Here's something!"

I ran to his side. Kneeling beside the bed, which he had moved out from the wall, he was gazing into an opening in the partition, evidently much frightened at the discovery he had made. The opening revealed a recess about one foot square.

" How did you find this?" I asked.

" I—I touched something or other; it must have been a spring, and a part of the wainscot rolled back."

As Nugent seemed utterly unable to proceed further, I gently shoved him aside. He fell sprawling as though I had struck him with a club. Putting my hand into the secret recess, I drew out a heavy wooden box open at the top. Bringing it nearer to the lamp I perceived almost at a glance that I was holding a fortune in my hands. Bank-notes of all values, gold and silver, every species of money. The missing treasure was found.

But who had placed it in this unknown hiding-place? It must have been my uncle. Could it be possible that he had deliberately secreted the large sum before committing suicide? This train of thought brought me back to Caggett.

Why had he thrown the awful suspicion of murder on Mrs. Dorne? Ah! it was true that he himself had wished to make away with the money. I turned to address him.

As I was about to speak, the clock in the hall, which, I had taken care to set early in the evening, broke into a peculiar whirring noise, at which sound Caggett gave a nervous start, and in moving his arm struck the shade of the student lamp. The shade moved several inches. It was connected with the wick, and in turning lowered it so that we were at once in a dim, ghostly light.

Caggett did not know that he was the cause of the darkness, and as the clock struck the first stroke of the hour of midnight he sprang to his feet with a low, horrible gasp and fell upon his knees, facing toward my uncle's bed.

Nugent, whose fears had been mounting with every moment since the discovery of the letter and the treasure, gave a wild cry, rushed to the door, and clattered down the stairs.

CHAPTER XXXIII.

IN WHICH CAGGETT MAKES A STARTLING DISCLOSURE, AND I PASS THROUGH THE GREAT CRISIS OF MY LIFE.

THERE beside the faint light of the lowered lamp, in presence of a kneeling man writhing with agony, I stood horror-stricken. It was a terrible moment—terrible in its present features, more terrible still in what it promised. Caggett was looking with a strained gaze not at the bed but at something on a line with it. His hands were alternately clasped, then thrown out from his body as though he were waving off some hideous vision. Inarticulate gasps and groans were laboring from his throat, gasps and groans beastlike in their sound, with the added human agony of a man beside himself with terror. I did not know it at the time; but I am now certain that, as Nugent had predicted, he was crazed with drink.

I would have come to his help; but I was no longer master of myself; and for what seemed a long span of time I stood motionless, gazing with awe upon this uncanny sight.

At last Caggett burst into speech:

"O Mr. Dee! Mr. Dee! You made me do it!

Go away—for God's sake don't look on me that way," and he waved his hands madly. I looked in the direction of the bed, almost expecting to see the luminous spectre of my uncle. But I saw nothing.

"It was all your own doing, Mr. Dee; you drove me to it. Didn't you tear up the will which made me your heir? I was listening, and I knew you had over forty thousand dollars with you. I couldn't help it—I didn't mean to kill you!"

Imagine my state of mind when I heard these words. It *was* a murder after all, and I was alone with the murderer.

"Before God, I didn't mean it! I stole up here, and tried to get your money without waking you. But you opened your eyes, and recognized me. Then I seized your knife and—oh! keep off—keep off——"

He gave a wild cry, and fell foaming at the mouth.

With an effort I freed myself from the spell which had bound me, and turning on the full light of the lamp I hastened to Caggett. There he lay, the embodiment of remorse and terror, his mouth still covered with foam, his eyes glassed in horror, every feature hideous beyond all human features I had ever seen. There he lay—my uncle's murderer. I could scarcely bring myself to touch this inanimate clot of crime. How my soul sickened as I put my arms about this dreadful man and placed him on my uncle's bed!

I returned to the table, and seated myself. Serious as I feared was the condition of that man of blood, I could not bring myself to touch his loathsome body again. Even his stertorous breathing filled me with disgust, and yet I realized that I would be obliged to spend several hours, at the very least, in his company; nor, as the time passed on, did my feelings of loathing lessen. To add to my disquietude, I found gradually that I was fascinated by that still figure on the bed. I could not withdraw my eyes from his face, though with every second that face seemed to take on additional repulsiveness.

At length, unable to endure the situation longer, I brought a chair to the table and set about counting my treasure-trove. I spent quite a time in separating the gold, silver, and the bills of various denominations; but presently I found that I was in no frame of mind to carry out my intention. Then I began pacing up and down the room, keeping my face turned from the bed, endeavoring to put Caggett out of my mind, and forcing my thoughts into lovelier channels. I thought of Percy; how I longed for the presence of that dear friend! I thought of Tom, our little Jesuit. By this time, Tom must have heard midnight mass, and it comforted me to think that his prayers were with me and helping me even now. *Now.* That one word brought back the ugly present realities; brought back Caggett and all the hideous train of thought I had endeavored to put aside. Yes; I was at length sure of the murderer; sure, too, of the money so long lost. But how about my uncle's note announcing his intention of committing suicide? How, too, did it happen that the money had been secreted? Certainly my uncle, as I knew from the data furnished me by Lang, had not been in the habit of hiding his money. Had he actually intended to commit suicide, only

to be killed by his villainous servant before he could
carry out his purpose? If so, why then had he concealed the money? But I scouted the thought that
my uncle had contemplated making away with himself. I remembered my last interview with him;
I remembered his kind words, and I felt convinced
that, if he had written the note directed to me, it had
been written previous to our interview in his bedroom; and that his intention had certainly been
changed.

For several hours did I ponder and consider, endeavoring vainly to piece these contradictory circumstances into a consistent whole. At length,
wearied and troubled, I paused in my walk, and
turned my face toward the open window which
looked out upon the east. The first faint gray
streaks of dawn were upon the horizon. I stood for
some moments gazing upon this joyous promise of
daylight. But I found presently that Caggett's figure was again asserting its horrible fascination: and
once more I turned my face to the wall, and, seating myself, I forced my thoughts to dwell upon the
sweetest memories of Christmas.

I believe that all boys take pleasure in thinking
of Bethlehem and the angels' songs. It is a series
of beautiful tableaux for young as well as old. At
all events, I became very interested in these tender
memories, and I actually made what Catholics call
a meditation. My imagination grew vivid, and I
almost saw the dear Infant, the sweet Mother, almost saw that multitude of the heavenly host prais-
ing and glorifying God; almost saw the great light
which cast such holy fear upon the shepherds; almost heard the heavenly chorus singing *Gloria in*

excelsis Deo—when suddenly (why I do not know, unless it be that I have a guardian angel) the vision faded, and by some impulse, which I do not attempt to account for, I turned my head sharply. I was not one moment too soon. As I turned, I noticed in the very act that it was sunrise, and the sun, bright and cheerful, was peeping over the eastern hills. This I noticed in a flash; but the fact of sunrise had no interest for me at that moment. The bed was empty! Caggett, on tiptoe, had advanced half-way across the room. His evil eyes were fixed upon me in a way there was no mistaking; in his right hand he grasped an open knife. The knife almost escaped my attention, but the eyes! I read in them that I was not to leave the room alive.

You may be sure I didn't stop to stare; for as I took in the situation I bounded to my feet, while Caggett, throwing aside his attempt at stealthiness, sprang at me with a fierce cry like the cry of a savage beast in its most savage moment.

Fear lent me agility. In a trice I had placed the table between myself and him. Oh, how I reproached myself that I had neglected to bring a pistol! I was face to face with a man stronger than myself and more accustomed, I had good reason for thinking, to deeds of violence; he was armed with a knife; I was unprotected. My heart sank within me, for I realized that the chances were in his favor. I thought of making a dash for the door, but it was evident that before I could turn the knob his knife would be in my back. Again I thought of picking up a chair, and fighting him with that weapon. But this would involve a hand-to-hand conflict—a thing I was resolved to avoid as long as possible.

For my great hope was in getting assistance from without. That cowardly law-clerk might, after all, have heart enough in his chicken-breast to return, once it was broad daylight. His return was my strongest hope. I resolved, therefore, by putting the table between Caggett and myself, to keep him at a distance as long as possible. What a tragic chase it was! With his eyes fixed steadily upon mine, Caggett played me as an angler would play a fish. With the coming of day his bravery had returned; and it was the fierce bravery of desperation. His terror had disappeared as completely as the shades of night. The deadly purpose which animated him could be read in his every feature, and most legibly in the rigid determination of his compressed lips and heavy lower jaw. Our actions, were it not for our facial expressions, might have impressed an observer with the idea that we were playing a game of "tag." Round and round we moved about the table, anon with guarded step, anon with sudden dashes. His every movement, slow or rapid, his every pause, was my guide. As he moved, I moved; as he paused, I paused. How long this grim game went on, I cannot say; it seemed at times to be of interminable length; it seemed at times to have gone on but for a few seconds. Whatever the length of time, we were soon breathing heavily. I could feel my heart beating in a way that under ordinary circumstances would have alarmed me; but placed as I was, I was too excited to be sensible of fear. It was in one of these pauses, when I stood stock-still, separated by the length of the table from my adversary, that there came upon the stillness, thus far broken only by our heavy breathing, a crashing noise; and with it the room grew suddenly quite dark. For the moment Caggett was disconcerted; he turned suddenly in the direction whence the noise came, and I took advantage of that one moment to seize the lamp from the table, and send it with all my force at his head. The noise that had alarmed Caggett so much was occasioned by the falling of the window curtain, which, owing doubtless to our violent motions, had broken from its fastening above the window. As I had been facing in that direction, I had taken in the circumstance, without being obliged to turn my eyes from my enemy.

But quick as I had been in hurling the lamp at Caggett, I was the least bit late. As he ducked his head, the lamp went crashing against the wall, within a few inches of the curtained window, and burst into a thousand fragments.

With a sharp hiss Caggett made a dash round the table: I was almost too late in recovering myself; and indeed, as I darted away, the blade of his knife touched my coat. The throwing of the lamp had given me a new idea. Upon the table there still remained the box, heavy with its store of coins. In passing around the table I seized it, determined to await my opportunity to throw it at his head. But here I made a fatal mistake. The box was heavy and cumbrous. Once in my hands, I discovered that I had to rid myself of it, or be caught in a few moments. I hesitated between replacing it or throwing it at Caggett. It was probably the hesitation of half a second, but my decision, as the sequel will show, was unfortunate. I threw it at Caggett's head. At once Caggett ducked beneath the table; and while the papers and notes went fluttering about the room, and with a thousand jingles the silver and gold fell and rolled in all directions upon the carpetless floor, mingling confusedly with the fragments of the glass; and while I stood motionless, waiting for Caggett's head to reappear—I suddenly felt a strong clasp upon my left ankle. Caggett had crawled under the table to my side.

On the instant I screamed out, "Help! help!" and with all my energy I broke away.

I succeeded in tearing myself from his grasp; but at what a cost! I lost my balance, fell headlong, and though I sprang to my feet without waste of a moment, there was a sharp, stinging pain in my left leg just above the ankle, where Caggett's knife had penetrated. At once my plans were changed. Delay on my part would now be dangerous, for the blood was streaming from the wound; and I grimly foresaw that with loss of blood I would presently become weak and dizzy—and then all would be over. The issue must be at once, and, therefore, as I gained my feet I turned and sprang upon Caggett, catching him above the wrist of his right hand, so as to prevent his stabbing me, and bearing him, with the force of my spring and the unexpectedness of the onset, heavily to the floor. Then there resulted a fearful struggle. He was under me, glaring at me with that same murderous look, and despite all my efforts prodding me here and there about the shoulders with his knife. I put both hands to his wrist, and held it firmly, while the blood came trickling down my arm and fell upon his upturned face.

And very soon what little confidence I had was gone; for I felt my strength leaving me. Strange

noises—did they come from within or without?—
broke like the beating of drums upon my ear. The
firmness of my grasp relaxed, and as a feeling of intense lassitude came over my frame the full horror
of my situation flashed upon me.

I endeavored to pray, and in the act heard, as I
fancied, quick footfalls without. Perhaps help was
nigh. The thought seemed to revive my strength;
and indeed I needed it all. Catching Caggett's
hand, which had just escaped me, I arrested what
might have been a fatal stroke. The struggle was
renewed; and as it went on I was certain that some
one was coming. I felt now that my grasp upon
him was losing its firmness—and then the door burst
open, and a figure, so dim had my eyes become that
I failed to make out who or what it was, bounded
into the room. I saw an arm strike out once, twice
—and then I slipped into unconsciousness.

CHAPTER XXXIV.

*IN WHICH PERCY WYNN THROWS ADDITIONAL LIGHT
UPON CAGGETT'S NARRATIVE, AND PUTS AN END TO
THE MYSTERY.*

"HALLO, Harry! Merry Christmas." Percy
was bending over me with a scared face.

"Thank God! thank God!" I whispered. "Is it
you, Percy, that saved me? I never counted on
looking upon your dear face again."

"Yes, Harry, without boasting I can say that I
saved your life. Caggett had you down, when I
struck out at him."

I attempted to rise from the bed on which I was

lying, but found I could scarcely lift my head, so stiff and sore was I from cuts, bruises, and loss of blood. I gave a gasp of pain, and sank back upon the pillow.

"Poor boy," said Percy, "you mustn't try to move again. I've spent over an hour bandaging you, and if you move my bandages will come loose. Be patient for a while; I've sent for a doctor for you, and a constable for Caggett."

"Where is he?" I inquired, trying to take a full view of the room, and noticing in the effort that the bed was stripped of blanket, coverlet, and sheets.

"He's in the room next this—the wretch! But you wouldn't know him. I've bundled him up in blankets and sheets—they were the nearest things to ropes I could get—till he can't move hand or limb. He's such an awful sight, though, that I thought it would be pleasanter for you to miss seeing him."

"But, Percy, you haven't told me how you came to save me."

"It's a long story, Harry. I went on the principle 'better late than never,' and took the evening train after paying your father a visit. I got to the depot beyond about three-quarters of an hour before sunrise; and I found standing there, solitary and stupid, an insignificant looking little man, who seemed to be in a state bordering on insanity."

"Oh, Mr. Nugent!" I put in.

"Yes; I got his name out of him in about the time that an ordinary dentist would have extracted all his double teeth. I plied him hard with questions, and I'm afraid I shook him a little roughly, poor fellow, before I could get the least inkling of the way things had been going on here. He gave me the idea that Caggett was dead because of the ghost, and that you were dying. I didn't wait for anything more, but set off for the house at a dead run."

" Six miles! did you run all the way?"

" Pretty much. When I got in sight, though, I was content to walk; I came on, getting nearer and nearer, when, as I was within three or four hundred feet of the house, I heard a cry, 'Help! help!'"

" You heard me, Percy."

" So I thought; and then you should have seen me run; I beat my record that time, and came bounding into the house, and up the stairs. I could hear an awful rolling and tumbling going on—and guided by the sound I made for this room. Caggett was just about to stab you. The two blows I gave him were cruel; he dropped over to one side like a log."

" But, Percy——"

" There now, lie still; you needn't get excited. I've lots more to tell you, you see. I know the whole story; Caggett told me everything."

" How?" I exclaimed incredulously.

" Oh, he didn't want to; but I persuaded him. At first when he came to, and found himself tied up in sheets and bedclothes, he wouldn't talk at all. But I saw that he was nervous, and I thought that by taking him on his weak point I might get all the news out of him. I took it for granted, of course, that he was the murderer."

" How did you work on his nerves, Percy?"

" Oh, it was quite simple. I cocked a pistol and put the muzzle against his ear, and said: 'Mr. Caggett, will you be obliging enough to answer a few questions?" And Mr. Caggett became very obliging all at once; for he professed himself willing and ready to answer any and all questions I might put to him. Tnen I took the pistol away from his ear, and began patching you up, poor boy, while I put him through a long examination. Would you like to hear the first and complete edition? He told me all that you know, and I'm sure you're puzzled still."

"Where did you get the pistol?"

"Right here in this room. I found it in Caggett's pocket, and it was loaded, too. I could see that by the way Caggett acted when I pressed it against his ear. By the way, Mr. Caggett, I believe, will never be hanged for the murder. What drinking has left undone in ruining his health the terror and the wounds and what-not of this night have accomplished. The wretched man will probably never leave his bed again."

"Tell me what he told you, Percy."

"Well, be quiet; you're weak. You know how, once upon a time, your uncle destroyed a will in your presence which favored Caggett, and read one in your favor. Your nurse claimed fifty thousand dollars from your uncle; said she'd have it, and made some remarks about your uncle's not living long. Caggett overheard every word. He had a trick of using a keyhole. He became very angry, and made up his mind to get something out of your uncle. He knew that Mr. Dee had a large sum of money on his person (forty-three thousand dollars), which he would place under his pillow at night, and he determined to get that money and fly the country. He did not make up his mind to kill your uncle—

18

that was an after-thought. At twelve o'clock he stole up to Mr. Dee's room, advanced on tiptoe to his side, and tried to get the money. But here began all the trouble. There was no money under Mr. Dee's pillow. Caggett examined very cautiously, and without disturbing the sleeper; he knew your uncle generally slept with it under his pillow; but on this particular night of all nights there wasn't a trace of the money."

"Was the dagger there?" I broke in.

"Yes; it was quite convenient to your uncle's hand."

"Where was the money?"

"In the place you found it," answered Percy. "You understand, don't you? It's plain that your uncle anticipated some danger or other that night, and hid those things away."

"Ah!" I exclaimed. "He suspected that Caggett might attempt to rob him."

"Precisely; knowing Caggett pretty well, it might have occurred to him that his servant had been eavesdropping and might attempt to visit him that very night. Anyhow, whatever was the reason of his suspicions, he was justified in the event. Well, to go on, Caggett began a systematic search of the room. Of course he didn't find the money; for, till a few hours ago, he didn't even know anything of that secret recess. Finally he approached the bed again, and was about to renew his search, when your uncle suddenly opened his eyes, gave a gasp, and whispered, 'Who's there?' and as he spoke he caught Caggett's arm. Caggett with a jerk released himself, and, as your uncle gave a cry for help, he caught him by the throat, choked him into silence, and grasping the dagger, which had slipped from your uncle's hand, plunged it into his breast. Would you believe it, Harry? that villain told me this as though he was speaking on the state of the weather. Having assured himself that your uncle was dead, the wretch walked over to the table, and turning up the light—your uncle, it seems, always slept with a light burning low—he wrote a note in imitation of James Dee's handwriting, announcing——"

"Ah," I gasped, "there's more light."

"You saw the note already, Harry; Caggett told me. But to return to our story. Caggett had just blotted and sealed this, when he heard a footstep without. Scarcely knowing what he was doing and certainly not knowing why, Caggett hastened over to the bed and pinned the letter where you found it. Then he brought out a pistol and, cocking it, waited. The steps drew nearer and nearer. Caggett waited motionless. Then, Harry, you appeared—a little boy in your night-shirt. You stopped for a moment on the threshold, and, as Caggett says, looked straight at him. That was very near the last of you, old boy. Caggett picked up a heavy walking-stick, and advanced with the intention of braining you. But, instead of drawing back, you walked right in. He remembered then that he had heard you were a sleep-walker, and lowered his arm. You kept on your course, walked past him and stopped at your uncle's bed. You passed your hands over your uncle's face and breast, and even touched the knife. In leaning against the bed, Caggett saw that you had dabbled your night-shirt with blood. This suggested a new plan to him. You were a somnambulist; it would appear that you in your sleep had murdered your uncle. Resolving to destroy the letter he had forged next day, Caggett stole on his tiptoes out of the room, and made his way hastily to his own sleeping-room, which was half-way down the hall."

"Ah!" I exclaimed, "his were the footsteps that my nurse heard."

"So I think, too. Well, he had not been in his room half a minute, when he heard some one else coming along the corridor. He put a chair beside his door—there was no light in his room—and looked through the transom. He saw your nurse, who was very agitated, carrying a lamp in her hand, and then he saw the meeting between you and her. He watched your nurse's movements until she left the house; and then he felt sure that no suspicion would fall on him."

"Did he give up the search for the money?"

"No, indeed; after Mrs. Dorne left the house he spent a part of the night in searching your uncle's room. Even when all else had deserted the place he continued his search for several days. On the last day he was severely frightened in some unaccountable way, and left precipitately, vowing never to come near the house again."

"He didn't keep his vow," I observed.

"No; the fact was, when you announced your intention to him of making a search for the money, he remembered how in the hurry of leaving he had neglected to destroy the forged letter. Then it occurred to him that, if the money were found, he was entitled to it. Mr. Caggett is a poor logician. These considerations, added to your promise of money, overcame his fear. He counted on destroyfng that note, to begin with; and in the next place, if the money was found, he was determined to make off with it."

"Have you seen the treasure, Percy?"

"Yes; after removing Mr. Caggett. I gathered up the scattered contents of that box. I never handled so much money in my life. It took me a long time to get it together; for I had to keep my eyes on you, and be on the lookout for some passer-by to get assistance. When I did get it all together, I brought the box by your side, Harry, and counted out the money, and watched you closely for ever so long a time. Do you know how much you've fallen heir to?"

"How much?"

"Forty-five thousand and some odd dollars."

"Isn't that a Christmas gift!" I exclaimed. "Within a week, Percy, those forty-five thousand dollars will be put in a bank; and there they'll grow to more in preparation for that great boys' and girls' magazine that is to be. Percy, allow me to return your first greeting—I wish you a happy Christmas."

And as we shook each other's hand we heard voices without, and people entering, and we knew that the mystery of Tower Hill Mansion was solved, that the problem had been made out, and that the shadow which had wrapped my life thus far had been lifted forever.

CHAPTER XXXV.

*IN WHICH HARRY DEE HAS SOME DIFFICULTY IN BRINGING
HIS STORY TO A CLOSE.*

IT is August 1st, one year and eight months since
the adventures related in the last chapters. Arrayed in all the glory of graduating costumes, several
very fine young gentlemen are seated in the parlor of
the Jesuit Novitiate. The reader knows them all.
He knows Harry Quip, grinning from under the first
hint of a mustache. He knows Percy Wynn, who
has taken the gold medal for excellence in the
various branches of the philosophy class. He knows
Frank Burdock, the only non-graduate present, now
quite tall, and with a face eminently intellectual.
He knows Will Ruthers and Joe Whyte—and as
there comes a quick patter down the stairs without,
and there enters, clothed in cassock and biretta, a
handsome, dark young man, with bright twinkling
eyes and merry face, he knows Mr. Playfair, S.J.,
who has taken his three vows and is now a religious.

What a chorus of babble and laughter arises, as
we shake our dear friend's hand, and congratulate
him on his happiness! For it was only yesterday
that Tom, impelled with the desire of serving God,
and trusting in His infinite sweetness and mercy,
vowed in presence of the most sacred Virgin Mary
and the whole heavenly court, poverty, chastity, and
obedience.

"It's the happiest day of my life, almost," said
Tom—I should say Mr. Playfair. "And if it were
not for yesterday, I think I could say it is the happiest. "Well, Harry, it's consoling to think that

Caggett after all died penitent. The poor fellow had a long year's purgatory in the hospital, and his sickness and suffering proved to be the greatest blessing of his life.   And how's the new magazine?"

"Strong *in spe*," I answered. "The money is safely invested, Tom; and it can wait better than Percy and I.   We feel like making a start at once; but we're determined to be prudent."

"I hope to be a member of the staff, Tom—I mean Mr. Playfair," said Quip, feeling for the down upon his upper lip. "You see, I'm thinking of taking to journalism—that is, if I take to anything."

"And I," said Joe Whyte, "intend to study law."

"Will Ruthers, who looks so mild and gentle, is going to be a sawbones," added Quip grimly.

"What are you thinking of, Frank?" asked Mr. Playfair.

"My present vocation," answered Frank, "is to graduate.   Then I think I'll marry."

"After which," put in Quip, "he'll look about to see how he can support a wife."

"I've got stock in a building association," said Frank seriously.

"These graduates are great fellows, Mr. Playfair," said Percy. "They're starting in at once, all except Harry Dee and myself."

"Don't believe Percy," said I. "He's doing the work of three, even now. He's the best friend of poor boys in the world. There's not a newsboy or a bootblack in Cincinnati who doesn't know and love him. He's studying up the lives and conditions of that class, and he intends giving much attention to bettering the poor fellows, and he's done ever so much good among them already, though he's only had a chance of making their acquaintance the last two months."

I did not add what was the fact, that Percy was looked upon by many a homeless lad as a saint. They loved him, but their reverence kept pace with their love. Percy had not forgotten his adventure with the dying tramp. His great heart was filled with love and compassion for God's chosen ones, for the poor and the outcast. He was determined to help them on, beginning with the little ones, on the theory that all reforms are best effected from below up.

"Very soon," said Percy, changing the subject, "Harry and I shall take a trip to Europe."

"What then, Percy?" asked Mr. Playfair.

"Oh, we'll settle down, and take a special course of literature and philosophy. You see we intend preparing *a longe* for the great magazine that is to be. Harry Dee purposes, in addition, to study finances. We've settled it between us that he's to be business manager and I the editor. We have concluded not to make any start till we're thirty years old or so; and in the mean time there's a big sum of money gathering interest."

"By the way, where is Mr. Keenan?"

"He's out on a walk," said Tom. "But I think he'll be back soon. But there's another friend of yours here."

"Who?" came the chorus.

"Guess," answered Mr. Playfair.

Before we could make answer the door opened and—

"Oh, Mr. Middleton!"

There stood our beloved teacher and prefect beaming upon us with his old-time smile. He had changed but little, though his face wore more markedly that expression which may be noticed in those whose thoughts have been constantly turned upon sacred things.

While we were still welcoming him, Tom called out:

"Boys, that's not Mr. Middleton. He's *Father* Middleton. He was ordained July 31st."

There was a solemn silence.

Each of us knelt, and Father Middleton, passing from one to another, gave us his priestly benediction.

What a delightful time of it we had that morning! Old memories—pleasant and fragrant they were—came back again. We fought our battles o'er, and talked and laughed with an abandon which sent time flying on the swiftest and lightest of wings.

Harry Quip presently mystified us not a little. He called Father Middleton aside, and went off with him, we knew not whither.

When he returned after half an hour he made up for lost time. He talked, and joked, and laughed till Frank Burdock brought him to a stand by saying:

"Harry, have you been drinking?"

"No," said Harry. "It's worse."

"Let's hear your confession, then," said Mr. Playfair.

"I just made it to Mr. Middleton—Father Middleton—a general confession of my whole life."

Harry was now quite serious; so were we; we saw that something more was to come.

"And besides I've had a talk with the novice-master."

"Oh, Harry Quip!" exclaimed Percy.

"He's of the same opinion as Father Middleton; and in a few days I'm going to join Donnel in the Baltimore Seminary."

"Well, Harry Quip," exclaimed Percy, grasping his hand warmly, "you always were a lucky fellow. Here you go and get one of the sublimest of calls, and leave Frank and Harry and Joe and me out in the cold."

Percy was smiling as he spoke, but there was sadness in both smile and voice.

"Well," said Harry, "you fellows deserve to be left out in the cold. When Tom went away you didn't throw an old slipper after him. I did, and now I'm thrown after the slipper." .

Perhaps the reader may think I am exaggerating; but it is a fact that before dinner Joe, Percy, Frank, and myself contrived to hold a secret interview with our saintly Father Middleton. But none of us came from it with the abounding joy that Harry had carried away; still all of us, I trust, were more at peace with ourselves and with God after our interview. We did not, like Harry, find a great vocation, but we received such advice as Father Middleton, who knew us so well, judged best for our interests.

When I returned from my conference with Father Middleton I found that another young religious had joined our little reunion.

"So this is Harry Dee," he exclaimed, with the most engaging of smiles, as he grasped my hand warmly. "I know you very well, Harry; though probably you have never even heard of me."

"Yes, he has, *Carissime*," put in Mr. Playfair.
"All my St. Maure's chums know you pretty well.
What a pity we're not allowed to have pillow-fights
here."

"What!" I burst out, "Arthur Vane?"

"The same," laughed Arthur. "I'm the youngest
novice in the house."

"He came to pay me a visit several months ago,"
said Mr. Playfair, "and fell in love with this place.
We could hardly get him out. He came back in
two weeks to stay."

"And now I'm happy," said Arthur, "and I look
upon the night I met Mr. Playfair as *the* night of
my life."

During the hour that preceded dinner Percy and
Arthur became warm friends. They struck me as
being remarkably similar in their tastes and
manners.

In the afternoon Tom rearranged the "Blue
Clippers." Our genial friend Mr. Keenan played
his old position, and, pressing into our service
Frank Burdock and Arthur Vane, we put out a full
nine which Tom as of old led to victory. The young
religious pitted against us played very well, but—
well, we played better.

The time came but too quickly for our departure.

"Boys," said Mr. Playfair, as we were about to
leave the parlor, "before you go, suppose we visit
the master of the house."

Somewhat mystified we followed Tom. He led us
into the presence of the Blessed Sacrament. Frank,
Harry, Joe, and myself kneeled upon the bench
farthest back in the chapel; Tom and Percy were in
front of us. Impressed with the occasion, I was

praying with more than usual fervor, when I felt a light touch upon my arm.

I lifted my head and saw Frank. "Look," he said reverently, "isn't it beautiful?" and he pointed to the kneeling figures of Tom and Percy. The evening sun was shining upon them, mingling the glory of earth with the heavenly glory that seemed to play about their faces. To look at them, as they then appeared, was as powerful an object lesson in prayer as this earth can give. Yes; before them, concealed by the tabernacle, was the one sweet secret to their sweet lives. It was the *Incarnation* that had made Tom our Tom, and Percy our Percy.

We were on the eve of separating, and taking different walks in life; but, different as were these walks, they were all to conduct us, we trusted, to the same goal—to an everlasting union with Him before whom we were now bowed in fervent adoration.

THE END.

PRINTED BY BENZIGER BROTHERS, NEW YORK.

www.ingramcontent.com/pod-product-compliance
Lightning Source LLC
Chambersburg PA
CBHW030628030726
47497CB00006B/1682